No\quad he
jack-i\quad th
some sort of shining silver-looking tabs on her shirt
collars. Neither man could quite make out what they
were. They looked like silver skulls. Nora stood smiling, but her smile was grotesque, filled with ageless
evil. She held out the box.

"Why are you doing this?" her father asked.

Nora's eyes glowed. "Because it's what I was born
to do."

She laughed at him and flipped the clasp on the
front of the box. The clown's head sprang out. The
hinged mouth worked up and down.

Phillip darted forward, grabbing the snake-like
spring neck in both hands. The jack-in-the-box
howled in rage as strong fingers closed around the
neck, choking the ugliness. The clown head dipped
down, the jaws opening, the yellow teeth snapping
and biting at Phillip's arm. He yelled in pain as the
teeth clamped onto flesh, drawing blood.

Wild, insane laughter sprang from Nora's mouth.
The girl seemed impervious to the struggling going on
around her. She calmly held the wooden box in her
small hands. Phillip tried to slap her, but she seemed
to be protected by an invisible field. She spat in her
father's face—an ugly, foul spittle. The jack-in-the-
box shrieked, twisting free of Sam's grasp. Laughter
rolled from its mouth. With blood dripping from the
bites and cuts on his arms, Phillip backed away. He
cursed the jack-in-the-box and Nora.

"Foolish man! Nora hissed at Phillip. "Now you
will die . . ."

TALES OF TERROR AND POSSESSION
from Zebra Books

HALLOWEEN II (1080, $2.95)
by Jack Martin
The terror begins again when it is Halloween night in Haddonfield, Illinois. Six shots pierce the quiet of the normally peaceful town—and before night is over, Haddonfield will be the scene of yet another gruesome massacre!

MAMA (1247, $3.50)
by Ruby Jean Jensen
Once upon a time there lived a sweet little dolly, but her one beaded glass eye gleamed with mischief and evil. If Dorrie could have read her doll's thoughts, she would have run for her life—for her dear little dolly only had killing on her mind.

WAIT AND SEE (1857, $3.95)
by Ruby Jean Jensen
"Don't go near the river," Kevin's aunt had said. But something dark and evil was waiting for him there, beckoning to him. Something that once freed, would exact a terrifying, unthinkable revenge.

ROCKINGHORSE (1743, $3.95)
by William W. Johnstone
It was the most beautiful rockinghorse Jackie and Johnny had ever seen. But as they took turns riding it they didn't see its lips curve into a terrifying smile. They couldn't know that their own innocent eyes had taken on a strange new gleam.

JACK-IN-THE-BOX (1892, $3.95)
by William W. Johnstone
Any other little girl would have cringed in horror at the sight of the clown with the insane eyes. But as Nora's wide eyes mirrored the grotesque wooden face her pink lips were curving into the same malicious smile.

Available wherever paperbacks are sold, or order direct from the Publisher. Send cover price plus 50¢ per copy for mailing and handling to Zebra Books, Dept. 1892, 475 Park Avenue South, New York, N.Y. 10016. Residents of New York, New Jersey and Pennsylvania must include sales tax. DO NOT SEND CASH.

JACK-IN-THE-BOX

WILLIAM W. JOHNSTONE

ZEBRA BOOKS

KENSINGTON PUBLISHING CORP.

ZEBRA BOOKS

are published by

Kensington Publishing Corp.
475 Park Avenue South
New York, NY 10016

First printing: September 1986

Printed in the United States of America

To the kid called Hollywood.

It's like a lion at the door;
And when the door begins to crack,
It's like a stick across your back;
And when your back begins to smart,
It's like a penknife in your heart;
And when your heart begins to bleed,
You're dead, and dead, and dead,
Indeed!

—Anonymous

Prologue

The antique and curio shop was dark. Traffic on the street in front of the small shop had dwindled to only an occasional vehicle. No footsteps of pedestrians tapped on the sidewalk. A light rain misted downward from the low-hanging clouds hovering wet and full and dark over the city. A dog stepped into the doorway of the shop, then suddenly bolted away, sensing danger and something very ominous—very close. The perception was nothing tangible, but terrifying in its unseen evil.

Inside the shop, the lid on a small wooden box sprang open. For a few seconds nothing appeared from the dark depths of the box. Then, like an awakening snake sensing food nearby, a jack-in-the-box slithered upward and out of the box. The toy was very old and the coiled spring in its canvas neck squeaked as the head snaked upward. The fabric neck was discolored and patched. The clown head and face grotesquely ugly, the paint chipped and splotchy. Music played from the tiny music box in the bottom of the case. But the gears were old and worn, the spring weak, so the music was just slightly out of tune—

draggy.

The music was the Funeral March.

The ugly head weaved and bobbed back and forth, very slowly, keeping in measure and meter with the somber, melodious dirge. The eyes were not painted on but glass, carefully set into the face of the ugly clown head.

Then the eyes moved. They shifted back and forth, inspecting the surroundings. The glass orbs flickered with an unnatural light and life. The eyes became slippery with moisture. They moved easier now, sliding from side to side.

The lower jaw dropped open with a rusty click, exposing dirty yellow teeth. Real teeth. Carefully removed from the mouths of cadavers and meticulously set in place. The jaws were hinged, enabling the mouth to move up and down. A curious humming sound rolled from the mouth, a harsh, guttural sound. The hinged mouth moved up and down, clicking with each slap shut. The humming changed to an unintelligible grunting. After a moment the grunting turned into understandable words. A macabre little ditty filled the curio shop:

"The worms crawl in and the worms crawl out. The worms play pinochle on your snout."

The jack-in-the-box laughed and laughed. Ugly. Evil.

The music slowed, becoming more discordant. Slowly the old wire in the fabric neck began to coil, the head sinking back into the cushioned depths of the case. Only the top of the blotched head and the eyes could now be seen. The eyes shifted, making one more inspection of the darkened interior of the shop.

The music ground to a halt. The head disappeared into the box. The lid closed.

Unseen fingers moved the brass clasp, locking the top of the wooden case.

Very low, muffled chuckling came from the scarred box.

The jack-in-the-box waited, as it had for many years, in many lands, for someone to come along and see it, like it, and buy it. Take it home, where the evil therein could be unleashed. Somebody would. Someone always did.

Part One

1

"Nora," the father said to his daughter, fighting to keep a lid on his temper, "why did you break that vase?"

"I didn't," the blond-haired, dark-eyed little girl replied, meeting her father's steady gaze with an unwavering stare. "I told you. It just fell off."

"The vase just fell off the stand? All by itself?"

"Yes sir. I was just walking by and it fell off."

The father sighed heavily. It had been a long day. The ride from the city to home had taken longer than usual, the commuters packed in like little canned fishies for much of the way. Then the drive from the station to home. A woman with a station wagon full of kids almost broadsided him, running a stop sign. Then *she* shot *him* the bird. He didn't need this immediately after opening the door. He was glad it was Friday. It had been a good but frustrating week at the law offices of Baxter, Sobel, Turner, and Weiskopf. Now this crap. Again.

Phillip Baxter stared in unbelieving silence at his daughter. As a parent, he knew perfectly well she was lying. She lied constantly. She lied even when the

15

truth would serve her better. But as an attorney, he knew he couldn't prove she was lying.

"All right, Nora," he said. "Pick up the pieces, and don't cut yourself doing it."

"Why should I pick them up?" she demanded. "I didn't break the vase."

"Don't argue with me, Nora!" He raised his voice. He calmed himself. "I'm not in any mood for it. Just do as I say."

"Let the cleaning woman do it."

"The cleaning woman, Nora, is gone until Monday. Now *do it*!" he snapped at her.

The child smiled, sensing in some small way she had bested her father, winning the verbal battle. Again. "Yes, father. Of course." Smugly.

He almost slapped her. He had never struck the child and prayed he never would. But this time he came very close. It was all Phillip could do not to hit her.

Phillip turned away and walked into the den of the large, two-story home, located just off the Merritt Parkway in Connecticut. Phillip loved the old house, which had been completely restored, but that trip to and from the city sometimes was a pain in the ass.

And so was Nora.

Phillip simply could not get close to his daughter. He couldn't reach her. And God knew he had tried; but he just couldn't understand her. There was something about the girl—literally *about*—her; she had wrapped some invisible cloak around her. And Phillip could not unwrap that deception.

Deception, he thought. Interesting description. But very apt.

"What was all that noise in the hall?" his wife asked.

"Nora broke the vase your aunt gave you and then lied about it."

"I did not!" the girl screamed from the hall. "It fell off. Stop picking on me. Leave me alone. You're always picking on me."

Jeanne Baxter looked at her husband. "If Nora says it fell off, it fell off. Accidents happen, Phillip. Why do you always doubt what she tells you?"

Phillip walked to the bar, loosening his tie as he walked. Here we go again, he thought. Ol' dad is the bad guy. Again. He fixed a drink and turned around, looking at his wife. "Because she lies, Jeanne. Nora . . ." He paused, detecting a slight movement by the archway separating hall from den. Nora was eavesdropping. Again. She was the sneakiest kid Phillip had ever seen. "Take the broken pieces and put them in the garbage, Nora."

"And be careful, darling," Jeanne called. "Don't cut yourself."

"Yes, mother."

When Nora was gone, carrying the dustpan as if it contained wet dog droppings, Phillip said, "She lies all the time, Jeanne. I've caught her countless times. I'm getting tired of it. The child has a problem, and we'd better be doing something about it. Before it's too late."

"That's ridiculous, Phillip. She's just a little girl."

There was no arguing with Jeanne— not about Nora. Nora was the baby, and there would be no more children. After a very difficult pregnancy and a rough time of it in the delivery room, the doctor had told

17

Jeanne that was it. No more.

Tube-tying time.

In Jeanne's mind, Nora was perfect. Faultless. Phillip picked on her, demanded too much of her. Jeanne could not see that the child was driving a wedge between husband and wife. Deliberately driving the wedge, Phillip thought. And the breech was widening.

Daddy Bad Guy.

"Go easy on the liquor," Jeanne cautioned him. "We're going out tonight."

Phillip had looked forward to a hot shower, several drinks, an early dinner, and a slob evening and weekend. Jesus Christ! he thought. "Where to now?" he asked wearily.

"The Gipsons. The party's been on for two months. I reminded you about it this morning, Phillip."

"I forgot. OK? So how about Nora?"

"A sitter is coming over."

Another one? he silently parried with her. How many does that make? The kid has run off more sitters than there were Indians at Little Big Horn.

Phillip tuned his wife back in. " . . . better shower and change."

"Right, Jeanne." The drive to New Canaan was not bad; it was Matthew and Judy Gipson that Phillip could not abide. Matthew was an overbearing jerk. About five feet seven, he wore the Little Man syndrome on his shoulder like a badge of honor. Matt always had something to prove, was always challenging the other guy's statement. Phillip had come very close, several times, to jacking Matt's jaw. Judy was just a plain out-and-out bitch. Period.

18

"Try to be civil this evening," Jeanne said, knowing what her husband was thinking. "Judy is my friend. In case you've forgotten."

"How could I forget? Both of you keep reminding me."

Jeanne rose from her chair. A tall, graceful, very pretty woman in her late thirties. Five years younger than Phillip. Short, honey-blond hair. A great figure. She could wear the same clothes she'd worn in high school, and did not have to work at keeping her figure.

Phillip, on the other hand, had to work to maintain a constant weight. But he had begun to believe it a losing battle. As the troubleshooting partner and head of the law firm, he had to travel extensively and was unable to keep any sort of regular schedule at his health club. Stocky to begin with, if he didn't work at exercise he would end up looking like a butcher's block. His thick hair was a light brown. Dark eyes. Big hands, more like a dock worker than a very successful lawyer.

"Are we about to have another of our famous semiserious discussions?" she asked.

"Not if I can help it," he said.

A loud crash came from the direction of the kitchen. Jeanne rushed from the room. Phillip used that time to freshen his drink. Jeanne returned and said, "The coffee maker fell off the counter. I cleaned it up."

Phillip knew he shouldn't say it. But he did. "The coffee maker fell off the counter? All by itself?"

"Nora said the coffee maker fell off the counter. I believe her."

19

"Right. Just . . . fell off." Ignoring the dark looks from his wife, Phillip took his drink and walked out of the den, trudging slowly up the stairs to their bedroom. He tossed his shirt and T-shirt to the floor, knowing it would irritate Jeanne. He deliberately sat his drink on the dresser, without a coaster. He kicked off his shoes like an angry child, the shoes sailing in opposite directions.

"Just fell off the goddamn counter. *Jesus!*"

Naked from the waist up, Phillip looked at himself in the mirror. He was still, at forty-three, a powerfully built man. He had boxed in high school and college, in the heavyweight division, and had given some thought to turning pro.

"The Fighting Lawyer," he said aloud, the old memories smoothing out his disposition, tempering his anger. He smiled as he looked around the room. He picked up what he had tossed on the floor and placed a coaster under his glass. It wasn't Jeanne's fault, but Nora was putting a big strain on a pretty good marriage.

He closed the bedroom door and stripped, stepping into the shower. He hit the cold water for a full minute, then cut it to hot, soaping away the grit and grime and tension of the city. He went back to cold, the hot and cold waking him, refreshing him.

Drying off, he dressed in underwear shorts and stood for a moment, wondering if this party was the jacket-and-tie type. "Hell with it," he muttered. He dressed casually in slacks, shirt, and sport coat. He chose a shirt he could wear a tie with, if it came to that. He turned as a knock came at the door.

"Come."

Phil Jr. stuck his head in and grinned at his father. "Sharp, dad. Sharp." The boy was built just like his father, right down to his big hands.

Phillip returned the grin. "Yeah. Pretty spiffy for an old man, hey?"

The boy groaned. "*Spiffy*, dad?"

"How about a cool dude?"

"Go back to spiffy."

"What do you have on tap for this evening, Phil?"

"Nothing that spectacular. Just going up the street to Alec's for a party. Spending the night. His parents are going to the same place you and mom are going."

"OK, boy, you know the rules. No boozing and no left-handed cigarettes."

"Few beers, probably," the boy admitted. "But the only one there with a car will be Jimmy, and he doesn't drink."

Phillip grinned. "Anymore," he said.

"Yeah, right."

Jimmy Hoover was sixteen, a year older than Phil. Jimmy had taken his mother's station wagon out joyriding when he was fourteen. The wagon and two six-packs of beer. He had plowed into a store front and ended up in the meat department, with lamb chops hanging from his ears and rolls of wieners around his neck. He had been very lucky; he was not seriously injured. Except for his butt when his dad got through with him. Jimmy was president of the local chapter of Students Against Drunk Driving.

"OK," Phillip said. "You know I trust you. And you know I'm not going to lecture you about drinking and driving when I'm going to be doing that very thing this evening."

21

"Yeah, but you're cool with it, dad. Dad? Have you ever been drunk?"

"Oh *hell*, yes. We'd come off patrol in Nam and get blasted."

"Over there I'd say you had a good excuse for doing it. How about in college?"

"Yes."

"High school?"

"One time. And that's the truth. Where is this line of questioning going, Phil?"

"No place in particular. I was just curious. Seems we don't get much chance to talk like we used to. Back when I was a kid."

Phillip didn't smile at that, even though he found it amusing. "Yes, and I'm sorry about that. I don't know why I work as hard as I do. I've got all sorts of junior eager beavers at the office who could be doing that. I've been very fortunate, Phil. You know that, don't you?"

"I guess so. You mean like at the office? Financially?"

"Yes. We've built a very profitable law firm in fifteen years. But I've been away from home about as much as I've been home. I promise you, though, we'll spend more time together next year." If I'm alive, that is, he thought.

Now why would I think that?

"Lookin' forward to it, dad. You and mom have a good time tonight."

"Same to you, boy."

Phillip went downstairs, meeting Jeanne on her way up

"They going to feed us at this shindig?" he asked.

"Party foods, lots of hors d'oeuvres. Things like that."

"Well then, I'd better fix a sandwich. You want one?"

"No. I haven't been drinking."

He watched her climb the stairs and wondered why so many cheap shots had been flung about between them—from both sides—over the past two years. Hell, he knew why: Nora. He shook his head and went to the kitchen, fixing a huge sandwich and a glass of milk. He knew that alone would cut way down on his drinking. He could not drink after eating.

Phil left just as the sitter arrived. She looked as though she had something to tell him, and Phillip had a pretty good idea what it was about: Nora. He had lost count of the numbers of sitters that had come and gone over the years. Just as the girl was about to speak, Jeanne came down and Phillip waited while the girl received her instructions on how to handle darling precious Nora.

Stop it! Phillip silently berated himself. You are the girl's father. You burped her and changed her diapers, held her while she puked, and loved her all the time. Stop thinking of the child as a kind of monster. You've just got to convince Jeanne the child needs some sort of counseling, and see to it that she gets it.

Yeah, he thought. Good luck.

On the drive to the Gipsons', Jeanne was silent for several miles. She finally broke the silence. "Nora is convinced you hate her."

"Are you serious, Jeanne?"

She was.

"That's ridiculous, Jeanne. Good Lord! You don't believe that. Do you?"

"I don't know what to believe," She was honest in her reply. "I know only that Nora is a little girl and you want her to behave as an adult. That is very unfair."

Going to be a swell evening, folks, Phillip thought. But if we have to hash it out, fine, let's do it, and to hell with the Gipsons. Both of them.

"Jeanne, that is just not true. I want the girl to stop telling lies. Honey, face up to something—please? Nora has no friends. None. The other kids don't like her."

"Of course not. That's because she's so much smarter than they."

"Are you *serious*?"

"Certainly. Nora is brilliant."

"Aw . . . *come off it*, Jeanne!" Phillip lost his fragile hold on his temper. "Both our kids are bright, yes, but not exceptionally so. Phil maintains a good grade average, sure, but he's no genius. And neither is Nora. Both their IQ's are above average, yes. But Nora's grades are terrible. Dammit, Jeanne, the girl needs some help."

"What are you suggesting?" she flared at him, her words icy.

"Nothing more than she see a good child psychologist."

"So now you think she's retarded!"

"I didn't say that, Jeanne."

"There is nothing wrong with Nora!" she screamed at him, her words bouncing around the closed car.

Phillip drove on in silence. There was no point in

pursuing the matter any further. Maybe Nora would grow out of it. Perhaps it was just a stage she was going through. But Phillip didn't believe that. Not for a minute. He had never told Jeanne about the time he'd found Nora torturing a bird that had some how been injured and landed in their backyard. She was enjoying it, laughing as she tormented the bird. By the time Phillip's revulsion had passed and he reached the child, the bird was dead. He had never confided in his wife that he was sure Nora had been the one who had poisoned their dog, old Lucky. Lucky had never warmed to Nora. Something about the girl caused the dog to shy away. Phillip had never told his wife about the rumors that persisted: the other kids didn't like to play with Nora because she was cruel and domineering and arrogant.

There would have been no point in talking with Jeanne about it.

She would not have believed him.

But something had to be done, for the child's sake. Only question was: What?

The party was a raging dud. With the exception of Carl Tremain, Alec's father, it appeared that Matt and Judy had invited everyone that Phillip could not abide. But he forced a party-goer's smile and struggled through the evening, making inane conversation and keeping his alcoholic intake very low. Phillip felt the tension between he and Jeanne was going to hit the breaking point before this night was over. And he certainly was not looking forward to that.

The party—if that was what all the social posturing

and jockeying for attention could be called—finally began to wind down. Phillip and Jeanne left as soon as it was socially acceptable to do so.

Jeanne opened on him before he had backed out of the Gipsons' drive. "What do you want to do, Phillip?"

"What are we taking about?"

"Us."

"There is nothing wrong with us, Jeanne. We've been married for eighteen good years. I have never been unfaithful, and no one could ever convince me you have. The problem is Nora. You want to hash this out now?"

"We may as well."

"All right. You've got to face up to the fact—and it *is* a fact—that Nora needs a little bit of help. It isn't some dreadful illness, baby. But it could develop into something very serious. I firmly believe that. Honey, Nora is a human being, and all human beings are very complex. I have my faults, you have your faults, Phil has his. Why can't Nora be flawed in some minor way? You know she tells lies, Jeanne. You know it. She lies to me, to you, to her brother, to her classmates—notice I didn't say friends, 'cause she doesn't have any—and she probably lies to herself. So let's find out why she lies, and do something about it. That's all I'm asking."

"You think she's crazy?"

Not going to be easy, he thought. "I think she needs help, Jeanne. And it's our responsibility to see that she gets it."

"Do you want a divorce, Phillip?"

"Who in the hell said anything about a divorce, for

26

Christ's sake?"

Jeanne turned her face away and looked out the window. "There is nothing wrong with Nora, Phillip. She is going through a stage, that's all."

"You really believe that, don't you?"

"Yes." And she would not speak another word on the long drive home.

Phillip paid off the sitter and called a cab for the girl. From the look on the teenager's face, Phillip knew Nora had pulled something. He braced himself.

The girl said, "I won't be back here, Mr. Baxter. You'll have to find another sitter."

Same old story, Phillip thought. Good Lord, how many does this make? And why won't any of them be specific as to what Nora does to drive them away? "All right, Lisa. I want to thank you for all the times you've come over. Care to tell me why you won't be coming back?"

The girl sighed. "I don't want any hard feelings, Mr. Baxter."

"I assure you, Lisa, there will be no hard feelings."

"Nora is . . . well, *weird*, Mr. Baxter. Frankly, I'm afraid of her. I don't wanna say no more about it. Here's my cab. See you, Mr. Baxter."

2

Saturday morning dawned dull and gray, with a sharp wind blowing. An early reminder that winter came quickly after fall. And Phillip wondered if this winter was going to be a bad one. They were overdue.

Rising early, leaving Jeanne asleep, Phillip dressed quietly in the darkened bedroom. Khaki trousers and flannel shirt and loafers. He went downstairs and fixed coffee. Phil had spent the night at Alec's, and Jeanne always slept very late on Saturday mornings. Phillip knew that as soon as he left the bedroom, Nora would slip into bed beside her mother. They would remain in bed most of the morning.

Phillip had deliberately left his briefcase at the office. He had vowed to cut back on the amount of work he brought home. Now he wished he had something to do. Anything to keep him occupied and out of another argument with Jeanne.

But he felt sure they'd have another blowup before the weekend was over.

Divorce. Jeanne had actually brought that up. Was it really coming to that? Christ, he wished he hadn't quit smoking. He could use a cigarette right now.

Maybe he'd take up smoking again.

He had to talk to someone about Nora. But who would it be? For all his talk about friends, Phillip himself wasn't overloaded in the true friend department. But who was? No one has that many real friends. Lots of acquaintances, but few friends. Sam Sobel and Bob Turner and Ed Weiskopf were his closest friends. College, Nam, then a partnership in what many in legal circles called the hottest and most successful law firm going. Odd, the four recently graduated law students all going into the service together, landing in the same unit, and all of them making it out alive.

They had formed their friendship as freshmen, and it had stood the test.

So it came down to which one Phillip wanted to confide in.

Sam was recently divorced; a rather messy affair. But Phillip was closest to Sam, a New Yorker born and reared. For all his complaining about the city, Sam would never leave it for a place "out in the wilderness," as he referred to anywhere outside of New York City. But Sam was a solid guy. You got a problem? Attack it! Maybe he would call Sam. Go into the city and have lunch.

Bob was the serious and studious one of the quartet. Absolutely no sense of humor. None. Business all the way, all the time. A brilliant lawyer, Bob was steady and prodding and meticulous. A good, solid family man, but not the one to talk with about Nora.

Ed was a clown. A natural actor and great courtroom lawyer who could have the jury laughing one minute and sobbing the next. But Phillip knew he wouldn't talk to Ed about Nora.

It came down to Sam.

Phillip suddenly felt eyes on him, that itchy feeling in the center of his back. Turning his head, he looked at Nora, standing a few feet away. Damn, she could move quietly. He wondered how long she had been standing there.

"Morning, honey," Phillip said.

"Good morning, father," she said formally. "I'm going with mother to visit Aunt Morgan in Bridgeport."

"Oh?"

"Yes. We'll be back sometime late tomorrow."

It was then Phillip noticed the child was fully dressed. Anger reared up white-hot within him. Thank you very much for telling me, Jeanne dear. "Well, then. You two have a good time." He fought to keep the anger out of his voice.

"Oh, I'm sure we shall," Nora said with a smile. She turned and left the kitchen.

Phillip gripped the edge of the table so hard his knuckles turned white. He stood up, shoving back his chair, turning it over. He left it there. He checked his pockets for keys and wallet and money clip and walked out of the house, slamming the front door. He went to his BMW and backed out of the drive without looking back at the house.

Had he looked back at the darkened den window, he would have seen Nora standing there, a smile on her lips.

Phillip drove the four blocks to the Tremain house. Carl Tremain was picking up the morning paper. Phillip braked and stopped, getting out and shaking hands with the man. "Enjoy the party last night?" he asked with a grin.

Carl laughed. "About as much as you did, Phillip."

"Yes. I don't suppose the boys are up?"

"Is it noon already?" Carl smiled.

"I keep forgetting. Look, Carl, Jeanne and Nora are leaving for the weekend and I've got to go into the city. Could I impose on you and Betty to look after Phil today?"

"Oh, sure. Consider it done. Just call when you get back and we'll send him home."

"Hey, sarge!" Sam said with a grin as he pulled Phillip into his apartment. Phillip had been promoted to buck sergeant just one week before getting wounded in the leg. Just one month before their tour of duty was over. None of the four partners had chosen ROTC in college.

Phillip looked around him at the large apartment. "I'm not . . . ah, disturbing anything, am I, Sam?"

Sam laughed, catching the implication. "Naw. No beauties parading around naked, ol' buddy. Hey! This is great. Let's have a slob Saturday. Wander around and get mustard on our shirts and talk about what heroes we were back in our younger days."

"Sounds great, Sam. But I have to talk to you. I got a problem. At home."

"Oh no, Phillip. Not you and Jeanne?"

"Well, that's sure part of it."

"Damn, I hate to hear that." Sam locked up the apartment and they went to a nearby restaurant and ate a huge breakfast. Phillip laid it out for his friend.

31

"She's a compulsive liar, Phillip. But you've caught it in time. A child psychologist can work it out. I don't see the problem."

"According to Jeanne, there isn't any problem. According to Jeanne, Nora doesn't tell lies. It's my fault. I'm picking on her."

Sam lifted his dark eyes, meeting Phillip's gaze. "Oh. Well, that muddies the water some, doesn't it?"

"Yeah. She asked me last night if I wanted a divorce."

"Phillip, you mind me being terribly blunt?"

"That's why I came to see you, Sam."

"I think they *both* need to see a shrink."

"You might be right. For damn sure one of them does." He paused while the waiter poured them more coffee and left. "I'm keeping Phil out of this. But I'm caught up in the middle and dammit, Sam, I just don't know what to do."

Sam sipped his coffee and said, "If you're looking for an easy answer, there isn't any, buddy."

"I know, I know. Maybe I've been kidding myself. Hoping you'd have a ready solution. I don't know what direction to take."

"I don't know what to tell you. I made a mess out of my marriage." He grimaced. "Deliver me from ever getting involved with another princess."

Phillip laughed, the laughter feeling good. "It wasn't all your fault, Sam."

"Oh, I know that. But fifteen years right down the drain. Well, it's ancient history."

"How are the kids?"

"Damned if I know. I can't find her or them. I know she's somewhere in the city, but where is up for

32

grabs."

"Where do you send her checks?"

Sam looked up, grinning. They laughed. Together they said, "To her lawyer!"

The jack-in-the-box heard stirrings in the shop. It waited, coiled in the darkness and safety of its wooden home. Its existence had been a long and varied one. Hand-carved and fitted in a small village in Germany, the jack-in-the-box was more than a hundred years old.

It had traveled from Germany to France to England, then to America. Its history was interesting. And very bloody.

It was about to get bloodier.

Phillip and Sam roamed about a part of the city, on foot and in taxis. They had a few beers and talked on a variety of subjects, with Phillip keeping his drinking to only a couple a beers, knowing he had to drive back to Connecticut later on that day. Sam, on the other hand, almost never drove, didn't own a car. He drove only when he was out of town on business. Besides, he was a perfectly awful driver.

"You and Jeanne always had, to my way of thinking, the ideal marriage." Sam spoke around a dripping hot dog. His third in an hour. Plus a garlic bagel. And a milkshake.

Phillip marveled, as always, at his friend's ability to eat anything he wanted and never gain a pound. "So did I. But when it started going downhill, it snowballed on me."

"How about another hot dog?" Sam asked.

"Good Lord, no! Those aren't kosher, you know." Phillip kidded him.

"Neither was the garbage we ate over in Nam."

"True. So, Sam, after mulling it over in that razor-sharp mind, you have any questions or answers?"

"One question."

"What?"

Sam burped. "You got a Tums?"

Laughing, the two buddies walked on, with Sam finally stopping in front of a curio shop. "Wanna browse?"

"Why not?"

They roamed the store for about fifteen minutes before Phillip stopped in front of a small battered wooden box with a brass clasp holding the lid tightly shut.

"What is this box?" he asked a clerk.

"A jack-in-the-box. Very old, sir. Supposed to be cursed. It was made in Germany, about 1875, we think."

"What kind of curse?"

"I don't know, sir."

"Germany, huh?" Sam said. "Open it up. Maybe a Nazi will jump out."

Sam had no way of knowing just how close he was to describing the evil therein.

Phillip looked at him. "Sam, sometimes I worry about that sense of humor of yours. It can really be sick."

Sam laughed.

"May I open the box?" Phillip asked.

"Sure," the clerk replied. He flipped the brass switch. The lid fell back. For a moment nothing happened. Then Phillip heard a weird whistling. But it didn't seem to be coming from the box.

He looked around. Sam was whistling the old G.I. tune. The words go, "There's a place in France, where the women . . ." You know the rest.

"Jesus, Sam!"

"I'm just trying to cheer you up. I could sing 'There's a Rose That Grows in No Man's Land.' "

"Spare me."

"Tin ear," Sam muttered.

Then both of them grew quiet as music began to drift out of the wooden box. They recognized it as the Funeral March. Then the grotesquely ugly clown's head began uncoiling ever so slowly, waving like a snake rising out of the box.

Phillip could not take his eyes off the macabre-looking clown's eyes. They seemed to pull at him. "Fascinating."

"If you find that ugly toy fascinating, it's time for me to start worrying about *you*!" Sam said.

The clown's eyes locked with Phillip's. He heard himself saying, "I want this."

"You have got to be kidding!" Sam said. "The stupid thing's cursed, all right. It makes grown men do crazy things!"

The clerk quoted him an absurdly high figure. Phillip and the clerk stood for fifteen minutes, haggling over price. They finally settled on a figure. Sam stood by shaking his head and clucking like a mother hen as Phillip paid his bill and requested the clerk put the jack-in-the-box in a box, with a cord, for easier carrying and to avoid breakage. He was charged a dollar for the box.

"No charge for the twine?" he asked.

"On the house." The clerk smiled.

"You have to be either out of your mind or your tastes run toward the grotesque," Sam said. "Jeanne is going to take one look at that ugly thing and toss you both out into the yard."

"Maybe. But something about this thing caught my attention . . . So what do you have on the burner for this evening?"

"I got this hot patootie coming over to the apartment for an evening of fun and games."

"Hot patootie?" Phillip laughed. "I've got to remember and tell Phil that."

They took a taxi back to Sam's building and went up. They chatted for another half hour. Phillip checked the time and realized it was getting late. He had to get Phil and fix dinner.

It was full dark when Phillip drove up to the Tremains' house. Up the street he could see lights blazing at his house. He drove on, fear gripping him. His first thought was something had happened to Jeanne or the kids. Leaving the box on the front seat, he ran up the sidewalk to the door, pushing it open. Jeanne was standing in the foyer.

"Thank God, you're all right. Is Nora all right? Phil? What happened?"

"Where have you been?" Jeanne shouted at him.

3

"What?" Phillip asked, stunned at the savagery in his wife's tone. "Huh?"

"I asked where have you been all day? How *dare* you storm out of this house and just leave, stay gone all day without telling anyone?"

Phillip slowly closed the door and stood leaning against it, looking at Jeanne. Was he going crazy? What was this, the Twilight Zone?

"Now just a minute, Jeanne. Hold on. I didn't start this going-away-without-telling-anyone business. You did."

"I did?"

"Yes. You did. Nora came down to the kitchen this morning while I was having coffee. She was fully dressed. She told me you were taking her up to visit your Aunt Morgan in Bridgeport. That you'd both be back late tomorrow. I'll admit that it made me hot. I guess I did storm out of the house. I spent the day with Sam. I bought an antique jack-in-the-box at a curio shop."

She glared at him for one long, hot moment. "Nora?" she called.

"Yes, mother?"

"Come down here, please."

"Right away, mother."

"May we please go into the den?" Phillip asked. "The doorknob is poking a hole in my back."

"You might not be staying that long," Jeanne told him.

Phillip felt the blood rise to his face and his temper soar out of control. "Hey, *goddammit!*" he roared, rattling the pictures in the foyer. "Don't you tell *me* where I will or won't be staying!"

Jeanne backed up several steps, her face pale. She knew Philip was a powerful man who really did not know his own enormous strength. While she had never had any reason to fear him, she had never seen him behave like this. She waved him toward the den.

"Thanks so much," Phillip said sarcastically, brushing past her.

In the den, Jeanne looked at Nora. Phillip didn't know where Phil was. "Nora," she said. "The truth now."

"Of course, mother."

"Did you tell your father that you and I were going to visit Aunt Morgan in Bridgeport this morning? That we would not be back until late Sunday?"

"No, mother," the child said, her face and eyes serious. "That's silly. Why would I do something like that?"

Both mother and daughter smiled victoriously.

Phillip stood, looking at Nora. His anger left him, replaced by a sadness. Sure, he thought. Now it all comes together. It's get rid of poppa time. That was it all along. I should have guessed it before now. Ol' dad scolds you when you're bad. Ol' dad sees right through your lies. Ol' dad knows that something is dreadfully wrong with you. And you know Ol' dad isn't going to put up with your antics much longer. So in your cunning little mind, you pit mother against father, knowing your mother will always take your side against ol' dad. You devious little . . . he mentally bit back the profanity. It would do no good. And, he thought with a sigh, there is no point in my challenging your lies, and you know it, Nora. Nasty little plan, kid. Your mother was right about one thing, though: You're a hell of a lot smarter than I gave you credit for being.

"Does counsel have any rebuttal?" Jeanne asked, sarcasm thick in her voice.

With a calmness he did not inwardly feel, Phillip said, "Would there be any point, Jeanne? Against your *perfect* child?"

"I really am sorry, daddy," Nora said. "But I won't lie for you."

"Thanks," Phillip said drily.

"Of course you wouldn't, baby," Jeanne said to Nora. "Now go to your room. Your father and I have some things we have to discuss."

Nora left, taking her dark-bordered innocence with her, and Phillip said, "You bet we have some things to discuss. And I'm not going to get angry; I won't rant and rave. I'm not even going to punish Nora for lying. Because I know now she can't help it. She's a very sick child, Jeanne. She has got to get some professional help."

39

Jeanne looked at him, contempt in her eyes. "I don't believe you, Phillip. How low! You're really going to place the blame on that little girl, aren't you?"

"There is no blame to place, Jeanne. The child is sick. Call Sam. He'll verify everything I told you."

"Your war buddy?" She laughed. "Are you kidding? Of course he'd lie for you. No way, Phillip."

"Carl Tremain wouldn't lie for me," he countered.

Her eyes narrowed in suspicion. "What do you mean?"

"I stopped by his place this morning. Told him about you and Nora leaving and my having to go into the city. I asked him if he'd look after Phil until I got back. Would I do that if I didn't think you and Nora were really leaving?"

She mentally wavered. "This time I'll trap you, Phillip. I'll call your bet." She walked swiftly across the room and punched out the Tremains' phone number, asking to speak to Phil. "What?" she blurted. "Oh . . . well. I . . . ah . . . decided not to go. I'm sorry I didn't call you. Please forgive me. And thank you for looking after Phil. Please. Yes, do that. Send him on home. Thanks again."

She slowly replaced the phone. She turned, looking at Phillip, confusion in her eyes. It was then that Phillip's rage bubbled over.

"Well?" he asked, his voice tight. "Since playing favorites is not limited to you, answer this, if you will: Would I do something like this to Phil, my favorite—deliberately lie to him? You know I wouldn't." He dug in his pocket and held out a slip of paper. "There is the receipt for the jack-in-the-box. It's out in the

40

car. I was so goddamned concerned that something had happened to you or the kids, I left it out there when I pulled in. See this stain here?" He pointed to the front of his shirt. "That's mustard, and probably ketchup, too. From the hot dogs Sam and I ate. Real swinging time in the big city, huh?"

"Oh, Phillip . . ."

"Aw . . . *shit!*" Phillip exploded, all the pent-up anger and frustration and disappointment and torn emotions finally erupting. "Don't 'Oh, Phillip' me. I've had it with that goddamned lying little brat upstairs."

Jeanne paled and stiffened where she stood. She put out one hand and touched the table, steadying herself against his verbal onslaught. She flushed with anger.

Phillip stood trembling for a moment, then his shoulders slumped. "I'm sorry, Jeanne. Forgive me for yelling. And I won't blame you if you don't. Nora isn't a brat. What she is is our creation and it's our responsibility to see her through to adulthood. And beyond, if it comes to that. Monday morning I'll ask around and find the best child psychologist in the city."

But his remarks about Nora being a "goddamned lying brat" had struck home with Jeanne. "You wait just a minute, Phillip. Didn't you say she was fully dressed?"

"That's right. Looked like a little doll."

"No."

"What?"

"I said no. That's impossible. She got into bed with me not two minutes after you left the room. I would

41

have heard her get out of bed."

"Not necessarily, Jeanne. That kid can move like a ghost. You're forgetting how spooky I am. Sam, Bob, Ed, and me are all Ranger-trained LRRP's. We worked right in the middle of the Cong. It's going to take a pro, even now, to slip up on me. But I would never have known she was standing there had I not sensed eyes on me. Wait a minute! Don't I remember you getting up about four-thirty and saying you had a headache and were going to take a pill?"

"Yes. So what?"

"What kind of pill did you take?"

She thought for a moment, then forced a smile. She nodded her head. "Valium. It would have hit me full strength about seven. That's when you got up, wasn't it?"

"Thereabouts."

"Oh, Phillip—why is she *doing* this?"

"Divide and conquer. And she came very close to succeeding."

Upstairs in her bedroom, where she had retreated after eavesdropping on her parents' conversation, knowing she had lost this battle but not the war, Nora sat in the center of her canopied bed. She jammed a long pin into a picture of her father until the eight-by-ten was poked and punched full of holes. Then the little girl spat in her father's face.

Phillip had been correct on all counts.

Nora was God damned.

She had been God damned since the moment of birth.

Outside, on the front seat of the BMW, in the cardboard box, in the wooden case, the jack-in-the-

42

box crouched, coiled, and laughed and laughed as the music played.

It was so good to be home.

Again.

4

The tension was still very thick in the Baxter house Sunday morning. There had been no making up between Jeanne and Phillip at bedtime. No touching, no sexual contact. It was too soon for that. Jeanne was still not convinced about Nora. One way or the other.

- The Baxters had stopped attending church a few years back. Again, the reason had been Nora. Her sixth birthday had fallen on a Sunday, January the sixth. From that moment on the child had rebelled against even entering a church. She cried, she threw tantrums, she grew feverish, she got sick and vomited.

The Baxters changed churches.

The same thing occurred.

They stopped going.

Phillip had been raised in the Catholic Church. He had broken from that church as a boy, when his parents had divorced. His father had been killed in an auto accident before Phillip reached his teens. His mother had dropped out of sight a short time later. Phillip had no brothers or sisters—that he knew of—and so he became a ward of the court. His mother was declared legally dead when Phillip was eighteen, and he had inherited his father's estate. The elder Baxter had been not rich but very comfortable, so Phillip had never wanted for anything. Except the love of natural parents; and that was something he could just vaguely remember.

Jeanne, the daughter of a very successful Connecticut farm family, had been raised a Presbyterian. Both her parents were dead. Her brother still operated the farm; her sister had moved to California after a big family fuss over the estate, and she had never returned. Jeanne was not sure where the sister, Dana, lived.

Since neither Phillip nor Jeanne was especially religious, backing away from organized churchgoing had not been that difficult. And since they themselves did not attend church, they did not force Phil to attend.

On this Sunday morning, sitting alone in the kitchen sipping coffee, Phillip reviewed it all in his mind, recalling that at first both he and Jeanne had dismissed Nora's tantrums as childish rebellion.

"That was stupid of us," Phillip muttered. He jammed out his cigarette butt in the ashtray. He had picked up a carton of cigarettes in the city, just after leaving the curio shop. Picked them up on impulse.

"You quit smoking years ago!" Sam had scolded.

"I felt like starting again," Phillip said.

Phillip lit another cigarette and poured more coffee. Where was his line of thinking going? He didn't know. Why think about Nora's attitude toward church at this time? Was there a connection? If so, what was it?

He smiled, then muttered, "Maybe it's the devil

45

making her do it."

Then he remembered the jack-in-the-box.

He went outside into a gray, windy morning. The air sharp. It reminded him that Thanksgiving was not far off. He wondered if they were going to Bridgeport, or was Aunt Morgan coming down to see them? Or were they driving up to get Morgan and then all of them going to Jeanne's brother's place? He just couldn't remember.

He opened the door to his BMW and reached across the front seat.

The cardboard box was gone.

He looked. He was sure he'd put it on the front seat of his car. Hell, he knew he had! He looked on the back seat. Empty except for the paper he'd bought and then forgotten to read. What was going on?

He looked down. There it was, on the floorboards between front and back seats. But how had it gotten there?

Oh well. He picked up the box and felt a very odd sensation flood him, grip him. A feeling of savagery and sudden hot lust. The memory of that awful afternoon in Nam came rushing back. That teenage girl they'd taken advantage of. He and Sam and Ed and Bob. Just after that search-and-destroy mission. She had popped out of a hole in the ground and shot—what was his name? Yeah. Lieutenant Rollins—right between the eyes with an AK. Sam had butt-stroked her with his own captured AK-47, and they had dragged her out of the hole. Pretty little thing. Spoke perfect English. Told them she'd killed dozens of Americans. Laughed about it. Hard to tell her age. Between fifteen and twenty-five. The four of them had looked in all directions. The rest of the battalion was way to hell and gone across a field, a good fifteen hundred meters away and moving farther away from the smoking, burning village. Or what was left of it.

So they stripped the VC, and all of them took a turn with her. John Rollins had watched it all, through dead eyes.

Then they didn't know what to do with her. As LRRP's they were supposed to bring back prisoners. But hell, they couldn't bring back this one. She'd tell on them. They couldn't have that.

She had solved the problem by grabbing up Bob's rifle. Before she could pull the trigger, Phillip shot her.

Standing in the cold fall wind, the cardboard box in his hands, Phillip felt the strange sensation leave him. He shook away the memories. He hadn't thought about that afternoon in years. He wondered if any of the others ever thought about it.

He laughed cruelly, sounding not at all like himself. War makes strange bedfellows, he thought.

He returned to the warmth of the house and put the box on a table. Jeanne came down the stairs, pausing at the last step, her slender hand on the polished railing.

Beautiful, Phillip thought. "You're up early," he said.

"I thought perhaps we'd better talk before the kids got up."

"All right. Good idea. I made coffee. You want some breakfast?"

"Later, perhaps. What's in the package?"

47

"That antique jack-in-the-box I told you about last night."

She tried a smile that almost came across. "Open it up. I could use a good laugh."

"You'd better brace yourself," he warned. "This thing is rather macabre."

"Oh?"

Phillip removed the twine and opened the cardboard lid, taking out the wooden box. "You're probably going to order me to toss this thing into the junk."

"Oh come on, Phillip. It can't be *that* bad."

"It's pretty gruesome, honey. Brace yourself." He flipped the brass catch.

The music began to play.

Jeanne listened, then an expression of horror passed across her face. "Phillip, that's the Funeral March!"

He grinned at her. "Yeah. Weird, isn't it." He laughed. "Just wait until you see this ugly thing."

The lid slowly opened; the music became louder. The grotesque clown's head seemed to slither upward, slowly inching out of the box, bobbing and weaving and grinning as it protruded out of its home. Its eyes rolled seemingly uncontrollably from side to side, making it look even more hideous.

"My Lord!" Jeanne whispered.

"I warned you." Phillip stared at the clown's face. It seemed . . . he searched for the word. Evil, he thought. Then all traces of the word disappeared from his mind.

He looked up at Jeanne, standing on the last step of the stairs.

"Phillip, put that thing away. It's hideous. Whatever in the world possessed you to buy it?"

Possessed, the word stuck in his mind. Odd, he thought. Why should that word provoke such a responsive cord within me?

"What's wrong, Phillip?"

He looked at her. "Eh? Oh . . . nothing." He glanced at the grinning head of the jack-in-the-box. "God, it is ugly, isn't it?"

"Oh no," Nora said. "It's beautiful."

Mother and father looked up and around. Nora was standing just behind her mother. Neither had heard the girl come down the stairs. And Phillip was facing the stairs.

Why didn't I see her? he thought.

"Beautiful?" Jeanne said.

"Oh yes. Did you buy it for me, daddy?" she asked.

"Why . . . ah, sure, honey!" Phillip stammered. "Sure. If you really like it."

"Oh, I love it!" She rushed across the room and came to the table where the jack-in-the-box sat, grinning insanely, evilly, always, at the mother and father and child. Nora threw her arms around her father's waist. "Oh, I love you, daddy. Thank you so very, very much."

Phillip looked at Jeanne. Both were dumbfounded at the child's reaction.

"May I take it up to my room and play with it? Please, daddy? Please?" Her dark eyes were shining with excitement.

"Why . . . sure, honey," Phillip said, just slightly embarrassed at his daughter's actions. For years she had stiffened whenever he tried to put his arms

49

around her. Now this. "If you like it that much, it's yours."

"Thank you, daddy." She tugged at him until he bent down and allowed her to kiss him on the cheek. "Daddy needs a shave," she said with a smile. It was a game they used to play. Nora had ceased playing it at age six.

Nora flipped a switch on the box that Phillip had not even noticed and the ugly clown's head slowly disappeared into the box. She closed the lid and locked it. "Now," she said, smiling. "Mine at last."

"What a strange thing to say, Nora," Jeanne said. "Whatever in the world do you mean?"

"I've always wanted one," the child replied, not taking her eyes off the scarred box. "And now I have my very own."

"I never knew you wanted a jack-in-the-box," Phillip said. "I never heard you say anything about it."

"I never did," the girl said strangely. "But I dreamed about having one. Over and over. The same dream."

Husband and wife exchanged glances, neither of them understanding what had happened.

Nora looked at her mother. "May I wear my new beige dress this morning, mother?"

"Why . . . I . . . certainly! But why would you want to wear that one today?"

Nora smiled, a peculiar light in her eyes. "Why, mother, it's Sunday. I want to go to church, of course."

5

"What church are we going to, dad?" Phil asked.

"I haven't the foggiest, son. I just wish I knew what has caused this total turnaround in your sister."

"She's always been weird," the son replied.

Phillip chose not to pursue that. Father and son were dressed in new suits, pinstripes. Jeanne wore an outfit she had recently purchased at Bonwit Teller.

Then Nora came down the stairs.

She looks like a little angel, Phillip thought. She is my daughter, but I can't deny the obvious. She is beautiful. Going to be even more beautiful than her mother, and that takes some doing.

Then doubt began once more to creep into his mind. What's she up to? he wondered. She's playing some sort of game with us—no, with *me*—but what is it? And why?

Well, we'll all soon find out. I hope.

But at church Nora's behavior was exemplary. She sat like a little doll, not once fidgeting in the pew, and paid close attention to the minister's words.

But Phillip noticed her little hands were balled into

51

white-knuckled fists. He wondered why.

It was his own attention that kept wandering, his mind constantly returning to Nora's flip-flopping, mulling it over and over. He mentally reviewed all the angles he could dredge up.

And he understood nothing of his daughter's new behavior.

The service was over before he realized it.

Nora was bright and bubbling after church. So much so that Phillip almost forgot his suspicions. Almost. As a treat, he took them out for lunch. Once again, Nora behaved as elegantly as a recent graduate from a British charm school. Her manners were impeccable. Phillip noticed several of the people seated around them smiling at the girl, commenting on how pretty she was.

Back home, Phil changed into jeans and sweat shirt and took off for Alec's house. Nora went up to her room. Phillip and Jeanne sat in the den.

"I'm as dumbfounded as you are, Phillip," Jeanne told him. "Shocked might be a better way of describing it. I don't know what to make of her."

"I don't either. But I'll tell you what I'll do. I'll make a deal with you."

She looked suspiciously at him.

He held up a hand. "No, hear me out. If her behavior stays anywhere near what it's been today, we'll just forget about a child psychologist. Maybe she's snapped out of that . . . stage, for want of a better word, she was going through. I don't know. But I'm real glad to see it."

Jeanne came to him and sat in his lap, putting her arms around his neck and kissing him. "You've got a

52

deal."

"Umm," Phillip said. "It's beginning to look like a very promising and interesting afternoon, young lady."

"Oh, thank you for the 'young lady' bit. What do you have on your mind, Mr. Baxter?"

He told her.

She said she thought that might be fun. It had been some time between . . .

Together, holding hands, they walked up the stairs. They looked in on Nora. She was asleep on her bed.

Or so they thought.

When her door had closed, Nora sat up quickly. She jerked off her pretty new dress and hurled it savagely to the floor. She spat on the dress. She changed into jeans and shirt and went into her bathroom, washing her hands twice. The minister's touch still lingered on her flesh. It was sickening.

She reached under her bed and pulled out the wooden box. She opened the clasp and waited for the music to begin. When the first notes of the somber march drifted from the base of the box, the clown's head peeked over the lip of the box, only the top of the head and eyes visible.

"I've been waiting for you," the girl said. "Waiting so long. I knew you would come."

The clown head emerged, bobbing back and forth, side to side, the eyes rolling.

"We have lots of time," Nora said. "Lots of time. "We'll have fun, just you and me."

Laughter rolled softly from the cruel hinged mouth.

"But we have to be careful," Nora cautioned. "Very careful. Do you understand?"

The hideous mouth snapped open and then closed with a pop.

"Good."

The head swayed back and forth, the jaw continuing to open and close.

"Very well," Nora said.

The girl walked to her dresser and sat down. She brushed her long blond hair away from her neck and looked at the birthmark there. When she was six years old it had begun to change, changing from a circle, slowly altering in shape. From that moment on, Nora had never allowed her mother to wash her hair. The girl knew she was different from other girls. But until recently she did not know just how different.

Her dark eyes looked up at the reflection of her face in the mirror, then lowered to the birthmark.

The tiny birthmark was in the perfect shape of a six.

"So how are things at home?" Sam asked.

Phillip looked up from the brief he had been studying. "Odd," he said. Then he told his friend and partner what had happened after he'd returned home Saturday.

Sam's eyes widened. He forced a smile. "That's not odd, buddy. That's just plain *weird*."

Phillip put his elbows on the desk top and his chin in his hands. "Sam, why can't I shake the feeling that Nora is pulling one of her little tricks on me—on Jeanne?"

"Because you're a lawyer. We tend to question everything."

"That's true. But besides that?"

Sam shook his head. "I think she is. Phillip, do you trust your daughter?"

Phillip sighed. "No," he replied, the word coming easily, without any feelings of guilt. "No, I really don't. And I'm wondering if it's possible she's a dual personality and doesn't know it?"

"Anything is possible, I suppose. But you'll never know until you take her to see a shrink."

"I can't do that. I made a deal with Jeanne." He told Sam about their pact.

"Well, you boxed yourself in. But I know why you did it. Keeping the peace at home, huh?"

"Yes. It's been a psychological battleground around there for longer than I care to remember. Yeah, you're right. I'm boxed in. But anything to keep the peace. Even if it means putting off something that obviously needs to be done."

"Nora."

"Precisely."

Both men were silent for a moment. Sam said, "Phillip, why don't you, without telling Jeanne, see a shrink, a child shrink, and lay it out for him? Hell, we have a half dozen right here in this building."

"That's a good idea, Sam. I'll go see him."

But it wasn't a him. It was a her. And the office was nothing like what Phillip had expected. He had thought there would be Disney characters on the walls, books about choo-choo's and friendly little mice. The office was pleasant, but not kiddy. And Dr. S. Harte turned out to be Sheela.

"Don't be uncomfortable, Mr. Baxter," she said, smiling at him. A very disarming smile from a very pretty lady. "Have you ever been to a psychologist before?"

"Psychiatrist. Couple of times after we got back from Nam. They were government people."

"I see. What branch of service were you in?"

"Army. I was a LRRP. Rhymes with burp."

She looked startled. "I beg your pardon?"

He grinned. "Long Range Recon Patrol."

"I'm not familiar with them. Was it dangerous work?"

He started to tell her that *any* place in Nam was dangerous. That anybody who served over there in any capacity deserved a medal. 'Cause they damn sure got their head warped. Instead he said, "Yes, it was dangerous."

"Do you dream about it?"

Phillip knew from speaking to others that when dealing with emotionally disturbed children, the doctors sometimes questioned the parents just about as much as the kids. "Not much. Not in years. I think about it."

"Often?"

"Yes."

"Did you kill, Mr. Baxter?"

"Many, many times, Dr. Harte. With guns, with knives, with piano wire, with my bare hands."

"What do you do with piano wire?"

"Silent kills. Wrap it around their neck, pull it tight, and hold on."

"Sounds fascinating."

"Oh, it is. Really helps one to get a job in the civilian marketplace." He grinned to soften that.

She smiled. "Tell me about Nora."

56

Where to begin? That was a very subtle perfume Dr. Harte was wearing, and he knew damn well Jeanne would smell it on his clothing when he got home. He'd drive with the window down when he got back to the station. "She was a very sweet, very normal—normal to a layman's way of thinking—until her sixth birthday."

It was there he picked it up. When he had finished, he was surprised to learn he'd been talking for almost half an hour.

Dr. Harte stared at him for a moment. "Mr. Baxter, I would very much like to talk with your daughter."

"She needs help?"

"From what you've told me, most definitely. When could I see her?"

"I'd like very much for you to talk with her. But for the moment, I'm afraid it's impossible."

"Is she physically ill?"

"Oh no." Then he told her of the arrangement he'd made with Jeanne.

"Mr. Baxter . . . "

"Phillip, please."

"All right, Phillip. Doesn't your wife understand it's very important to catch these things as early as possible? It's so much easier to deal with in a child."

"She won't even discuss it. Well, that's not true. We did discuss it, in a manner of speaking—or shouting. Then I had her convinced that Nora needed to see a shr . . . psychologist."

She laughed. "Shrink is fine, Phillip. Believe me, I've been called much worse."

"But then Nora pulled her turnaround act. That's

57

when I suggested the deal I just told you about."

"Act? That's interesting. You believe it's an act?"

"Yes, I do. Dr. Harte . . ."

"Sheela."

"Fine. Sheela, I believe my daughter is brilliantly . . . troubled." He could not bring himself to say insane. "She plays me off her mother, and I come out looking like the heavy every time. She has lied for five years. But this bit Saturday shows me, at least, that she is quite an actress."

"All children are actors, Phillip. Some better than others. All right now. Have you told me everything about her, about your situation at home?"

"I . . . think so. No!" He told her about the antique and supposedly cursed jack-in-the-box.

Did her interest perk up just then? he wondered. Yes, it did. But why? Why would a toy produce such an effect?

"Phillip, I strongly recommend that you bring Nora to see me."

"If she reverts to her old ways, I sure will. But Sheela, if I insisted on bringing her in now, it would probably cause a divorce."

"I'm sorry to hear that."

"So am I."

"All right, Phillip, as you wish. But will you please stay in touch with me?"

"Certainly. We work in the same building."

He watched as she wrote a number on a slip of paper and handed it to him. "That is my unlisted home number. If you ever need to talk to me, say at night, don't hesitate to call me."

He looked at the number. Lifted his eyes. "Why are

58

you doing this?"

"Because I think Nora needs help. And I'm hoping your wife will soon realize it."

Phillip felt she was holding back, but he couldn't possibly imagine why. He decided not to push it. "I certainly appreciate it, Sheela." He tucked the number into his wallet and stood up. "Do I pay the receptionist?"

She smiled that disarming smile. "No charge for this visit, Phillip. On the house."

"That's very kind of you. If you ever need any legal help, I'm a couple of floors up."

When the door had closed behind Phillip, Sheela took a private phone from her desk and punched out a number. "Father Joseph Debeau, please. Yes, thank you. I'll hold."

While she waited, she summoned her nearly total recall and jotted down everything Phillip had told her, writing in a small, very neat handwriting. She put down her pencil as the phone was picked up on the other end.

"Joe," she said. "I think I've found her."

There was no news to report to Dr. Harte. Nothing at all. The week passed uneventfully at the Baxter home, the tension finally disappearing completely when Nora's behavior did not change. She was still the sweet little girl she had now become.

On this day, Jeanne and Nora had gone to a local shopping mall to browse. Phillip sat alone in the den, drinking coffee and smoking and thinking.

Those lingering doubts would not leave Phillip's

59

mind.

Nothing made any sense.

People just did not change that abruptly. Unless . . . ? Unless what?

Phillip could not imagine the *what* of it.

The only thing that had happened to alter the Baxters' normal day-to-day routine had been . . . what?

Nothing that he could think of.

Then it came to him. The old jack-in-the-box. But what in the hell, or why, would an old toy have anything to do with a child's behavior?

He couldn't imagine. Unless the curse, whatever that was, was true. He chuckled at that. He wondered what the curse was.

He glanced up as the front door opened and closed. Phil looked in on his father.

"Hey, old man," the boy said with a grin. "You look like you're deep in thought."

"Kind of, I suppose. You busy, Phil?"

"Naw. Boring weekend. You want to talk?"

"Yes, I do. Come sit down." Phil did so and Phillip said, "I want you to level with me, Phil. OK?"

"Sure. What'd I do?"

Phillip smiled. Normal reaction for a kid. Serious talk meant someone was in trouble. Clear the air fast as to who was in dutch. "You haven't done a thing, Phil."

"That's a relief."

"Who poisoned old Lucky, Phil?"

The question caught the boy off guard. With hundreds of courtroom hours behind him, Phillip watched his son's eyes and knew the boy was about to lie. "Don't do it, Phil. I want the truth."

Phil shrugged and nodded his head. "Nora. But it wasn't poison. I got sick to my stomach when she told me what she'd done. It took her several months to do it. She crushed up glass into tiny bits and put in in his food."

Phillip felt his own stomach roll over. He loved animals, sent monthly contributions to the local animal league. "Why didn't you come to me and tell me about it?"

Again the boy shrugged. "Nora dared me to tell you. She said if I did, she'd tell mother I was lying and mother would punish me, 'cause mother always took Nora's side. I thought it over and reached the conclusion she was right."

"And Jeanne would have, too. I seem to forget how young we learn not to rock the boat."

"Yes sir. Especially when your sister is pos . . . weird."

"What did you start to say, Phil?"

"Nothing, sir."

"Come on, Phil. Level with me. Do you think your sister is mentally ill?"

"Yes sir. I do. I have for a long time."

"But that wasn't what you started to say, was it?"

The boy sat silent, looking at his father.

"What's wrong with you, Phil?"

The boy opened his mouth, then closed it. He shook his head.

"Phil, we've always been able to talk. Don't clam up on me now."

"You want the truth, dad? You want me to tell you what I really feel about Nora?"

61

"Yes. Very much. It might be very important. Your sister needs help."

"You're going to laugh at me."

"I promise I won't."

"I think she's possessed."

Phillip blinked. "Possessed? What do you mean, Phil? Possessed . . . how?"

"I think she's possessed by the devil."

6

Phillip stared at his son for a moment. He rose from his lounger and paced the den. He would occasionally pause to look at his son.

Phillip sat back down and said, "You want to elaborate on that, son?"

"I figured you'd laugh."

"I didn't."

"Dad, I was just a little kid when Nora was born. I remember, I really remember the day you and mother brought Nora home from the hospital. Lucky was just a puppy. Mrs. Mahoney was our housekeeper, remember?"

"You've got a good memory, son. Yes, I remember. I got angry because Mrs. Mahoney took one look at Nora and left. She never came back."

"Oh, she took more than one look, dad. She took several real good looks. I remember. I remember her looking down at me and saying, 'The poor child is marked. I will not stay in this house.'"

"Marked? I don't understand. But again, Phil, why didn't you come to me and tell me?"

"I tried, dad. I tried a lot of times. But you and mother were always busy with Nora. Finally I just gave up and shoved it back in my mind. Then . . . oh, I guess it was when Nora turned six, I began to notice things about her. The birthmark on the back of her neck, for instance. It began changing. And that's when she tossed such a fit about wanting to wash her own hair. Remember?"

Phillip slowly nodded his head. "Yes. And the fits she threw about going to church. What about this changing birthmark, son?"

"It's a number, Dad. A perfect six."

"A six?"

"Yes sir. That's it. I really didn't pay that much attention to it at first. I just figured it was caused by her growing, that's all."

Phillip sat quietly, trying to bring to mind what it was about the number six that refused to come to the fore in his mind. It would come to him. Something in the Bible, he felt. But he'd never been much of a student of the Bible. To tell the truth, he wasn't all that sure he believed very much of it.

All that was about to change.

"Phil, your mother and I have been remiss in some ways bringing you up. We didn't give you a solid church base. I apologize for that. Looking back, I can see where we leaned toward your sister's wishes. Catered to her whims. But from what you've told me, I can guess that you've given your sister a lot of thought. You really believe your sister is possessed?"

"Yes sir. The other kids are afraid of her. Animals don't like her. We can't keep sitters for very long. They're afraid of Nora. One told me she can make

. . . well, *things* . . . happen."

"What kind of things, son?"

"They won't talk about it. Adults don't seem to trust Nora. I've noticed that. And she is never invited to kids' parties. Never."

"I'll agree with what you say. But none of that makes your sister a prime candidate for devil possession."

"I know that, dad. It's just a . . . *feeling* I have. I've heard other kids talking. About Nora. Alec's little sister, for one. I've overheard her talking to her friends. They hate Nora, dad. They really hate her. They all say she's cruel and bitchy, she's selfish, she's mean—God, name it, Nora's been called it."

Phillip sighed. He could go along with his son believing Nora mentally ill; he believed that himself. But possessed by the devil? No. He didn't believe in all that baloney. Made for good books and movies, but it ended there.

Didn't it?

Sure it did! What in the world was he thinking?

"What do you think about your sister's turn-around?" Phillip asked.

"It's an act," the boy answered quickly and bluntly. "She's faking it. She probably overheard you and mother talking about sending her to a psychologist. She's playing with you, dad. She knows her mother will believe anything she says. She has mom wrapped around her little finger. It's you she knows has seen through her act."

Sharp boy, the father thought. Then something terrible in thought and scope struck Phillip. He tried to push it out of his mind. It would not leave. He stirred in his chair. He willed the awful thought to leave him. It remained. He shook his head, refused to accept it.

"What are you thinking, dad?"

"That little Donner girl. What was her name? Carla. That's it."

The boy's smile was not pleasant. "I was wondering when you'd put that together."

"Son . . . ?"

"That was no accident, dad."

"Do you know what you're saying, Phil? Carla Donner fell down the stairs."

"No sir. I will believe to my dying day that Nora pushed her."

Suddenly it was as if Phillip had been hurled forward in time. Scenes flooded his mind. He tried to push them out. They would not leave. It was cold in his mind. Dead, stark winter. Snow on the ground. He was hitting Jeanne with his fist. Phil was running toward him, shouting and cursing at him. The scene changed to some time later. He was stalking his son through the big house. Phil had a pistol in his hand. The father cornered the boy. Phil raised the pistol . . .

The scenes were gone.

Phillip could not remember any of them.

He came to the defense of Nora. "You have no right to say those things, Phil. You have no proof."

"Dad, there were three kids playing in the Donner house. Carla, Jenny Wright, and Nora. Carla hated Nora. A lot of kids remember her saying that. Including Jenny. And if mom would admit the truth, Nora told her she'd like to see Carla dead. I heard Nora tell mom that. Mother has just conveniently forgotten it.

66

Mrs. Donner stepped outside for two minutes at the most. When she got back, Carla was lying on the floor at the base of the stairs, her neck broken and her skull fractured. She died about twenty-four hours later."

"And Jenny was so traumatized by the . . . accident, she has never spoken a word since that day," Phillip picked it up. "The child is institutionalized."

"That's right. But none of it seemed to bother Nora, did it, dad?"

For a fact, Phillip thought, his daughter had shown no signs of remorse or grief. "No, it didn't, Phil."

"Dad, what ten-year-old kid keeps her room as spotless as Nora keeps hers? She has made her own bed, cleaned up, dusted, vacuumed—the whole bit— since she was about eight. I know, I know, that's what helped endear her to mother. Mother's little perfect child," he said bitterly.

"Sour grapes, Phil?"

"No sir. I know it sounds like it, but I don't mean it like that. Nora . . . well, dad, it's like she doesn't want anyone to *know* what she has in that bedroom."

Phillip looked confused for a moment. "Wait a minute, Phil. *Nora* does all that cleaning?"

"Yes sir. I thought you knew."

"I thought the housekeeper took care of Nora's room."

"Dad," the boy said patiently, "you're gone a lot of the time. When you're here, you leave for work before dawn and most of the time you don't get back home until after dark. Dad, you don't *know* what goes on in this house. Have you even seen the housekeeper we have now?"

"Of course I have!" Phillip said indignantly. "Mrs.

Horn."

The boy smiled sadly. He shook his head. "Dad, Mrs. Horn left here more than a year ago. Mrs. Carter takes care of the house."

"Oh. Oh really? I didn't know that. Your mother takes care of the household matters. Why did Mrs. Horn leave?"

The boy leaned back in his chair and looked at his father. "Three guesses, dad. And the first two don't count."

"Nora."

"Give the man a cigar. Or a cigarette," he said, looking disapprovingly at the cigarette in his father's fingers.

Phillip ignored that. "What did Nora do to make Mrs. Horn leave?"

"Dad, don't you and mom ever *talk*?"

"Not much in the last couple of years," Phillip admitted.

"Well, Nora did a lot of things. She wouldn't speak to the woman. Followed her around and stared at her. Sat and stared at her. The vacuum cleaner would come unplugged. Cleaning supplies would be moved. The air would be let out of the lady's tires. Furniture would be moved, and mom would jump on the housekeeper about it. When she would try to tell mom she didn't do it, Nora would tell mom the woman was lying. Then things began disappearing. Mom accused Mrs. Horn of stealing. Mrs. Horn really got mad and told mom off. Mom fired her on the spot. About six months later the missing articles were found up in the attic. Of course Nora put them there. I really felt sorry for Mrs. Horn. She was a nice person."

"Was?"

"She's dead. I heard she turned on the gas and stuck her head in the oven."

"How long after she was dismissed from here?"

"Not very long."

"Shit!" Phillip spat out the profanity.

Six six six! The numbers jumped into his consciousness. The Mark of Satan. That was it. He couldn't remember which book. "Sit still," he told Phil. He went into the kitchen for more coffee, his mind working overtime.

Carla Donner killed by Nora? Nora a killer? No. No, he couldn't accept that. The child was mean, yes; but a killer? No. Or was she?

Christ, he sighed. He didn't know what to believe.

He poured more coffee and returned to the den, taking his seat again. "I'm sorry to say, Phil, I don't even know where the Donners moved to."

"Vermont. They were both killed a year after Carla died."

Phillip lifted his eyes. "Killed? How could I have missed that?"

"You were overseas, dad. It was old news by the time you got back."

"How were they killed, son?"

"I think their car ran off the road. Plunged a couple of hundred feet into a creek or a river. Something like that. I remember the date, though. May the sixth."

Then it came to Phillip. That other elusive little worry-bug that had been prowling around the dark reaches of his mind.

Nora was born January sixth. Jeanne's parents died

69

thirteen months later, on February sixth. Fourteen months later, on March sixth, the kitchen in the Baxter home caught on fire. A neighbor saw the smoke and called the fire department.

Six six six.

Coincidence?

Maybe.

But there were just too damn many sixes popping up. Did that mean anything, though? Phillip just didn't know.

Father and son heard the front door open and close, the sounds of laughter drifting to them. Jeanne and Nora were home.

On Thanksgiving the Baxters drove up to Bridgeport to have the traditional dinner with Jeanne's Aunt Morgan. Jeanne's brother came down from his farm and for a few hours Phillip forgot about his daughter's strange behavior.

Aunt Morgan was one of Phillip's favorites. In her late seventies, the lady was spry and her mind sharp. Her home, located outside of Bridgeport proper, was a old Victorian-style house that had been in her family for more than a hundred years. Filled with expensive paintings and antiques and priceless china and vases, here, Phillip recalled, Nora had always been on her best behavior. She might be a holy terror on the way up, but once here, she epitomized Jeanne's perfect child.

And Phillip had never understood that.

But just as it had been for more than two weeks, Nora's behavior was faultless. She was indeed the perfect little girl.

And still Phillip could not bring himself to trust her.

Unknown to Jeanne or Phil, or to any of his partners except Sam, Phillip had asked one of the junior members of the firm to investigate the death of Carla Donner and the institutionalizing of Jenny Wright. Discreetly, of course. But so far it had produced nothing except slow going.

"What's the point of it, Phillip?" Sam had asked.

"The truth, Sam. As much of it as I can find out, that is. But damn, it's a cold trail."

"Nothing so far, huh?"

"Odds and ends and bits and pieces. But nothing I can tie together."

"You going to keep on it?"

"I don't know."

"What if Jeanne finds out?"

"She'll divorce me," Phillip said flatly and surely. "And do it without a second thought."

"Risky, Phillip."

"Yeah, I know."

Sam had walked away, scratching his head.

Aunt Morgan broke into Phillip's thoughts on this Thanksgiving day. "You look troubled, Phillip," she said. "Is everything all right?"

"I don't know, Morgan. Nora is . . . well, strange at times."

"She's a little brat!" the old woman said bluntly, surprising Phillip. "I set her straight a few years ago. I told her I saw right through her goody-goody act, and if she ever pulled any of her damned shenanigans around me, I'd use her butt for a broom."

71

Phillip chuckled for a moment. "I'm surprised she didn't run straight to her mother and tell on you."

"Oh, I'm sure she did. But Jeanne knows who controls the purse strings in this family. *Me!* Jeanne was cool to me for a time after that, but she got over it."

Phillip looked at Morgan and opened his mouth to speak, then closed it.

"Something else, Phillip?"

Phillip shook his head.

"Yes, there is. But you're not ready to talk about it. I'll be here when you get ready."

"I'll remember that."

"Please do."

After spending Thanksgiving day with the family, Phillip left Jeanne, Phil, and Nora and took the train back to Stamford and a taxi to his still and quiet home. He was just a few days away—he hoped—from wrapping up a long-running case, and was forced to work on it overtime. Jeanne accepted it without complaint. She'd been married to a successful attorney for too long not to know this was what bought the fine clothes, the expensive automobiles, the lovely home, and the security.

Phillip worked two twelve-hour days, spending a lot of time on overseas calls, and was deep in sleep when the phone rang on Sunday morning. He fumbled for the phone, dropped it, and finally hauled the whole thing into bed with him.

"Yeah," he said groggily.

"Your child is evil," a woman's voice said. "She is marked by the devil. She must die. Kill her before it is too late."

Phillip came wide awake and sat up in bed. "What? Who is this?"

"Your girl-child is marked by Satan. She must die before she kills you all and spreads her evil."

"Do you know what you're saying?"

"Perfectly well. You have been warned."

The connection was broken.

Phillip looked at the clock on the night stand. Nine o'clock. He felt rested and alert. And scared. The adrenaline pumping. He looked at the buzzing receiver in his hand. Slowly he hung up and swung his legs to the floor.

Sitting on the side of the bed, he thought: I know that voice. I've heard that voice before. But where?

It would not come to him.

He showered and shaved and made coffee. Just as he was sitting down behind his desk in the study, the phone rang again. Phillip clicked on the phone recorder and picked up the phone.

"Phillip Baxter," that voice sprang through the lines. "Your daughter is evil. She is just like your sister."

"My *sister*!" Phillip shouted. "I don't have any sister."

"Yes, you do. Her name is Jane. You never saw her. She was . . . put away the year you were born. She is evil, just like Nora."

A sister? "Who is this. Goddammit, tell me who you are."

"No. I cannot. That would serve no useful purpose. I shouldn't even be talking to you. It's dangerous. I've been watching Nora since she was born. The child is the daughter of the Dark One. She must be destroyed.

73

If she reaches the age of twelve, it will be too late. Then she will be almost impossible to stop."

"What do you mean?"

"Think about it, Phillip," the mysterious but somehow familiar voice said softly.

"I don't know what to think. Except that you're nuts!"

"You're forgetting your early training in the Church."

"Sixes?"

"Yes."

The age of twelve. "But that makes only two sixes." The Bible verse came to him: And his number is Six hundred threescore and six.

From Revelation. The Mark of the Beast.

"Add the six she wears hidden on her neck," the woman said.

Six six six.

"How do you know about that?"

"I know many things. Destroy the child before she destroys you. You must do as I say. Now I must go."

"Wait! Don't hang up. Tell me how a little girl could destroy me."

The woman sighed. "She can turn son against father, brother against brother. You must remember this: She has the power of Satan with her. She is very dangerous."

"Don't hang up. Please." Suddenly Phillip's head seemed as though it would burst as a raging headache struck him. He had a very quick and vivid glimpse of what he hoped was not the future. Again it was bitter cold outside, with snow on the ground. In the house Jeanne was lying on the floor, her mouth bloody.

Phillip was stalking his son through the house. The boy had a gun in his hand. Phillip was cursing his son. The boy raised the pistol, pointing it at him. The scene changed. People were milling about a funeral home. A coffin lay with flowers covering it. But Phillip could not see who was in the casket. It was a man, but he could not make out the face. People were crying. The scene changed again. A terrible sight filled Phillip's head. A young man was hanging from a banister, a rope around his neck. His neck was broken, his face dark, his tongue protruding from swollen lips.

Laughter exploded through Phillip's head. Then sounds of weeping overrode the laughter.

His headache eased. The terrible scenes faded away.

"I know what you're going through," the woman said. "And I'm sorry. You must be watchful of your sister. She is evil."

Phillip listened, not knowing what to believe.

The woman said, "You must burn Nora's companion. That must be done quickly. Before it is too late."

"What companion? What are you talking about? You're speaking in riddles."

"I cannot be more specific. To do so would mean my death. I have been hiding from the Dark One and his followers for years. Burn it. But be careful. It will know you are coming to do it harm. Be careful."

"What are you talking about? What companion of Nora's?"

"Then you must call a priest. Together, the two of you must destroy Nora. It has to be done. I know it's a terrible thing to say. But it must be. Goodbye."

Before Phillip could protest, the connection was broken.

Phillip thought he heard laughter in the house. A shuffling sound coming from above him.

He lifted his head, listening. But the sounds were gone.

Was it real? Had he really heard the sounds?

What was going on?

7

Sam listened to the tape recording Monday morning in Phillip's office. He listened to it twice before he spoke.

"And you don't have any idea who this woman is?" Sam asked.

"I feel as though I should know. Yes, I *do* know that voice. But I just can't quite put a name to it."

"Your sister?"

Phillip shook his head. "Sam, I don't *have* any sister."

"Are you sure?"

Phillip sighed. A man totally frustrated. "Not . . . entirely. No."

Sam smiled. "You'll have to forgive my ignorance of the New Testament, Phillip. What about this Beast you told me about?"

"Six six six. The Mark of the Beast. It's in Revelation. A lot of people believe that Satan's children are born marked."

"And you?"

"Hell, Sam, I don't know what to believe. I'm not a religious person. I know practically nothing of the Bible."

"Have you played this tape to Jeanne?"

"God, no!"

"Dr. Harte?"

"No."

"I'd like to play with Dr. Harte," Sam said with a grin, trying to lighten the moment. "I'd let her psychoanalyze me any time she wanted to."

"You're just horny."

"You got that right."

Phillip leaned back in his chair, glad to have something on his mind other than idiot phone calls from crazy women. "What about your hot patootie?"

"She turned out to be a codfish."

Phillip struggled through the morning, finding he could not concentrate on his work. Luckily for him, his long-running case was over. The other party had just that morning agreed to settle out of court.

The other partners would occasionally walk past Phillip's office, looking in, seeing their friend staring into space, or breaking pencils in his big hands, or sitting with a look of frustration on his face. The junior partners and secretaries stayed away from Phillip that morning.

Ed Weiskopf stuck his head into Phillip's office just after lunch. "Got a minute, Phillip?" he asked.

"Lots of minutes, Ed," Phillip said, disgust in his voice. He threw his pencil on his desk. "I can't get with it today."

Ed sat down, looking at his longtime friend. "Phillip, you haven't taken a vacation in five years. You're tired, buddy."

Phillip opened his mouth to protest, knowing what was coming. Ed waved him silent.

"No arguments, Phillip. We've all talked it over. You've logged more air travel time, both stateside and overseas, than the rest of us combined. Man, you're *tired*. We haven't spoken of it, but I can sense that you . . . well, have some personal problems. You want to talk about it—fine. If not, that's fine as well. But you are going to take a vacation. There won't be any problem shuffling around your case load. A month, Phillip. That's what we want you to take. You know we're going to shut it down in a couple of weeks anyway. We've agreed on that. So come back after the first of the year. OK?"

Ed was right. He was tired. Beat. Phillip felt as if his brains were bowlegged. He was not mentally alert. And that was dangerous for any lawyer. He nodded. "You're right, Ed. Thanks for seeing it where I couldn't."

"No problem. One more thing: If I'm to handle this Jenny Wright case of yours, I need to know more about it."

"It's a nothing case, Ed. One I'm doing for a friend. But it's a dead end. I'll tell Ballinger to stop his snooping. I might pick it up when I come back."

"You sure?"

"Yeah. It's OK." Phillip smiled. "You guys are right, Ed. And I appreciate your concern."

"No sweat, sarge. Enjoy, and don't worry about the office. I promise we'll only take your most lucrative cases away from you."

The friends enjoyed a good laugh at that.

"You're going to think I have lost my mind, Sheela," Phillip said.

She smiled across her desk. "Well, you have certainly come to the right person if that's the case."

"I'm sure. Sheela . . . I have uncovered some, well, information you may find pertinent."

"Oh? Pertaining to Nora?"

"Ah . . . yes. And then again, you might want to call whatever institution you use and have me committed."

"Oh, I don't think so. Well, I'm intrigued, Phillip. Are you going to leave me in suspense?"

Phillip took a deep breath. "My son Phil seems to think, believe, that his sister is possessed by the devil." He dropped it into her lap and waited for some reaction.

She did not change expression or bat an eyelid. "Oh? Well, that's interesting. And what do you think?"

Phillip opened his mouth, closed it, then finally said, "I don't know what to believe."

"What happened, Phillip? Talk to me."

He told her everything Phil had told him. He wrapped it up by using her cassette player to play the tape of the last phone call he had received Sunday morning.

Sheela listened intently. She lifted her eyes to his. "Have you discussed any of this with your wife?"

"Good God, no."

"Your son?"

80

"No. Only with one of my partners at the office. Sam Sobel."

Sheela leaned back in her chair and looked at him. She seemed undecided as to what she should do. She took a deep breath and said, "I think there is someone you need to talk with, Phillip. His name is Father Joseph Debeau."

"Why do I need to talk with him?" Phillip had not left the Church with any good will behind him. He still harbored many bitter feelings.

"Because his field is—well, how to put this? It would be unfair to Joe—Father Debeau—to call him a mere exorcist. He is much more than that. He has studied Satan and his methods for most of his life. During my years as a psychologist, I have called on him several times."

"Possessed children?" Phillip was very doubtful about that, and it showed in his tone.

She shrugged and smiled at that. "The children were helped, nonetheless. Besides, didn't the woman tell you to get a priest?"

"Sheela, as far as I'm concerned, this whole thing is a ugly joke."

"Do you really believe that?"

Phillip stared at her for a moment. "No. I guess not. But how in the world would I explain my seeing a priest? To my wife, I mean?"

"I don't see why you should have to explain. I'm not asking that you take the girl. Just that you talk with Father Debeau."

"Well, maybe that way. Sheela, why do I get the feeling you're not leveling with me? And I think I'm correct in feeling that during our first meeting you

81

paid much closer attention when I mentioned that old jack-in-the-box—right?"

"Very astute of you. Yes, I did. I collect antiques. That is how I met Father Debeau. At an antique shop. We became friends. He is really a fascinating man. After a time, he told me about this old jack-in-the-box that is supposed to be cursed. Tragedy always seems to befall its owner. I could not help but think this may be the jack-in-the-box Joe told me about."

Phillip waved her silent, as the same time shaking his head. "Sheela, this is getting a bit mumbo-jumboish for me. Now, as a professional person, I should think you would dismiss curses and hobgoblins and zombies and such as nonsense."

"I can't dismiss evil, Phillip. Evil is very real. Evil is more than just morally wrong or injurious. It's more than imputed bad character or conduct. It is a *sin*. And what is sin? It's the transgression of divine law."

Phillip remembered something Sam had said one day. He smiled. "I have a friend that says some sin is downright delicious."

She laughed. "Stop trying to evade this, Phillip"

"Oh? You don't agree with my friend?"

"No comment."

"Sheela, I can't take this seriously. I'm sorry, I just can't."

"Won't you even talk with Father Debeau?"

Phillip expelled a breath of air. "Well, I have to come back to the city tomorrow to wrap up some matters at the office. I'm taking some time off. You gather up your priest and we'll have lunch. You like *frutta di mare* salad?"

"That depends on what's in it," she said.

He smiled. "All sorts of things. Squid, octopus, shrimp—whatever you like. Mussels vinaigrette, tripe, mushrooms. I'll meet you both at Felidia's."

"We'll be there."

The man sitting at the table with Sheela rose and extended his hand. Phillip shook hands, inspecting him.

The priest was dressed in a pinstripe business suit, a light blue cuff-link shirt, dark tie. His hair was silver gray, his face tanned. His handshake was firm. About six feet tall, Debeau looked fit, solid, and rugged, more like a retired boxer than a priest. Midfifties, Phillip guessed. An inner strength seemed to flow from the man, touching Phillip with invisible force.

Phillip saw that the man's nose had been broken, probably more than once. And at least once badly set.

"Forgive me for asking, Father," Phillip said. "But did you used to box?"

"Call me Joe," Debeau said with a smile. "And I'll call you Phillip. OK? Fine. Yes, I still work out with the heavy bag whenever possible. Sheela tells me you were quite a boxer."

Phillip did not recall mentioning his boxing days to the psychologist. So how did the priest know about that? Odd.

"Yes, I did, Joe. I entertained—briefly—the thought of turning pro."

"What changed your mind?"

"My wife."

They all laughed at that.

Phillip added, "Plus a right cross from a welter-weight that knocked me cold as a hammer."

Debeau chuckled as the men sat down. "And where did that happen, Phillip?"

"In a honky-tonk outside of Fort Benning."

"Good place for it," the priest said.

The three of them ordered coffee. The maitre d' had, at Phillip's call-in reservation, placed them at a table offering relative privacy, enabling them to talk freely.

"Forgive me for being blunt, Phillip. Are you Catholic?"

"No. I was raised in the Church, however. I broke away from it as a boy." Phillip waited for the priest to pursue that. He did not.

"Sheela told me about Nora. Why do you think she objected so strongly to entering a church?"

"I don't know, Joe. To be honest with you, neither my wife nor I are especially religious, so we didn't attach much significance to it. We wondered about it, but passed it off as a childhood stage."

Joe nodded his head. His eyes remained unreadable. "Would you please describe the jack-in-the-box, Phillip?"

"It's . . ." Phillip struggled for a one-word description. He could not find any one word. "It's hideous. It's grotesque. It's . . ." His eyes met Sheela's. "Evil," he concluded.

She smiled.

"If you feel that way," Debeau said, "why don't you get rid of it?"

"I don't know."

"Why did you buy it?" the priest asked.

84

Phillip forced his thoughts back to the curio shop. That day. He struggled to recall exactly what had prompted him to purchase the old jack-in-the-box. But the memories were cloudy, distorted. He shook his head.

"I can't seem to think," he said. "Ed was right. I've been working too hard."

"No, Phillip," Debeau said softly. "You're being manipulated."

"Manipulated? I don't see how that could be. Manipulated by whom?"

The waiter approached the table, interrupting any reply the priest might have been ready to offer. When they had ordered, Phillip again asked, "Manipulated by whom?"

"Satan," Debeau said softly.

Phillip leaned back in his chair. "Joe, I don't believe in all that cra—nonsense."

"Then I feel very sorry for you, Phillip. For Satan is most assuredly alive and well."

"If that is what you choose to believe, Joe."

"You didn't believe it as a child?"

"I suppose I did. I don't remember. I've deliberately blocked most of that out. But that still doesn't change my position on the subject."

"Yet," Debeau said.

Phillip shrugged noncommittally.

"Why did you leave the Church, Phillip?"

"My dad was killed, my mother took off for parts unknown. I haven't seen nor heard from her since. I was undergoing terrible doubts and fears. The priests laid tons of drivel on me, meaningless platitudes. I may have been only a boy, but I knew lies when I

85

heard them."

"We're only human, Phillip. We don't have all the answers. Priests, preachers, rabbis are not instant problem solvers. Most of us—but not all, certainly—know the Bible, at least in the way each of us was taught to interpret it. We understand, or profess to understand, divine law, and what the Bible teaches on dealing with human problems. But we are still frail human beings."

"Susceptible to mistakes?"

"Of course." Joe replied. "Unfortunately, some of us won't admit to any mistakes. But I'm not one of them. I have a bad temper, Phillip. And I tend to speak my mind. I am something of a maverick."

Phillip put down his coffee cup and laughed. "I get your message, Joe, and I think we're going to get along. I really do."

8

They were alone in the school's dressing rooms, and Nora had left her sweetness in the darkness of her mind. She was glad to be free of the pretense.

"Nigger, nigger!" she taunted the black child, speaking softly, just loud enough for the girl to hear her.

"You leave me alone!" the child said. "You leave me alone or I'll tell on you, Nora Baxter. You're *evil*."

Nora laughed at her. "No one will believe you. Nigger, nigger," she taunted again.

Gloria started crying.

"Ugly!" Nora hissed at her. "You're so ugly you belong in a zoo."

Tears running down her face, Gloria rushed toward Nora, running into her, knocking her down. Nora kicked at the girl.

"You're crazy!" Gloria gasped.

Nora fell, then pulled herself up, sitting on the concrete floor of the dressing room. Her dark eyes glowed with evil and hatred. "No one touches me unless I want them to. No one! You'll die for that."

The black girl turned and ran down the aisle between the rows of lockers, tears nearly blinding her.

Nora sat on the floor and stared at the retreating back of the tormented girl. Then she heard muted laughter and strange voices in her head, and music playing.

Nora smiled. Her dark eyes glowed with a strange light, glowing fiercely.

The running child began screaming as her hair burst into flames. Blinded by fear and fire, her face blistered and peeling, the child slammed into a locker, bounced off, and fell to the floor, shrieking in pain, kicking and jerking as the flames reached her clothing and she burst into a human fireball.

Nora sat where she was, some distance from the burning girl. She smiled as she listened to the girl's screams of agony. At the sounds of running feet and excited voices, Nora suddenly began crying, the tears coming on mental request. She jumped up and reached into her locker, jerking out her coat. She ran to the ball of fire that once was a human being and began beating at the flames that now covered Gloria, from her smoking, cooked head to her shoes.

Nora carefully placed her foot close to the flames, allowing her jeans leg to smoulder a bit. "Help, help! she screamed. She beat at the flames. "Somebody please help us!"

Gloria had slipped into unconsciousness, burned over most of her body. The flames had destroyed her eyes, melting them. Gloria was now a charred mass of once-human flesh.

Several teachers, a counselor, and a coach reached the smoking scene, pulling Nora away, beating at her ankles, putting out the flames that were threatening to consume her. They wrapped Nora in a blanket and the coach swept her up into his arms and ran toward the school's small infirmary. A Vietnam combat vet and former Navy corpsman, the coach had seen many, many burn victims. After taking one look at Gloria Waltham, lying sightless and charred on the concrete, he knew the child had no chance. He knew that in all probability, her brains would be cooked.

And suddenly little Nora Baxter was a media heroine, having risked her life in an attempt to save another child. TV, radio, and print journalists interviewed her, standing in her smoky jeans, her dark eyes shining. She was a real-life heroine.

Almost everyone believed her. She was a good little actress. With her blond hair and pretty face, she suckered nearly everyone.

"Nora hates black people," Phil reminded his dad that evening, after dinner. "You remember the black ladies we've had in here as maids? How Nora treated them? There is no way she would have risked her life to save a black child, dad. No way."

"People do change, son. Perhaps your sister is growing up."

The boy just sat and looked at his father, open doubt in his eyes.

"How is the little girl?" Phillip asked finally.

"Dead. She died about two hours ago. I heard it on the news. Nora set her on fire, dad. I don't know how

89

or why, but she did."

"You have no proof of that, son. And don't ever say it where your mother can hear it. We are all going to try very hard to pull this family back together again. You understand?"

"Yes sir. Dad? You know this goody-goody attitude of Nora's is an act, don't you?"

But Phillip would not reply to his son's question.

A few miles away, Nora's school counselor said to her husband, "Nora Baxter hated Gloria. Gloria came to me many times, complaining about the way Nora treated her. She told me Nora called her filthy names."

The coach, who was the counselor's husband, only shook his head. "You were there, Bette. You saw the girl beating at the flames with her coat. Hell, Nora's *own* clothing was on fire."

"I know, Rich. But it still doesn't wash. The police could find nothing flammable or combustible in that entire locker room. Absolutely nothing to create that kind of intense heat. And they searched every locker. And I went over every inch of Nora's clothing while she was in the infirmary. No matches, no lighter. No nothing."

"Then how could she have started it, Bette? And more important, *why*?"

"I don't know. But she did. I just know she did. There is something very wrong with that child, Rich. I've heard rumors about her for the past several years. The other kids—up until now—have never liked her."

"We've been over this before, Bette. Get off the kid's back, will you?"

But the memory of Gloria's charred little body

would not leave the counselor's mind.

Phillip awakened, his heart pounding, sweat beading his face. He did not know what had awakened him in such a state. He had not been dreaming, although from time to time he did still dream about Nam. As did, he suspected, anyone who had served over there. Or over anywhere, in any war, for that matter.

He looked at the clock on the nightstand. The numbers glowed at him. Twelve-one.

The witching hour, that thought came to him.

Nonsense! he thought.

Then he heard it, very faint but very real. Laughter. A man's laughter, and then a woman's laughter. No. No, that wasn't quite correct. It sounded more inhuman than anything. But the genders were definitely different. It was that same laughter he'd heard the other day. Or thought he'd heard.

No mistaking it now. It was real.

He looked through the gloom at Jeanne. She had been so upset over Nora's very minor burns, she'd taken a sedative before retiring. She was deep in drug-induced sleep.

Then Phillip remembered: Nora had encouraged her mother to take the pill. Daughter consoling and counseling mother.

Phillip lay still, controlling his breathing, listening to the sounds of the night. There it was again. That haunting laughter.

He slipped softly from the the warmth of the bed and found his slippers. He put on his robe and walked quietly to the bedroom door, putting an ear to the

91

wood, listening. The laughter was real, no doubt about it. He gently opened the door and stepped out into the hall to stand for a moment, trying to locate the source of the strange laughter.

It seemed to be coming from Nora's room. No . . . well, yes. In part. Or was it echoing around the house? Some of the laughter seemed to be coming from above him. In the attic. But that was impossible.

Phillip padded down the carpeted hall until he reached his daughter's room. He listened at the door. There the laughter was much more audible. But surely that wasn't Nora laughing? Couldn't be. This laughter was . . . inhuman sounding.

Phillip lifted his head as the laughter seemed to shift, coming from above him.

Then that faded away.

He tried the doorknob. It turned easily in his hand. He pushed the door open. He stood in open-mouthed shock and bewilderment, staring at the sight on the floor.

The jack-in-the-box was out, snake-like, its long canvas-covered spring neck swaying back and forth to the strange music playing from the depths of the box.

But it wasn't playing the Funeral March. Phillip struggled to place the tune. He could not. But he was sure it was a German marching song.

Was that possible?

He looked at the jack-in-the-box. The hinged mouth was opening and closing, laughter rolling from the mouth. Nora was seated on the floor in front of the snake-like jack. She was dressed in the filthiest clothing Phillip had ever seen, the dirt and crud crusted on the jeans and blouse.

The music stopped abruptly.

The eyes of the jack-in-the-box shifted, clicking as they moved, stopping and staring at Phillip.

"Du bist mir immer!" the jack-in-the-box said. Then it laughed.

Nora slowly turned her head to look at her father. Hate sprang from her eyes. She began cursing him, the vocal filth rolling from her mouth. The breath from her mouth stank, filling the room with a foulness that was almost unbearable.

"Get out!" Nora spat at him. But the voice that ripped in his direction did not belong to Nora. This voice was like none Phillip had ever heard. It was deep and hollow-sounding. And very menacing.

Phillip backed away from the hate-filled voice and angry eyes.

He blinked his eyes in disbelief. Had that jack-in-the-box actually spoken to him?

He looked at the swaying clown's head. The mouth opened, laughter rolling.

"Get out!" Nora hissed at him. "Don't you *ever* again set foot in my room without my permission. Get out!" she screamed at him.

Phillip's doubts and shock were replaced by a hot anger. He stepped toward his daughter.

"Fool!" she shouted at him. "Get out! Leave me be!"

The room turned unbearably hot; sweat streaked Phillip's face. Nora laughed at him, that sickening foulness once more lashing from her open mouth, enveloping him in its stench.

The jack-in-the-box laughed and laughed and swayed side to side. The jaw popped open, the laughter taunting and evil-sounding, hate-filled and worse. Ominous.

"No!" Phillip said. "This is not real."

Nora looked at her father, an evil smile curving her young lips. Then her eyes began rolling around and around in her head. Phillip stared in horror. That was impossible. Humanly impossible. She could not be doing that.

The heat in the room increased as Nora turned her head around. *Completely* around. Her neck seemed made of rubber.

"No!" Phillip whispered.

His daughter howled at him, a savage animal howling, only the whites of her eyes showing. That foulness once more covered him with its stink.

Some sort of slime leaked from Nora's mouth. The sight sickened Phillip. He backed away in disgust. The slime rolled from her mouth, dripping onto her filthy shirt.

Phillip backed further away.

Nora spat at her father, the spittle a muddy bloody brown, staining the carpet where it landed, stinking globs of it.

Phillip fought to keep from vomiting.

"Get out!" Nora howled at him.

"*Rasch, rasch!*" the jack-in-the-box said.

Phillip backed out of her room, into the hall. He closed the door behind him and stood for a moment trembling. He heard the laughter again, but this time it was coming from above him. He ran down the hall to Phil's room and burst in. The boy was sleeping soundly. Good Lord, Phillip thought. *Surely* he'd heard it.

But the boy was deep in sleep.

Phillip left his room, closing the door. He walked back to Nora's room. He was afraid, really afraid to open the door. He took several deep breaths to get calm, and he forced himself to open the door. He looked in, not knowing what to expect.

The room was dark except for a nightlight plugged in across the room. The jack-in-the-box was nowhere to be seen. Nora was sleeping in her canopied bed. She wore a soft white nightgown. The room smelled faintly of a young girl's perfume.

Phillip backed out of the room, into the hall, closing the door. He didn't know what to believe. Had it all been a dream? A nightmare? Surely it must have been. There could be no other explanation for it.

That's what it was. Just a dream.

He walked slowly back to the master bedroom and slipped in beside his sleeping wife. She stirred, and then settled down. She murmured something Phillip could not catch.

Surprisingly, sleep came swiftly to Phillip, almost as soon as he closed his eyes. When he awakened, hours later, his memories of that awful few moments were jumbled and confused. That was one terrible nightmare, he concluded. He wondered what had brought it on.

Then he put on his robe. A foul odor drifted to him. He lifted his arm, sniffing the sleeve of the robe. His nose wrinkled in disgust.

"Time to wash this thing," he muttered. He tossed the robe into the dirty clothes hamper. He didn't know what had caused the odor, but he was convinced Nora had nothing to do with it. Nothing human could have done the things Nora did in his nightmare. And old toys don't laugh and speak.

He did not believe in ghosts or hobgoblins or the supernatural. All that stuff made for exciting books and movies, but other than that . . .

He had suffered through a very bad dream, and that was all it had been. Sam would tell him it had been something he'd eaten.

So Phillip put it out of his mind.

Almost.

An entire month with nothing to do. That's what Phillip was thinking as he listened to the sounds of the house. He was wondering what he was going to do with a month's vacation. He hadn't had a month with nothing to do since college.

He had the house to himself. Jeanne had gone into the city for some early Christmas shopping; Nora and Phil were at school. Gloria Waltham's funeral was to be held today, and then Nora's school would be dismissed early.

The nightmare returned to him. "What a dream," he said. "Crazy, crazy."

Phillip decided he'd start by cleaning out the attic. More than ten years of junk was piled up there. Everything from worn-out clothing to unwanted presents and broken furniture.

And a few surprises that Phillip didn't know about.

But first he'd have another cup of coffee, sit in the den, and read the morning paper, read it in leisure, a luxury that for years had been confined to Sunday mornings. If then.

He fixed his coffee, took his favorite chair, and was getting into the lead story when he heard the laughter.

He remembered that laughter. This time the insaneness seemed to be coming from above him.

He laid his paper aside and listened, sure he'd been mistaken.

No, there it was. Very faint, but very real. Laughter.

"What the hell is going on around here?" he said aloud.

He rose from his chair and walked into the hall, standing for a moment at the base of the stairs, listening. The laughter came again. It chilled Phillip with its evil sound.

He began slowly climbing the stairs, following the sounds of evil. Down the hall to Nora's room. He listened at her door. No, it wasn't coming from in there. He lifted his head and strained all his resources, attempting to pinpoint the location.

The attic. It had to be coming from the attic. Phillip wondered if someone was playing a cruel joke on him. He dismissed that thought.

He walked on down the hall to the short flight of steps that led to the attic of the old home. There he paused.

And the evil laughter stopped.

Then his head felt giddy as he thought he heard someone calling his name.

He leaned against the wall as his knees threatened to buckle.

He knew there was no one else in the house. So was this his imagination?

Sure—it had to be.

"Phillip," the faint call drifted to him.

"I'm going mad," he muttered. "I must be losing my mind."

"Phillip. Come to me, Phillip,"

The voice faded, replaced by a hissing sound. That changed into a whine, then a soft moaning. More laughter.

His dream returned to him. Nora's hissing at him. He shook that away. Pure craziness, he thought. It was a dream, a nightmare. And that's all it was.

The laughter returned.

Phillip climbed the steps to the attic door, putting his hand on the doorknob.

The laughter stopped. Now it was a whining, yowling sound. He put an ear to the door. It definitely was coming from behind that door.

"Now it's your turn," the voice whispered. "I've paid. And now it's your turn to suffer, just like I suffered."

Phillip heard himself ask, "Who are you? What do you want with me?"

This is ridiculous! he silently chastised himself. None of this is real. It's my imagination working overtime, that's all.

"They locked me away." The voice floated from the other side of the door. "And now you're going to pay for that."

"Who locked you away?"

But insane laughter was all that greeted his question.

A foul odor drifted from behind the door. Where had he smelled that before? It came to him. In his dream.

He turned the knob and pushed open the door.

Something dark and angry and ugly came flying and howling at Phillip. Phillip yelled as the back of his head exploded in pain. He was hurled into darkness. He fell forward, splintering the door as his full weight struck it.

9

Phillip opened his eyes. He looked up into the face of Father Joseph Debeau. The priest's face seemed to be covered with a mist. Phillip blinked his eyes. The mist disappeared.

"Don't try to get up," Debeau said. "You've had a pretty nasty crack on the head. Just lie still for a moment."

"Joe," Phillip said, his voice thick. He cleared his throat. "Where did you come from?"

"I came calling. Just as I was about to ring the doorbell, I heard you yell and then fall. The front door was unlocked. I came in. You were lying at the top of the stairs. You seemed unconscious. That woman knocked me down when she ran out the front door."

"Woman?" Phillip sat up, leaning against the wall. "What woman?"

Debeau shrugged. "I don't know who she was. The woman who attacked you, I suppose. She ran around the side of the house, into those woods back there."

"Jesus Christ! I never saw any woman. Did you

100

call the police?"

"No."

Phillip's head had stopped its spinning. His vision had cleared. He had a headache. He blinked his eyes and said, "Why not?"

"I haven't had time."

"Good point."

"I don't notice you rushing to call the police, either."

"Yeah. Another point. What did she look like, Joe?"

"Hideous. Her eyes were mad. She was a . . . a hag. Hair all matted and dirty. Her clothing was ragged and filthy. She appeared to be half-starved. That was all I could see. To tell the truth, she just about frightened the life out of me."

Phillip slowly got to his feet, Debeau steadying him. He stood for a moment, felt his strength returning to shaky legs, and said, "I'm OK now. Wait a minute! The woman was in the attic. That's what came jumping and screaming at me. But then . . . No, she couldn't have hit me in the back of the head. So who did?"

"I haven't any idea. Perhaps you turned?"

Phillip shook his head, and was immediately sorry he had. "No. I crouched defensively, but I didn't turn around. I remember that. But that's all I remember."

"I neither saw nor heard anyone else."

Phillip remembered the laughter, someone calling his name. "Someone was laughing at me, calling my name."

Father Debeau's eyes narrowed. "Are you sure of that?"

"Positive, Joe. I . . ." He sighed. "Come on. Let's get some coffee. I really think it's time for us to talk."

"Yes," Debeau said. "I believe it is."

The back of Phillip's head was sore and tender to the touch, but the skin had not been broken. And no, he did not wish to go to the hospital.

"If I start getting blurred vision and severe headaches, then I'll go," he told Debeau.

Before he could tell the priest about his strange dreams of the night before—and he was still sure that was what they had been—the phone rang. Mrs. Carter, the housekeeper. She was not feeling well and would not be in for several days.

"That's perfectly all right, Mrs. Carter," Phillip assured her. "I'll tell Mrs. Baxter. Hope you get to feeling better soon."

"I forgot about the housekeeper," Phillip said. "I don't even know what she looks like." He glanced at Debeau. "I don't remember telling you where I live, Father."

"You didn't. But you did tell Sheela. She told me."

"I see." Phillip wasn't too sure he liked that.

The priest smiled. "I can be very persuasive."

"I'm sure." Then Phillip told him about his dreams.

The priest sat quietly. When Phillip had finished, he said, "And you believe it was a dream?"

"Of course. It is physically impossible for a human being to do those things."

"And the voices that called you?"

"Obviously that was real."

"Tell me about the child that was burned at Nora's school."

102

"You do get around, don't you?"

"I read the papers and watch TV. Your daughter is quite the little heroine."

Phillip said nothing. He found the aspirin bottle and took two painkillers. He looked back at the priest. "You don't believe Nora tried to save the child's life?"

"I was not there, Phillip. I don't know what to believe."

"I see. And today you just happened to be in the neighborhood?"

"Oh no. My being here is no accident. I came to see you."

"Why?"

"Because I'm worried about you. I think you are in danger."

Phillip nodded his head. The pain had lessened. He glanced out the window. Spitting snow. Early in the season for snow, he thought. Then he recalled his glimpses into the future. He told Debeau about them.

The priest shook his head and sighed. "What can I say? What can I tell you? What do you *want* me to say?"

Phillip sat down. "I don't know, Joe. You think I'm hiding from the truth, don't you?"

"Honestly, yes, I do. If you had not thought something was dreadfully wrong with your daughter, you would not have sought Sheela's professional help."

"I think Nora is . . . perhaps mentally disturbed, Joe. But I do not believe the girl is possessed by Satan."

"Oh, neither do I."

Phillip stared at him. "You *don't*?"

"No. I think she is the child of Satan."

Nora's entire class was bused to the church for Gloria's funeral. The kids had carried a change of clothing to school for the services, changing in the dressing rooms of the gym. At the church the minister referred to Nora several times during the service, calling her a friend of Gloria's, an unselfish human being, and a true heroine.

Nora sat like a little angel doll during the services, paying close attention to the minister's words. She especially enjoyed all the other kids looking at her, admiration in their eyes. The other kids had forgotten all the bad things they had said about Nora. They had forgotten all their parties that had excluded Nora. The kids had forgotten how they all, every single one, had shunned Nora.

But Nora remembered it all. She had forgotten nothing. While the minister spoke of unselfish love, Nora's head was filled with the blackest hate; thoughts of dark and evil revenge boiled in her brain. She fought to keep the laughter from spilling from her mouth during the services.

Now she would get the others, one by one. They would pay dearly for taunting her. Oh my, yes.

And now, Nora thought—time for a little fun.

Nora stared at the closed casket, her eyes glowing. A cracking sound interrupted the minister's words. He fell silent. The bier shifted, the casket trembled. The metal legs collapsed, the casket tumbling to the floor, the lid springing open. Gloria's charred little body rolled out, sprawling in death on the floor.

The church was filled with screaming people, adults and kids alike. People were running all about, not knowing what to do. Some were being sick on the floor of the church.

To Nora, the sight was hysterically amusing. She could scarcely contain her laughter.

"You can't be serious!" Phillip blurted. "Nora the *child* of Satan?"

"To my way of thinking, Phillip, all signs point to it. I've confronted this before."

"I should order you out of my house!"

"I would leave."

Phillip waved that off. "You know I don't mean that. What signs are you talking about?"

"What she did last evening is a good starting point."

"I was dreaming all that." Phillip stubbornly stuck to his story.

"I doubt it."

Phillip said nothing.

"How about that woman calling your name?"

"What has she to do with Nora?"

"She's involved."

"I don't believe it. That . . . person simply broke into this house, and I caught her. She is probably an escapee from some institution."

"That's what the voice told you, wasn't it?"

"In a manner of speaking. Locked up, she said."

"And . . . ?"

Phillip shifted away from that. "I know one thing

I'm going to do. I'm going to burn that damned jack-in-the-box."

"Then you do believe the old toy is playing some part in all this?"

"I . . . suppose, Father. I don't know what to believe. I am going to destroy it, though."

"We must be very careful attempting that, Phillip," Debeau cautioned him.

Phillip picked up on the *we*. "It's just a toy, Father."

"It is much more than that, Phillip. According to legend, the old jack-in-the-box was at one time a major element in satanic worship. It once belonged to a commandant of a Nazi death camp. It can cause evil in otherwise innocent people. It has a long and very bloody history."

"If it's the same jack-in-the-box as described in the legend."

"It is," the priest stated. "I felt the evil when I approached the house."

The house! Phillip thought. Could it be the house? Nonsense! he mentally brushed that from his mind. It's just a house. He looked at Debeau, looking at him. Somehow he felt the priest was reading his mind.

Phillip expelled breath in a long sigh. His head still ached, but the pain was abating. In his mind the jack-in-the-box was secondary. He wanted to know about that woman in his attic. and who had hit him from behind? He said as much.

"I don't know who struck you. But could the woman have been your sister?"

"Joe, don't you think I would have found out if I had a sister? My father left me a very comfortable estate. It was never contested. I have never found any papers pertaining to a sister being institutionalized anywhere. Monies would have had to be paid to keep her in any kind of facility. Believe me, I have gone over dad's papers many, many times. I simply do not have a sister."

"Then why don't you call the police and report the attack?"

It was just the beginning of a day of long sighs for Phillip. He added another to his mounting score. "I don't know," he admitted. He knew; he just didn't want to say it. And he knew he wasn't fooling the priest. He was afraid. He began pacing the den. He knew he had to start checking birth records. He had to talk to people who had known his father and mother. But that was going to be difficult, if not downright impossible. Phillip could barely remember the old neighborhood in New Haven. If he had a sister, there would be a record of it. Somewhere. He told Father Debeau of his thoughts.

"Yes, I agree. And I'll help you. Right now, let's take a look at this jack-in-the-box."

They searched Nora's room thoroughly. The jack-in-the-box was not there.

Or was not visible.

That was in the mind of both men. But neither wanted to put it into words.

They shared a silent look and continued their searching.

Phillip found the filthy clothing Nora had been wearing the previous evening. He was hesitant even to touch the filth-encrusted garments. When he looked up at Father Debeau, there was sadness in his eyes.

"Truth time, I suppose, Father."

"Yes. I am so sorry, Phillip. Please believe me."

Phillip nodded his head. He was so confused. He did not know what to believe or what to do. "I saw Nora leave for school. She did not have the toy with her."

"It's hiding from us."

"Joe, it's . . . it's just an *object*. It can't hide all by itself."

"Legend says it can do anything it wishes to do. Providing it has someone to do its bidding. We're not going to find it until it is ready for us to find it. What are you thinking?"

"Let's look outside. Try to find where that woman went."

Father Debeau and Phillip tracked the mysterious woman's trail as she had torn through bushes and thick underbrush in the woods behind the Baxter house.

But the trail ended abruptly at a small creek. Debeau went south along the bank, Phillip heading in the other direction. They could not find where the woman had left the cold waters of the creek. By the time they met back at the starting point, the snow had intensified. The men trudged back to the house, neither of them being dressed for any prolonged outside winter activity.

Unanswered questions were strong in Phillip's mind. He worried them about in his aching head. Who was the woman in the attic? How long had she been up there? And why? Where did she fit into this puzzle? Surely she fit in somewhere. Was the unknown woman on the phone correct? Was the woman his sister? Did he have a sister? Was all this some sort of sick joke being played on him? My God, who would do such a horrible thing?

No, he answered some of his silent questions. No, it was no joke. He was sure of that. He could think of no one who would do such a thing. And Nora . . . what about her? He had almost convinced himself it had all been a nightmare. But finding the filthy clothing had proven that to be only wishful thinking.

Back at the house, Father Debeau declined Phillip's invitation to come in. "I have to return to the city. When do we start checking birth records?"

"In the morning."

"Can you meet me at the station in Stamford?"

"Second train?"

"I'll be on it."

And once more Phillip was alone in the big house.

He prowled the attic, flashlight in hand, the strong beam touching the dark pockets where the unshaded light bulbs did not reach, creating pockets of deep shadows.

What he found nauseated him.

Whoever the woman was—or *what*ever she was, the odd thought came to him—it was obvious she had been living in the Baxter's attic for some time. Months, at least. Phillip found a pile of dry gnawed-on bones, taken, he guessed, from their garbage. Behind several wooden crates—Phillip had absolutely no idea what might be in the crates—he found where she had been hiding and sleeping. A heap of disgustingly filthy blankets, a dirty, tattered old dress, and a pair of old torn tennis shoes. An old coat of Jeanne's. He remembered that Jeanne had discarded it . . .

109

God, more than two years ago. He had put it out for the trash pickup.

Two years ago!

Had the woman been living up in the attic for two years? Obviously so.

He cast the beam of light around the odious living area of the stranger. On the wall by her blankets, tacked above the floor at eye level, was an upside-down cross.

Never much of a fan of horror movies and books, Phillip nonetheless knew what that symbol meant.

Devil worship.

The house creaked. Phillip froze, listening. He raised the beam of the flashlight. A sigh of resignation passed his lips.

Just above the cross was tacked a small photo of Nora.

10

He was sitting in the den when he heard the sounds of Jeanne's car pull into the drive. He knew Judy Gipson had gone with her into the city; he hoped Jeanne had dropped her off at her own home. He didn't feel he could tolerate any of Judy's gushing, breathless conversation.

Jeanne was alone. She breezed into the den, her arms filled with packages.

"Need any help?" Phillip asked.

She shook her head. "No, this is it. Did you have a good day?"

He grunted. "You're back early. I didn't expect you until this evening."

"Oh, we went to the mall in Stamford. Found some darling things."

"That's good." Then he told her what had happened that day, leaving nothing out. He did not tell her about his encounter with Nora the past evening. From the look on her face, she was having a difficult enough time accepting even a part of what he was not telling her. And Phillip couldn't blame her.

She listened, her face first paling, then reddening

from ill-concealed anger. "You're crazy!" she blurted. "You're *lying*!"

Her reaction did not surprise him. He gingerly touched the back of his head. "Then come over here and feel this. But please do it carefully, darling."

She gently touched the bump on the back of his head. She grimaced and said, "How did you get that?"

"I just told you, Jeanne." He stood up. "Come on. I'll show you."

He had left the door as it was, broken at one hinge. "Good Lord, Phillip!"

He led her through the attic to the spot where he had discovered the blankets, the upside-down cross, the small photo of Nora. He was afraid it would all be gone, vanishing as mysteriously as it had appeared, like most of the events in his life during the past few days. But it was all in place. He shone the flashlight beam on the filthy blankets and clothing, the small pile of gnawed bones.

Jeanne gasped and backed up, her face reflecting her disgust.

"Still think I'm crazy or lying?" Phillip asked.

She shook her head, her lips pressed tightly together. "I want you to . . . please get rid of that disgusting stuff!"

"I don't think so."

"What?"

"I want her to come back."

"Now I really think you've gone off the deep end. This . . . person is obviously insane. And you want to entice her back here, endangering us all? Phillip, be reasonable. Get rid of this junk. Did you call the police?"

"No."

"No? For God's sake, why not?"

He wasn't ready to tell her the real reason he hadn't called the police. Not yet. "Because I want the truth, Jeanne. All of it." He pointed to the blankets. "This person, Nora's behavior, everything weird that's been happening, it's all tied in. I have no proof of that, none at all, but I know it is true."

"Oh, I see now. Oh yes," Jeanne said, her initial anger returning. "It's always back to Nora, isn't it, Phillip?"

"Jeanne, I didn't say any of this was her fault. I just said it's all tied in. Give me credit for a little intelligence, will you? You're thinking like an over-protective parent while I'm trying to reason this out. Work with me on this, Jeanne. Please?"

She stared at him, refusing to reply.

"I'm not blaming Nora, honey."

"Oh yes, you are! Now wait a minute, Phillip. Just hold on. You said the woman came at you out of the attic, right?"

"I was wondering when you'd put that together."

Neither of them heard Nora enter the house. She climbed the stairs and stood very silently, listening to her parents.

Jeanne said, "Then who hit you on the back of the head?"

"I don't know."

"*Two* crazies living up here?"

"God, I hope not." He wondered what she would say if he told her about his encounter with Nora?

"Then . . .?"

113

"I don't know, Jeanne." Then he decided he would level with her as much as he could. He told her about the phone calls, the voices insisting he had a sister. He told her about Father Debeau, and that the priest had seen the woman as well. He did not tell her about seeing Dr. Harte.

"And you taped the phone call?"

"Yes, I did. The second one. But you are not going to like it."

"Why?"

"Because of the content," Phillip said, hedging somewhat.

"I'm sure part of it concerns Nora. You're always picking on her."

Ever since the tension between them had increased, Phillip had noticed that Jeanne would sometimes avert her eyes when speaking to him. He wondered about that.

On the landing Nora listened to every word, her dark eyes shining with raw hatred. She had implanted the dream-thought into her father's mind last night, so she felt sure she was safe on that. But her friend had been discovered and was gone. And that angered her.

Now she knew what she must do. It was early, and she had planned on having more time. But she couldn't wait much longer.

Nora slipped quietly down the stairs and reopened the front door. Cold wind blew in. This time she slammed it shut.

Phillip had just asked if Jeanne was having second thoughts about Nora when the door slammed. Was that relief on her face at not having to answer the question? He thought so.

"Nora?" Jeanne called.

"Yes, mother."

"Go into the den, darling. Mother will be down in a minute."

"Yes, mother." Nora went into the den and looked at the twin eight-by-ten pictures of her mother and father on the mantel. Both of them were early photos of the couple. The girl leaned close and spat into her father's face, the spittle dribbling down the glass front. She hunched her hips obscenely toward her mother's photo. Then she smiled.

"Answer my question, Jeanne," Phillip said.

Again, Jeanne would not meet Phillip's eyes. "Are you going to tell the kids?"

"Not yet."

"But you're especially not going to tell Nora, are you?"

"That is correct. Why are you refusing to answer my question?"

Jeanne turned around and walked away, her back stiff with anger. She walked down the stairs, leaving Phillip with more unanswered questions than before mulling about in his mind. She's hiding something from me, Phillip thought. She isn't lying, as I originally felt, but she is hiding something from me. But what in the world could it be?

The dream, the vision, that propelling thrust and glimpse into the future hit Phillip hard, striking him with much more force than ever before, numbing him.

A child was laughing. Phillip felt sure it was Nora. Parts of the house were a wreck, furniture smashed and broken, some drapes torn down, lying wrinkled on the floor. As before, Jeanne was down on the floor, her mouth bloody. "I'll kill you!" Phil was shouting at his father. The boy held a gun in his hand. "I'll kill you, Dad. Leave me alone, goddamn you."

"You no-good little bastard!" Phillip snarled at his son. "I'll kick your goddamned head in, boy!"

Phil raised the gun. The gun looked somehow familiar to Phillip.

The big house seemed to sigh.

Nora's wild, insane laughter was joined by that awful dirge from the jack-in-the-box.

The vision faded.

Phillip stood in the attic, gently rubbing the back of his head. He sighed and walked out of the attic, cutting off the lights. As he reached the foyer, the doorbell rang. He opened the door. A woman he did not know stood on the snowy steps, looking at him.

"Yes?"

"Mr. Baxter?"

"Yes. May I help you?"

"I'm Mrs. Strassel. Mrs. Carter has been hospitalized and will be out for some time. The agency told me to come over and introduce myself. If I am acceptable, I will replace Mrs. Carter."

Phillip opened the door wider and motioned for the woman to come inside. "Please come in out of the weather, Mrs. Strassel." The woman inside, Phillip closed the door and looked at her. "I don't mean to be rude, Mrs. Strassel, but aren't you . . . well . . ."

She smiled at him, her eyes twinkling. "A bit too old for housekeeping work?" she finished for Phillip.

Jeanne joined her husband in the foyer just as he was saying, "Well, to be perfectly frank, yes, that's

116

what I was thinking."

"I'm sixty-three, Mr. Baxter, and fit as a fiddle. I come with excellent recommendations. I don't do heavy housework and I don't do windows. I am not just a good cook, I am a superb cook. I can work the month of December and perhaps a week or so into the New Year. I am an expert pastry chef and can fix main courses that I guarantee will put twenty pounds on you in a month."

Both Phillip and Jeanne smiled. Jeanne said, "Well . . ."

Nora joined them. "Hi!" she said brightly. "I'm Nora. Are you going to be our new housekeeper?"

"My, what a pretty little girl," Mr. Strassel said. "Well, I might be your housekeeper. Would you like that?"

"Oh yes. I can see we're going to be friends right off."

"That settles it," Jeanne said. She looked at Phillip. "We have parties planned for this month, plus that New Year's Eve thing that it's our turn to host. We must hire someone." Phillip shrugged. He never got involved in matters concerning the domestic help. Jeanne looked at Mrs. Strassel. "Are you married?"

"Call me Else. No, I'm a widow. Mr. Strassel passed away some years ago."

"Would you consent to live in for a month, Else?"

"I usually do, Mrs. Baxter."

"Oh, that's wonderful. The housekeeper's quarters are just off the kitchen. They're not large, but they're very comfortable. Your salary . . ."

Else waved that away. "Standard agency rate, Mrs. Baxter."

117

"Fine," Jeanne said. She looked down at the woman's suitcase. Funny, she hadn't noticed that before. "You came awfully sure we'd hire you, Else."

"Eh?" Phillip said, not understanding his wife's remark.

Else smiled. "I have never been turned down, Mrs. Baxter. I don't know why, but it's true."

"You're keeping your record intact. Come on, I'll show you to your quarters. Would you get her suitcase, Phillip?"

"What suitcase?"

"That one." Jeanne pointed.

Phillip looked down, eyeballing the large suitcase. He hadn't noticed it. Must be the bump on my head, he thought, picking up the suitcase. Christ, what did she have in the thing—lead bars?

And neither Phillip nor Jeanne thought to call the agency to check on Mrs. Else Strassel.

After settling in, Else inspected the kitchen and the pantry, then sent Phillip packing off to the supermarket with a grocery list about a foot long. As he was backing out of the drive, Phil came in from school. Phillip waved him over and they drove to the store together.

On the way, Phillip told his son most of what had transpired that day. "Wow!" the boy said, shaking his head.

"Yeah."

"Oh, dad? Did Nora tell you what happened at the funeral?"

"No. She didn't say anything to me."

"The, ah—what do you call it?—the thing the casket sits on?"

"The bier?"

"Yes sir, that's it. It collapsed. The casket hit the floor and sprang open. The little girl's body fell out."

"Oh Lord! Horrible! What a terrible thing for the girl's parents to see."

"Yes sir. But the funeral people say it couldn't have happened. Those things lock in place. They said—and this is street talk—somebody heated the legs, weakening them. Investigators found where the legs had been subjected to extreme heat, causing them to collapse."

"And it couldn't have been done a long time ago, the stress just now affecting the legs?"

"They don't believe so. Someone would have noticed it. And it couldn't have been done during the last twenty-four hours. A member of the family was with the little girl constantly from the moment the morticians got through with her.

"Then how . . .?" Phillip let that trail off as suspicions grew in his mind.

"No one knows, dad. But it sure happened."

Phillip thought of Nora's eyes whirling around in her head. The intense heat he had experienced while in her room. Her entire head turning around and around as if made of rubber.

"What are you thinking, dad?"

"Nora."

"Yes sir. Me too."

11

No doubt about one thing, Phillip thought, sitting down with a contented sigh after dinner. Else Strassel certainly knew her way around a kitchen.

She had served *rouladen*: braised stuffed beef rolls, prepared with hot mustard, chopped onions, bacon, pickles, celery, leeks, and parsnip. She had prepared *spatzle*: tiny dumplings very slightly flavored with nutmeg, quite delicious. And *pilze mit tomaten und speck*: mushrooms with tomatoes and bacon.

And everybody had eaten too much.

Then Else received quiet cheers and won Nora's heart by serving a dessert of *lebkuchen hauschen*: a lovely gingerbread house. It was so beautifully decorated, Jeanne hesitated to cut into it.

Sam had called just before dinner. He had hit a minor snag with one of Phillip's cases. Phillip told him about Else and what she was fixing for dinner.

Sam had grunted. "You come back into the office goose-stepping, and I'll personally shoot you." Then he laughed. "It sounds delicious. I wish I'd been there."

"Well, you're aware of the time of year and what

I'm going to do this weekend. So come on out and spend some time.

"Saturday all right?"

"Perfect."

"Good. I'll rent a car." Sam knew what reaction that would bring from Phillip.

"Oh no, Sam. Don't do that. The last time I rode with you I nearly lost all faith in automobiles. I'll pick you up at the station. Call me Friday and tell me what train you're coming up on."

"OK," Sam said, when he finished chuckling. "Talk to you Friday."

Jeanne came into the den and sank onto the sectional. "I ate so much I feel absolutely miserable."

"I know the feeling. Where are the kids?"

"Nora is with Else. They really hit it off well. Phil is up in his room, studying. Phillip?"

"Umm?" He pretty well knew what was coming.

"I don't want to hear that tape."

"As you wish, Jeanne."

"You're not angry?"

"Not in the least." He was rather relieved, not looking forward to more arguments with Jeanne. He had made up his mind to go this alone; he felt he could get more done that way. He glanced at Jeanne. She was definitely worried about something.

"What do you have planned for your month off?" she asked.

"A little genealogical work." Not quite a lie. But he was not prepared for the shocked look on his wife's face. For some reason, that remark really shook her. But why?

"Well, that's . . . interesting, I guess. Your family

or mine?"

"Mine." She was very relieved at that, and it showed on her face. Was there something hanging on her family tree she would prefer to keep hidden? If so, what? "I'd kind of like to know about my ancestors."

"Your mother or father's side?"

Phillip paused for a heartbeat. "Mother's side of the tree."

She chewed on her lip. "Well, don't dig too deeply, you might find a pirate hanging from a yardarm." She tried a smile that turned out to be a grimace.

What was going on? "We all have our black sheep, darling."

"Yes," she said softly. She took a deep breath. "I'll be at Judy's most of Thursday and Friday. The country club bash, you know?"

"Yeah," he said drily. He endured the things every year. He hated them. "I'm going up to New Haven and start there. Leave about seven forty-five, I guess. Be back when you see me."

Her stare held a curious flavor, one that Phillip could not read. Was that fear in her eyes? Phillip thought it was. But fear of what?

"Have fun," she said flatly. She left the room.

Phillip and Father Debeau definitely did not have fun. They struck out all the way around in New Haven. Lots of babies had been born in 1940-41, but none to Elizabeth and Phillip Baxter. There was not a single family still living in the old neighborhood who was there when Phillip was a boy. The doctor who had delivered Phillip was dead. Everywhere they turned, they hit a dead end.

Over lunch Debeau said, "I have a suggestion."

"I'm certainly open."

"It will probably be expensive, but I would suggest hiring a private detective."

Phillip groaned. "Now why didn't I think of that? The firm uses a very reputable agency. Sure. That's the way to go with this matter. I'll call him right now."

"Phillip? Have him check on your house while you're at it."

"What do you mean?"

"I told you I felt evil when I looked at your house, remember? I would say that is a very old house."

"Between eighty and a hundred years old. I think that's what the realtor told me."

"Have him check its history. You might be surprised at what he finds."

Phillip and Debeau met with Paul Weaver the next morning. Paul was average in height, weight, complexion, hair color, and dress. Nothing about him stood out or attracted attention. But Phillip knew the man was one of the best P.I.'s in the city. He had worked in various branches of military intelligence for twenty years, pulling the pin after his twenty.

Phillip told Weaver everything that had happened, then played the tape for him. He leaned back and braced himself for laughter from the P.I. It did not come.

"Interesting case," Paul said. "Finding out if you have a sister won't be all that difficult. I'll just check birth records in a five-state area. It's all computerized now; it won't take long. But odds are she was born in Connecticut. I would say the phone call probably came from your mother, Mr. Baxter."

"My *mother*?"

"Yes. That would be my first guess. The woman in your attic was probably your sister—if you have a sister, that is. If anything weird happened in or around your house, that won't be hard to find out. I'll be a free-lance writer doing research on old homes in the area. People love to talk. I should have something for you in a couple of days. A week at the most."

"You make it sound awfully easy, Mr. Weaver," Debeau said.

"Well, it involves a lot of good contacts and a lot of legwork and snooping, Father. I've been doing this most of my life. I went into the army right out of college, straight into the ASA. Then into, well, other areas of intelligence work. I've operated in most of the free world countries. Spent two years working covertly behind the Iron Curtain. Believe me, this case is a piece of cake."

Phillip and Sam spent most of Saturday gathering up and untangling Christmas lights and decorations, checking them out, and replacing bulbs. Sam got a kick helping out, keeping up a steady stream of wisecracks. Else Strassel frowned at Sam's wisecracks.

"Are you Jewish?" she asked.

"Yeah," Sam grinned. "*Un*orthodox."

Else shook her head and walked off.

Over coffee Phillip asked, "Don't you believe in anything, Sam?"

"I don't know," Sam replied, turning slightly serious. "I used to. Kind of like you, I suppose. Certainly

124

there is a higher power. I think it would take an arrogant fool not to believe that. Has the Son of God already walked on this earth? I don't know. Neither does anybody else. Except God. And I'm not exactly His confidant. Our time in Nam kind of turned me around, so to speak. Got me to thinking about a lot of things. We used to talk about it, remember?"

"Yeah, I remember. Seems like a million years ago." He looked around him. "Sam? You ever think about the VC girl we raped?"

"Yeah." His reply was soft. "Funny you should ask about that. I hadn't thought about it in years. Just completely forgot about it. Then . . . oh, 'bout two-three weeks ago it just popped back in my head. Hell, I *know* when it was. It was the day we—you—bought that jack-in-the-box." He raised his eyes and stared at Phillip. "That's it, isn't it? That thing is evil, right?"

"Yes. As ludicrous as it seems and sounds." Phillip told Sam about his hiring of a private detective. He leveled with his old and dear friend about everything.

"This is *wild*, Phillip."

"Tell me."

"You know, I've joked and kidded most of my life," Sam said. "I once reached the point where no one would take me seriously. My father was about ready to disown me. Really! But I'm deadly serious about this . . . situation you're in. It frightens me. And I'll tell you why. Outside of my family I have never told this to anyone." He paused, collecting his thoughts. "When I was a kid I used to dream, have nightmares, about a jack-in-the-box. It came close to unhinging me. I used to hate the night; I was afraid to go to sleep. I fought sleep. Almost became very ill because of that. I was,

125

oh, a good thirteen years old before the dreams finally faded."

"You know what brought them on?"

"Sure. I have—had—a couple of aunts who made it out of Belsen. They used to tell stories about one of the camp commanders and his jack-in-the-box. The man was totally perverted and insane. He used to carry the jack-in-the-box out to the line-ups. He'd flip the switch and the thing would jump out, grinning and bobbing and rolling its eyes. Whoever it looked at got gassed. I was joking back in that curio shop to keep from screaming. And I'll tell you something else, Phillip."

Phillip thought he knew what was coming. He braced himself.

Sam's hands were clenched into white-knuckled fists. "That's the same jack-in-the-box."

Phillip walked around the house, trying to collect his thoughts. He felt like an innocent man in a jail cell. He did not know what to do. He felt Sam was correct in thinking the jack-in-the-box had once been in the hands of a Nazi. And the devil.

Was there a difference?

He thought not.

But what to do?

When he walked back into the den, Sam was holding a book and looking at Phillip strangely.

"Sam?" Phillip said. "What's the matter with you? You look ill."

"Looks like you had us all fooled, ol' buddy." Sam's voice was odd sounding, strained.

"What do you mean?" Phillip was sure he detected

some . . . *force* in the room, working its evil.

"You're quite an actor, Phillip. I wasn't snooping into your personal effects, but I just found it odd that you would have something . . . this hideous in your library."

"What is that book?"

"Come on, Phillip. Don't try to lie your way out of this. Anyway, if the book is bad, the dedication is even worse."

"What are you talking about, Sam? Let me see that book."

Sam tossed the book to him. Phillip had never seen it before. If he had, he would have burned it. It was a book defending what the Nazis did to the Jews during the thirties and forties. "Sam, I have never seen this book before in my life."

"Yeah, sure. And I guess you don't know about the dedication either?"

Phillip opened the book. The handwriting jumped out at him.

TO MY GOOD AND DEAR FRIEND, PHIL-
LIP BAXTER: MANY THANKS FOR YOUR
LEGAL HELP AND THE MONIES YOU'VE
SENT OVER THE LONG YEARS. YOU
HAVE BEEN A GODSEND. PLEASE AC-
CEPT THIS BOOK AS A SMALL TOKEN
OF MY GRATITUDE.

J.MENGELE

"Mengele!" Phillip blurted. "Oh, come on, Sam. You don't believe I would help that creature, do you?

And if I did, would I leave this book out in the open? Think about it, man. You've known me for a quarter of a century. You know me better than any living man."

Sam glared at Phillip. Then his shoulders slumped as Phillip felt that odd force leave the room. Sam's eyes changed. He laid the book on an end table and rubbed a trembling hand across his face.

"What is happening here, Phillip? Of course I don't believe any of that. Why did I say it? I felt like I, well, wasn't in control. What is going on?"

Debeau's words came to Phillip. "We're being manipulated, Sam. Divide and conquer, I would say."

"Gee, Phillip, I feel like such a *fool*. I feel as though I've been in a trance." He looked at the table. "Where did I put that book?"

"Right there on the table. I watched you put it there."

Both men looked at the table.

The book was gone.

In its place lay a tiny silver swastika.

Sam looked at what had been the most hated symbol in the free world. He lifted his eyes to Phillip's. "Phillip you wanna know something?"

"Sam, I'm just as scared as you are."

"No, you're not, buddy. And I don't have to tell you why."

Sam sat straight up in bed. He was soaked with sweat. His face felt hot, feverish. His heart was beating so fast he thought it might explode in his chest.

That dream. That evil-looking jack-in-the-box with

that horrible clown's face. Swaying and laughing. He hadn't had that dream in almost thirty years. But he sure had dreamed it this night. He was certain that lousy swastika had brought it on. He looked at his watch. Twelve-one.

But had it been the dream that had awakened him? Sam didn't think so. He didn't know why, but he didn't think it was. He mentally willed himself to calm down, take deep breaths. He lay in bed, his heart slowing. He listened. There! There it was. Someone was calling his name.

"Samuel," the whisper came to him, a harsh and guttural sound. "Samuel? Are you listening, Samuel?" The whispering changed to an ugly laugh.

"Yeah, I'm listening," Sam returned the whisper. He sat up in bed. He hit his forehead with the heel of his hand. "What am I saying? What am I doing? This isn't real. I'm still dreaming."

"No, you're not dreaming. Listen," the voice said.

Voices filled Sam's head. Screaming and crying and begging. Men and women and children. Screams of pain as someone was being beaten. The thudding of clubs striking living flesh. A harsh voice yelled, "*Achtung, achtung, schwein-gesicht. Lassen, lassen.*"

"No!" Sam whispered. "I won't listen to this. I won't!"

"What's the matter, Samuel? Are you afraid? Would you like to take a trip, Samuel? Back to 1941, perhaps? I can show you some lovely sights and sounds."

Hysterical laughter boomed in Sam's head, almost blocking out the weeping and screams of pain.

"Hear that, Samuel?" the harsh voice whispered.

"They're going to the gas chambers. Would you like to see it?"

"No!" Sam roared. Screaming his rage, he jumped from the bed and flung open the door, almost running into Phillip, who was racing up the hall.

"What's the matter, Sam? I heard you yell."

"Voices, Phillip. Terrible voices. Someone was talking to me. And I dreamed about that jack-in-the-box."

"I can't rouse Jeanne. It's like she's in some sort of trance. I looked in on Else. She looks like she's in a coma.

"Phil?"

"There's his bedroom." Phillip pointed.

Sam threw open the door. Phil was sleeping on his back, his mouth open. He appeared to be unconscious rather than sleeping.

"Phil!" his father shouted.

The boy did not move.

The men looked at each other, neither of them having any idea what might be coming at them next.

A strange, glowing light appeared at the far end of the hall, close to the short flight of steps leading to the attic.

Both men stared speechless as the light became brighter.

Then they both heard the music. That somber dirge that came from the base of the jack-in-the-box.

"We're dreaming all this, aren't we, Phillip?" Sam asked, a hopeful note in his voice.

"I wish we were, buddy."

Something stepped out of the bright light.

"Phillip. Look! It's Nora. But what is that thing

behind her?"

Everything Phillip had ever read or seen concerning the occult leaped into his consciousness. He glanced up the hall, averting his eyes quickly as the form behind Nora became more distinct. The . . . *thing* was shrouded in a red mist.

Phillip grabbed Sam by the shoulders and flung him to the carpet. "Don't look, Sam. For God's sake, don't look."

"What is it?" Sam asked, his voice muffled, his face pressed against the carpet.

"I think it's Satan."

12

The red glow faded with the dying echoes of Phillip's words. The hall was plunged into darkness that was broken only by a tiny night-light plugged in at the other end of the hall.

Phillip sat up, releasing his grip on Sam. Both men stared in unbelieving horror at the sight that confronted them.

Nora stood holding the wooden case containing the jack-in-the-box. She was dressed all in black, with some sort of shining silver-looking tabs on her shirt collars. Neither man could quite make out what they were. They looked like silver skulls. Nora stood smiling at the men. But her smile was grotesque, filled with ageless evil. She held out the box.

Both men scooted backward on the carpet.

"Poor daddy," she said. "Are you afraid, daddy dear?"

Phillip stood up, Sam rising with him. They moved toward the child.

"Nora," Phillip said. "Let me help you, baby. Please? Tell me what that thing was standing behind you a moment ago."

"My master, daddy. Too bad you didn't look more closely at him. I would have been saved a lot of trouble."

Phillip remembered that no mortal could look upon the face of Satan and live. "Won't you let me help you, baby?"

"*You* help *me*?" The child laughed. "That's funny. Daddy is funny. But soon daddy will be dead. Dead, dead daddy."

Her words chilled both men. Sam moved with Phillip toward the girl. "Nora," Sam said. He held out his hands to the girl. "Why are you doing this?"

The question seemed to confuse the girl. She tilted her head to one side. Then, as the men watched in fascination and revulsion, she turned her head completely around and laughed at them. Both men heard a faint whispering. They could not make out the words. Nora's eyes glowed. "Because it's what I was born to do."

Sam stopped in the hall. Suddenly he was filled with an anger that had been suppressed for years. He walked toward the girl. "I'll slap the smugness off your face, Nora. And then I'm going to destroy that damned filthy toy."

She laughed at him and flipped the clasp on the front of the box. The clown's head sprang out. The hinged mouth worked up and down. "*Du!*" The guttural sound erupted from the mouth as the eyes stared at Sam. "I choose *you*!"

Screaming his rage, Sam darted forward, grabbing the snake-like spring neck in both hands. The jack-in-the-box howled in rage as strong fingers closed around the neck, choking the ugliness.

133

"You Nazi son of a bitch!" Sam yelled.

The clown head dipped down, the jaws opening, the yellow teeth snapping and biting at Sam's arm. Sam yelled in pain as the teeth clamped onto flesh, drawing blood.

Phillip ran toward the macabre scene. He was stopped abruptly as a force struck him in the chest, knocking him backward, sending him sprawling on the hall floor. He struggled to rise. He could not. It felt as if a giant foot were on his chest, pinning him. He could do nothing except lie flat on his back and watch as Sam battled the snake-like jack-in-the-box.

The eyes of the clown head rolled and glowed as the jaws dipped and struck again and again, reddening Sam's arms with blood. Sam screamed in pain as the mouth closed down hard on his arm, the teeth sinking in, the head twisting like an attacking shark.

Wild, insane laughter sprang from Nora's mouth. The girl seemed impervious to the struggle going on around her. Calmly she held the wooden box in her small hands. Sam tried to slap the girl, but she seemed to be protected by an invisible field. She spat in Sam's face. An ugly, foul spittle, that muddy, bloody brown. It leaked from Sam's face, dripping onto his pajama top, staining it.

The jack-in-the-box shrieked, twisting free of Sam's grasp. Laughter rolled from its mouth. With blood dripped from the bites and cuts on his arms, Sam backed away. He cursed the jack-in-the-box and Nora.

"Foolish man!" Nora hissed at Sam. "Now you will die as well!"

"Devil-bitch!" Sam panted the words, his chest

heaving from near-exhaustion.

Nora laughed at him. She cursed the man in rapid-fire German, speaking so fast Sam could make out only a few of the words.

Sam roared his rage and lunged at Nora. The same inexplicable and invisible force that had knocked Phillip down and held him to the floor struck Sam, slamming him to the carpet, pinning him there. That red-tinted glow once more enveloped Nora and the jack-in-the-box. The light brightened, becoming too fierce for the men to bear. They turned their heads and closed their eyes. Neither knew what to expect. They braced themselves for the worse.

Both men were plunged into darkness and unconsciousness.

Phillip and Sam awoke on the carpet in the hall. They were stiff and sore and confused. With a groan Sam sat up, looking at his arms. The sleeves of his pajama tops were caked with dried blood.

"I thought it was all just a bad dream, Phillip."

"Would that it were," Phillip said, getting to his feet and extending his hand to Sam. "Come on. We've got to treat those bites on your arms."

"How could a *toy* do those things?"

"I don't know. But we can't deny the fact that it's dangerous."

"By itself, or does it have to have help?"

"You're asking me questions that I have no answers for, buddy."

The bites were painful, but not deep. After washing them, Phillip put iodine on the cuts, Sam wincing as the medication was applied. Both men were startled to see dawn breaking over the horizon, dull gray fingers probing the shadows.

"Do you remember what time it was we hit the hall?" Phillip asked.

"I looked at my watch when I woke up. It was twelve-one. I don't think I'll ever forget that. Or that damned voice, those pitiful voices in my head."

"Twelve-one. That's the same time I was awakened the other night."

"The witching hour." The joke fell flat.

"That's the same thought I had. What was that outfit Nora had on, Sam? It looked familiar to me."

"Yeah, me too. It was a goddamned storm trooper's uniform, Phillip. SS shit. Did you see those death's-heads on the collars?"

"That's what they were?"

"In living color. A Nazi jack-in-the-box, Phillip?"

"Just an evil one."

"One and the same. No point in going back to bed now. But it's going to be interesting to see how Nora behaves this morning."

"She'll be all sweetness and light, Sam. Bet on it. We can't prove anything that happened last night. Jeanne and Phil and Else were all out cold. So it'll be our word against Nora. And you know who Jeanne will believe."

Sam was thoughtful for a moment. "Phillip, what in the hell are we going to do? We can't go to the police. They'd laugh us both right to the nut house."

"Play it by ear. We have the tapes and that swastika for evidence. We'll write down everything that happened to us last night. We've got to tell Father Debeau and Weaver about it. As for today, we behave as if

136

nothing happened."

"And then . . .?"

"I don't know. I just don't know."

But the swastika was gone, disappearing as mysteriously as it had appeared.

"You're sure this is where you put it?" Sam asked.

"Positive. It's just gone."

Jeanne, Nora, Phil, and Else dressed and went to church. Jeanne was miffed because Phillip elected to stay behind, and she did nothing to hide her irritation.

Sam was wearing a long-sleeved shirt that hid the bite marks.

Nora stood with a slight smile on her pretty face. She said, "Perhaps father did not sleep well last night, mother."

Sam had to struggle to choke back his grunt of disgust.

"Perhaps not, darling," Jeanne said. "Come along. We don't want to be late."

The echo of the door closing had not died away before Sam said, "If somebody gave an award for evil, she wouldn't have any competition." He looked at Phillip. "Sorry, Phillip. I keep forgetting she's your daughter."

Phillip shook his head. "No, Sam. She is my flesh and blood. But she is the daughter of the devil."

Sam could not suppress a shudder.

The men searched Nora's room. The jack-in-the-box was gone. They could find no trace of the black uniform she had been wearing.

Exasperated, Sam said, "Well, the goddamned box has to be around here someplace."

"It's hiding from us." Phillip glanced at his watch. "Christ. I forgot the time. Come on. You'll miss your train."

"You're going to stay here? Alone? Come on, buddy."

"I don't have any choice, Sam. None at all."

Returning from the station, Phillip called Father Debeau at his residence, telling the priest all that had happened.

"You're sure it was a storm trooper's uniform, Phillip? The black gestapo-type uniform?"

"Sam says it was."

"He was very brave, attacking that devil's toy."

"He was the most highly decorated man in my outfit, Joe. Sam's got a lot of brass on his ass, believe it."

"It's coming to a head, Phillip," Debeau said. "Consider yourself in very grave danger from now on. She's made her move, exposing her true self and her intentions. She knows there is nothing that you alone can do to stop her."

"That's just it, Joe. What can I do?"

"Do you have a Bible in the house?"

Phillip's silence gave the priest his answer.

"Not even a small pocket Bible? The New Testament will be fine."

Phillip started to say no. Then he remembered the small Bible he'd been given in the service, just before shipping out. Or flying out, as it were. "Yes, I do, Joe. I just remembered. If I can find it, that is."

"Find it. Keep it with you until I can get out there and bless the house. My blessing is no guarantee, but it will slow Nora down some. I'm leaving now."

138

Phillip slowly replaced the receiver. He tried to remember where he'd put the little Bible. He knew he would never throw a Bible away. It was in his war trunk, probably, up in the attic.

He looked up, not wanting to go back into that attic. But he knew he had to do it. He looked around the room. He felt ashamed that they did not keep a Bible in the house. Fine parents we turned out to be, he thought.

But they had owned Bibles before. Phillip remembered them. Several Bibles. One large Bible that used to be right there on the shelf. A beautiful Bible. Leather-bound.

Of course, he thought. Nora had disposed of them, in her own quiet little way. Naturally she would not want something that repugnant anywhere near her.

Have we been blind all this time? he asked himself as he slowly walked up the stairs toward the attic. Or has there been some sort of—he searched for the word—*power* insidiously working in this old house? He guessed the latter.

He stopped at the door he and Sam had repaired. Not very well, but at least it was staying up. Then another thought hit him: Jeanne had not made much fuss about his being attacked. Everything about her, *everything*, seemed to be centered and focused around Nora, as if the mother was shielding the child, not so much against from what might be coming from without, as from within.

Or was he just imagining all that?

Christ, he didn't know.

But the thought would not leave him. You don't suppose, he thought, Jeanne and Nora are . . .?

139

"No," he said. "No. I don't—won't—believe that."
I can't, he silently added.

He opened the door and held it while he propped it up to one side. He found the light switch and flipped it. Nothing. He felt a hard surge of fear. The attic remained obscured in darkness. He went back down the stairs and found a flashlight.

Returning to the attic, Phillip got a firmer grip on his emotions and entered the darkness, the narrow beam of light leading the way. He found his trunk under several boxes and managed to wrestle it out into the hall. Opening the trunk, he expected a musty odor to rise from inside, but the trunk smelled fresh. That was odd, he thought, for it had been years since he'd looked through it. He pawed through field clothes and his class-A's. Then his hand touched the butt of his .45. He'd forgotten he had the thing.

He had found the pistol after a major battle and had carried it for several months. When he'd turned in his gear from his hospital bed, the sergeant had winked and said, "Hell, Baxter, it wasn't checked out to you. I didn't see a thing."

Phillip inspected the Colt. It wasn't in that bad shape, nothing a few drops of oil wouldn't fix. A box of ACP's was next to the leather holster. He laid holster, .45, and shells to one side. He found his Bible and opened the pages. Disgust filled him.

Someone—Phillip didn't have to do much guessing to know who—had taken a red marking pencil and profaned the pages, every one of them. Filthy words and phrases were scrawled all over the little Bible. He closed it and put it back into its canvas case. He tossed the trunk back into the attic and picked up his gear. He headed back downstairs, stopping as he recalled his visions. The pistol in his hand. That was the pistol Phil had pointed at him in those terrible visions.

Prophetic? He hoped not.

In the den, he fieldstripped the weapon and cleaned and oiled it. He inspected the ammo for signs of corrosion, and loaded the clip. Six rounds. He left the chamber empty. He holstered the weapon and put it aside. He waited for the priest.

Debeau had told him he lived in New Rochelle. But Phillip didn't know if the man was driving up, or what. Driving, probably.

Phillip felt tired. He leaned back in the chair, behind his desk. He was confused and scared, and did not know what course of action to pursue. He thought of and immediately discounted the police. Sam was right. The cops might have both him and Sam committed if they told them what was happening. And Phillip wouldn't have blamed them for it.

Laughter drifted down from the second floor of the house. Phillip gritted his teeth and gripped the arms of his chair.

"Want to see what the future holds for you?" the voice said tauntingly.

That same force that had pinned him to the hall floor the night before placed an invisible hand on his chest, pushing him back in this chair and holding him there. It felt as though a steel band had been placed around his head and was slowly tightening. Phillip slipped into unconsciousness as the pain overwhelmed him.

Phillip was in a closed box, sealed in, in utter

darkness. He could not get out. He was trapped. He screamed silently, knowing he could not be heard. He beat his fists against the top of the narrow box. The box was lined with softness. Narrow box! He was lying on satin, a small, soft pillow under his head.

Then he knew where he was.

In a casket.

The scene shifted. He could see Jeanne running through the house, her face all bloody. She was screaming and crying. Nora was standing in the open doorway of her room, holding the swaying, grinning, evil jack-in-the-box. She was laughing and laughing. Phil had stopped running and was standing with his face pale, his mouth open, his eyes wide. He leveled the pistol and pulled the trigger.

Phillip heard a scream of pain. Himself screaming.

The invisible force pinning him to the chair pulled away. Phillip returned to consciousness. He was coughing and choking, tears nearly blinding him. He smelled smoke. His flesh seemed to be on fire. He lunged from the chair, expecting the room to be blazing.

He controlled his breathing, slowing his racing heart. He looked around the room. A small fire burned in the fireplace. The room was brightly lit by lamps. Nothing was burning that wasn't supposed to be. No smoke, no flames leaping around the room. He had a terrible headache.

He was more confused than ever.

Laughter rolled from the second floor of the home. A muted whispering followed the taunting laughter. Phillip could not make out the words.

The phone rang, startling him. He picked it up.

"Mr. Baxter?"

"Yes."

"This is Paul Weaver. I'm sorry to be bothering you on Sunday."

"It's no bother, believe me. You have some news, Paul?"

"Plenty of it, sir."

"Hold on, Paul. I want to record this." He turned on the cassette-corder by the phone. "Go."

"You definitely have a sister, Mr. Baxter. Her name is Jane. She's a couple of years older than you. She was placed in a home for severely retarded children when she was four. But that was a cover-up. She isn't retarded. She's brilliantly evil. She had to be kept in isolation constantly. Hard lockdown. I don't have all the details yet, but I'll get them.

"Now let me tell you about your house. Mr. Baxter, I would advise you to vacate that place as quickly as possible. The house is just slightly over ninety years old. It was built by a man named Gunsche. When the First World War appeared imminent, he left and went back to Germany. He was a bad one. But his son wrote the book on evil. His name is Otto Gunsche. He was one of the commandants of Belsen concentration camp. No one knows whether he is alive or dead. Military intelligence seemed to think he's alive and living in the New York City area. Otto was one fruitcake Nazi. No telling how many people he killed. Thousands. Most after he was shifted to another camp. Otto collected jack-in-the-boxes. Believed very strongly in the occult. Practiced it religiously. Used to use Jews for human sacrifices. Offering them up to Satan."

143

"Good God! Why hasn't any of this ever come out in the press?"

"Because Gunsche was small potatoes, comparatively speaking. That, plus he was supposed to have been killed before the war ended."

"Another cover-up?"

"Probably. A lot of military intelligence units got in too deep before they realized who they were dealing with. Then they couldn't back out."

"You mean they wouldn't back out, admitting their mistakes." It was not a question.

"One way to put it. Dozens of families have tried to live in that house you're living in, Mr. Baxter. Something tragic and terrible happened to at least one member of every family who ever attempted to live there. A lot of people have died in that house, sir. It was empty before you bought it. Naturally the real estate people wouldn't tell you what I just did."

"Yeah. All right, Paul. Do you know what happened to my sister?"

"She escaped from the institution three years ago. It was her third escape since childhood. Same institution. The reason you could never find any paperwork about her is because someone other than the Baxter family has been picking up the tab for her care."

"That's odd," Phillip said. "I'm curious as to the how and why of that."

"I don't know the why of it, yet. But I can tell you the who part. It's the Vincinci family out of Bridgeport."

Phillip sat very still and shocked at that news. Vincinci was Jeanne's aunt Morgan's married name. The Vincincis were a very old and highly respected

144

family, with roots that ran deep in Connecticut. Going back to the 1700s. What was the connection here? Phillip couldn't figure it.

"You still there, Mr. Baxter?"

"Yes, I'm still here. You threw me a curve with that last bit, Paul. Give me some details."

"The Vincinci family paid the bills for your sister's confinement. Up until she broke out, a Mrs. Morgan Vincinci was signing the checks."

13

"All these years, and Morgan never told me," Phillip said to Father Debeau. "But *why* is the Vincinci family involved? Where is the connection? I don't understand it. None of this makes any sense. All this information does, to my way of thinking, is complicate an already twisted matter."

Debeau had blessed the house, the grounds, the contents, and prayed with Phillip. He had looked at the profaned Bible and burned it.

Debeau sat up straight in his chair and snapped his fingers. "Monsignor Vincinci! Sure. I knew that name was familiar. He hasn't been active for a long time; I haven't heard him mentioned in years. Let me think. Ah! Yes. About forty years ago, between forty and forty-five years, when he was a young priest, the story goes that he performed an exorcism. I seem to recall hearing that he failed to follow church procedure and got in a lot of trouble. I believe he was attempting to exorcise a young girl. Maybe, oh, three or four years old."

Phillip glanced at the priest. "You said he was *attempting*?"

"Yes. He failed. So the story goes. But he was eventually forgiven for stepping out of bounds, so to speak, and became a well-respected priest. But . . . I don't believe he ever again held a parish church. Yes, that's right. He became a scholar. Kept to himself, so I'm told. Became rather a mystery."

"Do you know the man?"

"No. I've never met him."

"Could the girl have been my sister?"

"It's possible, I suppose."

"Where did the exorcism take place?"

"I . . . really don't know. Somewhere in Connecticut is all I ever heard. Really, not too much has ever been said about it. An exorcism is something one simply does not talk about."

Phillip nodded. "What relation is this Monsignor Vincinci to Morgan Vincinci?"

"There again, I'm not sure. Brother-in-law, I believe."

"You're not leveling with me, Joe. What's the matter? Could it be that a little hanky-panky went on between a priest and a woman?"

Debeau sighed. "Rumors, Phillip. Vague rumors are all I've ever heard."

The clunking of car doors put an end to the conversation. The family was back from church. "How do I introduce you, Joe?" Phillip asked the Catholic priest.

"As what I am, Phillip. I believe enough lies have been told."

"A priest?" Jeanne said. She looked at Phillip. "I thought you told me you'd never again accept the Catholic faith."

"Joe is a friend," Phillip said. He looked over at Nora. She was backed up against a wall, her face pale, her eyes glowing raw hate mixed with fear at Debeau. Debeau was smiling at the child. Phillip sensed a silent battle being waged between the man of God and the child of Satan. Nora trembled and dropped her gaze. "Nora, you and Phil go to your rooms and stay there, please. Mrs. Strassel, would you fix lunch?"

"Right away, sir." She left the room. She seemed glad to go.

Phillip wondered about that.

A lot of things were swiftly returning to Phillip's mind. Jeanne had never liked the Catholic Church. They of course had friends who were Catholic, but religion was never discussed. And what was that remark of Morgan's some years back? Phillip dredged it up from the recesses of his mind. "We broke with the Catholic Church years ago, Phillip. The Vincincis, the Garrisons, several families. We had our reasons." And she'd never said another word about it.

Jeanne said, "If this is about Nora, I don't wish to hear it."

"It's about a lot of things, Jeanne," Phillip said. "But we'll start with my sister. I think you know all about her."

Did she pale just a bit? Yes, she did, Phillip thought, watching his wife's face closely.

"Truth time, Jeanne," Phillip prodded. "No more lying or dodging. Why did your family leave the Catholic Church?"

She refused to meet his eyes. She shook her head. "I have no idea, Phillip. And I resent this inquisition."

Again his courtroom years came to the fore. He knew she was lying. "Jeanne, the time for half truths and deceit is over. Let's try honesty for a change. Tell me about my sister."

Jeanne sat down heavily on the sectional. She breathed a deep sigh. She looked at Debeau. "Why couldn't you stay out of this? Why did you have to come along and drag all this out into the open?"

"Joe didn't drag out anything," Phillip told her. "I hired a private detective. He found out about my sister and about the Vincinci family paying for her being institutionalized. Would you please explain that?"

"Your father was not killed in a car wreck, Phillip," Jeanne said. "Nick Vincinci arranged that after your father was killed."

"No?" Phillip's voice was soft. "Then how did he die?"

"Your sister killed him. She escaped from the . . . asylum and hid in the back seat of his car. Just so happened he was going out of town that day. She cut his throat right outside of New Haven. One of the truck drivers for the Garrison Lines spotted your father's car and called in. Morgan was contacted, and she called Nick. He took it from there."

Phillip sat down hard. "My mother?"

"Jane—that's your sister—came after her. Cut her up very badly. Your mother was hospitalized for a long time. She . . . lost her mind. So the doctors thought. She broke out of the institution and ran away. Years ago. Before we were married. No one knows where she is."

Phillip started to say something. Jeanne held up her hand. "Wait. Phillip, do you remember how we met?"

"We've known each other all our lives. Ever since we were kids, babies."

"That was no accident, Phillip. You might even say our marriage was carefully arranged, and you'd be correct. The Garrison family, the Baxter family, and the Vincinci family go back a long, long way. You and I, Phillip, are fifth cousins."

Before Phillip could recover from his initial shock and speak, Else stuck her head into the room. "Will any of you be dining?"

"No, Else," Jeanne said. "Feed Nora and Phil. And close the door. We don't wish to be disturbed." She looked at Debeau. "I'm sorry, Father. Would you care for some lunch?"

"Thank you, no."

"That will be all, Else."

"Yes, ma'am." She closed the door.

"Fifth cousins, Jeanne?" Phillip asked.

Again she sighed. "Maybe fourth. We . . . like to keep it in the family, so to speak."

"Keep *what* in the family?" Phillip raised his voice.

"Don't shout at me, Phillip. I'm trying very hard to maintain my composure."

Debeau stepped in. "Then the rumors are true, Mrs. Baxter?"

"Yes," Jeanne said, meeting his gaze. "Including the unspeakable ones." She looked at her husband. "This is not easy for me, Phillip. I want you to know that. But it's going to be very bad for you."

"It gets worse?"

150

"Oh yes."

"I'm listening."

Her sigh was almost painful to hear. "Your mother had an affair. The affair produced a child. Jane. Your father forgave your mother's . . . indiscretion and accepted the girl as his own. It was a mistake. Morgan tried to convince your mother to have an abortion. She refused." She paused and dropped her eyes.

Phillip said, "The real father?"

Debeau picked it up. "Has to be a young priest by the name of Vincinci. Oh, god*damn* these cover-ups."

Jeanne's eyes turned hot. She flared at the priest. "You people make me *sick*! You think you're so holy. Mrs. Baxter was in love with Mark Vincinci, and he with her. Haven't you ever sexually desired a woman?"

"Many times," Debeau remained calm. "I may be a priest, but I'm still a man. But I have never violated my vows."

"Hurray for you," Jeanne replied sarcastically.

"What did you mean by that remark about keeping it in the family?" Phillip asked.

"The Garrisons, the Baxters, the Vincinci family— well, we seem to have some sort of curse, or hex, or whatever you choose to call it, on us. Every generation seems to produce at least one babbling idiot. That's my choice of description, since I don't believe in demonic possession. That's the reason my family broke from the Catholic Church. Before I was born. Morgan tried to get your father to split with the church. He refused."

"What happens to the children who are born

marked?" Debeau asked.

"I never said they were marked."

"You didn't have to say it," the priest told her.

"Some have been helped," Jeanne admitted. Reluctantly. The words seemed to contain a sour flavor by the way she spat them out. "Yes, by priests. The others are put away. Institutionalized in a . . . home up near the Massachusetts state line. Near Canaan."

"Let me guess," Phillip said. "The Vincinci family owns the institution."

"Very astute of you, Phillip," Jeanne told him. "Yes, that's right. A very profitable place, so I'm told. I've seen it several times. I have a brother there."

"I didn't know that," Phillip said.

"Among other things you don't know."

Phillip ignored the sarcasm. "How—well—thick are the blood ties between our families?"

"We've been inbreeding for two centuries, at least. One of these days it's going to catch up with us, and the entire crop of babies will be born deformed and insane. It's happening now, isn't it?"

"I . . . well, I don't accept all you say, Jeanne," Phillip said. "I don't mean to imply you're not telling the truth, just . . . well . . ." Then he got it. After his father had been killed and his mother had left, he'd had no one else. He had never questioned why he had been taken in so readily by the people who had raised him after he'd lost his parents. Now he knew. They were all related.

Gunther. Gunsche. Sure. He let that lie for a moment. "Happening now?" Phillip asked. "You mean like Nora?"

"Nora is a perfectly normal child!" Jeanne shouted

at him. "Goddammit, she is."

"She isn't, Jeanne. And you know it. I think you've known it for years."

She stubbornly shook her head.

"Where is Monsignor Vincinci?" Debeau asked.

"At the Center," Jeanne said.

"He's insane?"

"No. Not at all. He just doesn't track very well. His mind tends to wander. He has good days and bad days. So I'm told."

"How about the family who helped raise me, Jeanne? The Gunther family."

Her eyes became hooded. "What about them?"

"I think I'll have my P.I. do a little checking on them."

"Why would you do that?"

"I think he'll discover their name was originally Gunsche. Right?"

She said nothing.

"You pushed for this house, Jeanne. You. You could have had any house you wanted. But you pushed me to buy this one. Why?"

Jeanne sat silent for a moment. "Something . . . well, pulled me to this place," she admitted. "I can't explain it. The first time I saw it, I was drawn to it. It's just as simple as that, Phillip. I had no other motive."

He believed her. Both men did. Phillip knew his wife was not a pathological liar, and only a practiced liar can lie that easily and smoothly. But what had pulled her? And why?

"And you know nothing of the Gunther family?"

She shook her head. "Very little. Only that we are

153

all related, the Gunthers very distantly. But I never heard the name Gunsche before."

Phillip then played his wife both tapes, telling her everything. He told her about Sam and the jack-in-the-box. About his own dreams and visions. About the dead child tumbling out of the casket. And about Otto Gunsche.

She sat in open-mouthed shock.

Leaving his wife with the priest, Phillip went outside to the garbage, where he'd thrown Sam's bloody pajamas. He brought them inside and showed them to Jeanne.

She cringed at the sight. Phillip said, "Now tell me again that Nora is a perfectly normal child."

The tears spilled from her eyes. Long overdue, both men thought. When she was cried out, she lifted her tear-streaked face.

"I thought love would be the cure," Jeanne said. "I was wrong. I guess I knew it all along but wouldn't admit it. I knew I had produced a . . . a monster when I saw that birthmark. That's why I had the doctor tie my tubes. Not for health reasons—I'm healthy as a horse. Aunt Morgan sensed during the pregnancy that I was bringing forth a monster. That was the reason I had a hard time of it. Morgan said that was always the first sign. Some women have died giving birth to . . . well . . . one of *them*. But we, Morgan and I, thought we could save Nora. I think it almost worked, too."

"I commend your spirit," Father Debeau said. "But you tried it by yourselves. You should have sought help."

Jeanne looked at him. "From a *priest*?" She spat

out the words.

"If you find one rotten apple, do you throw out the entire crate?" Debeau countered. "Of course not. You and the others, you're blaming the Church for your misfortune. This cycle of Satan can never be stopped until we find the root cause for the curse? Do you agree with me on that point?"

Reluctantly, she did.

"Then blaming the Church all this time has been rather illogical, correct?"

But Jeanne had more salvos to fire. "What has the Church done for this family?" she challenged him. "For more than two hundred years we've been cursed. You people haven't found out why as yet. You and your kind have perhaps helped one out of ten. That's not a very good average, is it, Father?"

"No, it really isn't. Dismal, I should say."

"Your honesty is disarming," Jeanne admitted. She looked at her husband. "Now what?" The question was put very defensively.

"We take first things first. Joe, what are the chances of helping Nora?"

The priest sighed. He shook his head. "Truthfully, Phillip?"

"Yes."

"The odds are weighed heavily against us. But there is always hope. I must warn you that it is going to be very ugly and very trying for you both. Satan is very near. We could all die attempting an exorcism."

"Is there no other way?" Jeanne asked.

"No, Jeanne. None."

"You've done this before?" she asked.

"Yes. Many times."

"Successfully?"

"Sometimes. Certainly not always."

Jeanne shrugged her shoulders.

"Don't you have to get Church's permission to do this?" Phillip asked.

"According to protocol, yes. But I have permission in a manner of speaking. I have spoken with my bishop about this matter."

"I thought all this mumbo-jumbo stuff was done at night?" Jeanne said, an open sneer in the question.

Debeau only smiled patiently. "Is there a place where your son can go to spend the night, Phillip?"

"Yes. I'll send him up to Alec's. How about Mrs. Strassel?"

"She knows what is going on."

"What do you mean?" Jeanne asked.

"I sent her here. We've worked together for years. Her name is not Strassel. It's Gunsche. She's a nun."

14

"You're quite an actress, Sister," Phillip said to Else.

"Sister is not quite an accurate description," Else said. "I was thrown out of my order ten years ago. I was branded a heretic and a militant. The Church, I believe, is decaying from within. We've got to come to grips with modern-day reality if we are to combat the evil all around us and meet the needs of the people we are to serve." She smiled. "But I'm here to assist, not to preach to you."

"Oh, I agree with you, Sister. I'm curious. Do nuns often help in exorcisms?"

"This one does."

"Your name is Gunsche?"

"Yes. I am distantly related to Otto Gunsche. The Gunsche name is a fine, old, very honorable one. Otto was an evil man—*is* an evil man. My family has been attempting to locate him since 1945. We believe him to be in the New York City area."

"And he is involved, somehow, with . . ." Phillip waved his hand. "The devil?"

"Yes."

"Stay away!" the heavy, hollow voice rolled down the stairs. "Stay away!"

Jeanne stepped into the room. She looked upward. "Who is that?"

"Nora," Else said.

"That isn't Nora's voice."

"No, you're right. It isn't. It belongs to the demon inside the child." Else signed herself.

Instinctively, Phillip did the same. He was not conscious of his action.

A howling came from upstairs.

"Won't that bring the police?" Jeanne asked.

Else shook her head. "Unless Satan desires it, no one outside of this house can hear it."

The howling intensified. There was nothing human sounding about it.

The noise brought chill bumps on the arms of Jeanne and raised the short hairs on the back of Phillip's neck.

Phillip looked outside. It was snowing, and this time the snow was sticking. He recalled his terrible visual thrusts into the future. He shook them away.

Phil had not questioned his father's request that he spend the night with Alec. He had looked curiously at Father Debeau, but kept silent.

"Sister Else?" Phillip asked. "Will you be needing our assistance?" He looked at Jeanne.

"No," the Sister replied. "Not at first. If at all. Please, neither of you really want to see this."

"I certainly do want to see what you'll be doing to my child!" Jeanne said.

"No, Mrs. Baxter." Else stood firm. "You really don't. If we need either of you, we'll let you know."

"Are you ready?" Debeau asked from the doorway.

"Yes, Father."

Debeau and Else began walking up the stairs. They stopped when Nora appeared at the top of the stairs, holding the closed jack-in-the-box in her hands.

The girl was dressed in black. All in black. Right down to her gleaming, polished boots, the trousers fitted into the top of the boots. She wore a storm trooper's cap, the death's-head insignia on the peaked Prussian cap. Her blond hair stood out against the black uniform.

"The perfect Aryan child," Phillip muttered. "Hitler would be so proud."

Jeanne's eyes flashed sudden hate at her husband. She started toward the stairs. Phillip pulled her back and held her.

"You are both far too late," Nora told the priest and nun. Her voice was deep and hollow-sounding, a man's voice springing out of a child's mouth. "There is nothing either of you can do to stop me."

"We'll see," Debeau said.

Nora laughed, the sound filled with thousands of years of evil. "Oh, but *I* have already seen. I warn you both. Don't come any closer to me."

Debeau and Else started the climb up the stairs. Nora moved one hand nearer to the brass clasp on the front of the wooden box.

"Foolish, foolish people," Nora said. She looked at her mother and father. "Don't worry, mother. Nothing will happen to you. I promise you."

Jeanne stood and stared in silence at her daughter. Her eyes simply would not accept what she was witnessing. She started to speak. Phillip's quick hand

159

over her mouth blocked any words.

"By everything that I believe in," Nora said to her father, "I despise you!"

The priest and nun moved closer. Debeau held a large cross in his hand. He lifted it and began praying softly.

Nora laughed at him. "Eat shit, man," she said.

Neither man nor woman of God changed expression at her profanity. They knew it would become much worse than that. They began praying. The snow was coming down harder, in large, wet flakes. Debeau and Else reached the top of the stairs. Nora suddenly lunged at the Sister, knocking her backward, sending her tumbling down the steps. She banged her head several times on the way down. Her head smacked wetly against the floor, blood leaking from her indented forehead. Her neck was twisted at an impossible angle. She did not move.

Debeau stepped back a few steps, looking at Else. He brought his gaze back to Nora. She stood smiling at him. "You filthy little spawn of Hell. I was wrong. Wrong about you."

Phillip and Jeanne stood very still, listening to the priest and the girl.

"Oh?" Nora said, in that hollow man's voice.

"You're not possessed. You are the essence of evil. The epitome of evil."

Nora howled, her breath stinking and profaning the air. She spat in the priest's face.

"Back off, Joe!" Phillip shouted. "Back off. We've got to get Else to the hospital. Leave Nora."

"You don't know what you're saying," Debeau said, never taking his eyes off the girl. "It has to be right now, Phillip. Now. Look at Else, man. She's dead."

Phillip knew with a sinking feeling that Joe was right.

Else's neck was broken.

"The bitch stank of death anyway," Nora said. "I just relieved her of more suffering. Now she can go happily to sit and simper at the feet of your so-called God."

"Nora!" Jeanne said. "You don't know what you're saying."

The child gave her mother a look of pity.

"What does she mean?" Phillip called.

"Cancer," the priest said. "Else had less than six months to live. But she deserved a better death than this one."

"Hadn't you better go to her and work your after-death mumbo-jumbo, witch doctor?" Nora said with a nasty laugh.

"You filthy little demon!" Debeau said, considerable heat in his voice.

Nora laughed. "Aww!" she said sarcastically. "What's the matter, dads? Did I take your steady sex away from you? Come on now. You weren't really humping that old bat, were you?"

Jeanne listened in disbelief. It could not be her child saying those horrid things.

Nora placed the wooden case to one side. "Let's make it more interesting, Debeau. You see, I don't need my friend here. He needs me. Shall we play a game, tall, dark, and pukey-looking?"

Debeau reached into his pocket, taking out a small vial of clear liquid. He slowly unscrewed the cap.

Nora chuckled, that odd evil sound rolling from her young mouth. "Holy water, Zorro? Really now! Don't you think we've progressed past that stage? You don't think I can be harmed by that, do you?"

Debeau doused the girl with holy water. She stood smiling arrogantly at him. "Is that your best shot?"

Debeau's shoulders slumped slightly. He looked back at Phillip. *"Parlez-vous français?"*

"Oui," Phillip said. *"Lentement, s'il vous plaît."*

"What are you saying?" Nora screamed. "What are you plotting?"

The men switched to French, Debeau saying, "We've got to restrain her physically. Tie her to a bed. Then we might, and I stress *might*, have a chance at saving her."

"Oui, en effet," Phillip said.

"You scummy bags of shit!" Nora screamed. "What are you saying? If you touch me, you'll die. Give it up. You're whipped. *Lassen Sie mich allein! Schweinekobens."*

Phillip began walking slowly up the stairs, his eyes fixed on Nora.

"I told you you would soon be dead, daddy," Nora said. "You must be anxious to die."

Phillip walked past Debeau and faced his daughter. He whipped his hand across Nora's face and knocked her backward, the blow bruising her face, bloodying her lips.

"No!" Jeanne screamed. "Damn you, Phillip, she's just a child!"

As Nora was sliding down a wall and before she could recover from the stunning backhand, Phillip hit her a short, vicious chop to her jaw. Her eyes rolled back in her head. Blood leaked from one side of her mouth. She was out.

Jeanne ran screaming up the stairs. Debeau grabbed her and manhandled her to the landing. "Quick!" the priest said. "Bind the girl securely to a bed. Not her room. Hurry!"

"You son of a bitch!" Jeanne screamed, neither man knowing whom she was cursing. She cleared that up promptly. "Goddamn both of you! I won't have you hurting Nora!"

Phillip considered punching her out.

The wooden box jerked and rocked back and forth on the floor. Muffled guttural cries came from the box. The men ignored it.

Phillip jerked up Nora and carried her into a guest bedroom, tossing her on the bed. The black polish from her boots smeared dark on the sheets. He jerked the boots off her and hurled them to the floor. He found linens and tore a sheet into strips, securing Nora's hands to the head posts, her feet to the footposts.

Phillip screamed in pain as sharp teeth clamped down hard on his forearm. Nora was awake and hanging onto his flesh.

Every parental instinct in him rebelled against striking the child. But he knew he had no choice in the matter. He popped her hard on the jaw with a big fist, returning the girl to unconsciousness. A chunk of meat was ripped from his arm as she fell back. Jeanne was screaming and kicking and fighting Debeau in the hallway. Phillip checked Nora's bonds and ran out to help the priest contain his wife.

Phillip wrestled Jeanne to the floor and held her.

"In her medicine cabinet," he told the priest. "A bottle of Valium. Get it. That door there."

Debeau was back in a moment. Phillip took three of the Valiums and forced them into Jeannes' mouth, holding her mouth shut until she swallowed them.

Nora was awake now, howling her fury, screaming and cursing. The lights in the big house dimmed, flickering off and on. A foul, slightly sulfuric odor wafted through the house. The lights dimmed to a low output and remained at low wattage, casting shadows and creating dull concavities in the hallway.

Phillip, not liking it but knowing it had to be, tied Jeanne's hands behind her and carried her into their bedroom, placing her gently on the bed.

"You're going to kill her, Phillip," she sobbed.

"Maybe so," he said. "But better that than what she is."

"She's just a child. Please. Phillip, she can be helped."

"That's what we're trying to do, Jeanne. Dammit, you saw her kill Sister Else."

"That was just an accident. She didn't mean to. She was scared, that's all."

Phillip left his wife with her naiveté—if that was what it was, he reminded himself—and rejoined Father Debeau in the hall. "Nora's too strong for us, isn't she, Joe?"

Joe poured iodine on Phillip's arm and said, "Probably." The men walked out into the hall. Debeau said, "Call the detective, Weaver, and tell him what has happened. I met him a few years ago, through Sheela. When I started to say something about it to you, Paul indicated I shouldn't. I don't know why. I suppose he has his reasons. I can tell you he is a Nazi hunter. Anyway," he said with a sigh, "tell him about Else. I'm sure he knows how to arrange to remove her body without involving the police."

Phillip wondered about that request, but did as Debeau asked. Weaver had listened without comment. He said, "Yeah. It'll take me about two hours, Mr. Baxter. But I'll take care of it. Do you want me to notify the Center to make preparations for Nora?"

Phillip was brought up short by that. "The Center? You mean up near Canaan?"

"Yes sir."

"How do you know about that?"

The P.I. chuckled grimly. "For a very successful attorney, Mr. Baxter, you are not very well informed about certain matters. But perhaps you and your firm haven't handled many quiet nut cases."

"None that I can remember." Except this one, Phillip thought. "About Nora, no. We'll talk about that when you get here."

"Rolling." He hung up.

Phillip rejoined the priest. Debeau said, "I just looked in on your wife. I doubt the pills have had time to work, but she's resting comfortably."

"They won't take long with her. Any kind of sedative has a powerful psychological effect on Jeanne. Nora?"

"That's quite another matter," the priest said, in a classic understatement.

That muddy, bloody slime was leaking from the child's mouth. She had fouled herself, and the room stank. Her eyes had rolled back into her head—or to one side. Phillip wasn't sure.

165

"Double her bonds," Debeau said. "I've seen much smaller persons pop leather restraints effortlessly. Remember, their strength is aided by Satan. And be very careful of her teeth."

As he worked, Phillip said, "You said she was the essence of evil. What did you mean by that?"

"Pure evil, to use a contradiction. I don't believe there is any hope for her. But I have to try."

Phillip took leather belts and secured Nora's wrists and ankles. She hissed and spat and cursed him. When he had finished, Phillip thought: Arnold Schwarzenegger would have trouble getting out of this.

"No!" Nora spat the word in that hollow man's voice. "No! Don't do this to me. Don't do this to me."

"Why?" Phillip asked her.

"You are guaranteeing your death," Nora said.

Phillip stepped back, away from the stinking bed. Debeau said, "This is going to be very unpleasant for you. But I have to have your help. Are you a Christian?"

"What? Yes. Yes, of course."

Debeau signed himself, Phillip, and then Nora with the sign of the cross. Nora cursed him passionately and profanely. He sprinkled holy water on Nora, Phillip, and himself.

"You will be my witness," he told Phillip.

Phillip nodded his head. He had absolutely no knowledge of the workings of an exorcism.

He was about to find out.

As if reading his thoughts, Debeau said, "This is the *Rituale Romanum*. Some of this will be spoken in

166

Latin, some in English. Do what I tell you, when I tell you. Do not hesitate. Our lives are in very grave danger. Do you understand that?"

"Yes."

Nora howled.

"Are you ready, Phillip?"

"I . . . guess so, Father."

"Be sure!" the priest said sharply.

"I am ready."

"Let us begin."

15

Phillip had lost all track of time. He was not even sure what day it was. He had never heard such profanity in all his life, nothing like the verbal filth that rolled from Nora's mouth, none of it in her voice. The child was bathed in sweat. The bedsheets were wet from it. Nora had slung her head from side to side, that slime from her mouth and nose fouling the room, sticking to the walls and the carpet and on the men's clothing. She switched languages half a dozen times, some of them totally unfamiliar to Phillip.

Neither man heard Weaver enter the house. They knew he was there only when Phillip happened to look up and saw him leaning against the door frame, watching the proceedings through expressionless eyes, a lighted cigarette dangling from his lips, the smoke curling upward. He did not appear to be in the least shocked by what he was witnessing.

When Nora lapsed into one of her rare quiet periods, Debeau waved Phillip out of the room and into the hall. Both were very tired.

"Having any luck, Father?" Weaver asked.

"I don't know," the priest admitted. "No," he said.

"I'm not. Else?"

"All taken care of. She'll turn up in a car accident in New York State."

"Thank you."

"No sweat. I'll just bill Baxter's firm."

"Aren't you afraid of witnessing this?" Phillip asked the P.I.

"I've seen it before," Weaver said, lighting another cigarette. "Sometimes it works, sometimes it doesn't. Where's your wife?"

"I knocked her out with sedatives and put her in our bedroom."

"Your son?"

"I didn't tell him what we were planning, if that's what you're driving at. He's up the street at a friend's house. Why?"

"Just curious." He glanced at Debeau. "You're running out of time, Padre."

"I know," Debeau said.

"What do you mean, running out of time?" Phillip asked.

"Your daughter is getting stronger while we are getting weaker."

"So what do we do?"

"Put a bullet in her head before it's too late," the P.I. said flatly.

Phillip looked at the man. "Are you serious?"

"I don't have much of a sense of humor, Mr. Baxter." He shifted his cold eyes to Debeau. "What do you say, Padre?"

"It's too late for that. The . . ." He hesitated. "It would not be permitted. You'd die before you could pull the trigger. You'd better get out of here, Paul."

Some strange light Phillip could not pinpoint flick-ered through the P.I.'s eyes, vanishing as quickly as it came. His eyes slid to Phillip, back to the priest, then back to Phillip. "You're willing to die for that little she-devil in there?"

"If I have to," Phillip told him.

"Your ass," Weaver said. He looked at Debeau. "You're sure about this, Padre?"

"I'm sure. Paul, whatever happens here this night, don't drop this case. See it through. There is more here than we see on the surface."

Phillip didn't have the faintest idea what was going on between the two men.

Debeau looked at Phillip. "Call your friend Sam. Tell him what is happening here, and to keep Mr. Weaver paid for as long as it takes. Would you do that, please?"

"Joe, *I* fully intend to keep the bills paid."

Debeau glanced at Weaver. "You'd better leave now, Paul."

The P.I. nodded. "You guys take 'er easy." Then he was gone, walking down the stairs. The front door opened and closed.

"What's going on, Joe?"

"Phillip, Satan's presence is growing much stronger. Anything could happen. *Anything!*" he stressed. "Now call your friend. Do it now, please."

"Joe, you act like . . . well, like I'm not going to be around to take care of matters."

"You might not be, Phillip. Let me put it this way—no! First let me say this: Your daughter hates you much more than she hates me and what I stand for. With me, as far as she is concerned, this is a

170

game. I don't think she can or will kill me. But she will kill you. Now then, we could both leave this house and remain safe and well. If we stay here, in this house, surrounded by the growing evil, we're going to lose the battle. Not the war, just the battle. Do you understand what I'm saying Phillip? The choice is yours to make."

The full impact of it all struck Phillip. "I'm going to die, is that it?"

"Yes," the priest said softly. "I am afraid that is the bottom line. What is your decision?"

"I'll call Sam."

"Jesus, Phillip!" Sam mumbled. "What time is it?"

"Very early, or very late. Depending on your point of view." He told Sam what was taking place.

Sam came wide awake. And scared. "Are you *serious*?"

"Yes. Sam, if . . . anything happens to me—and it probably will—keep Weaver on the case. No matter what, keep him on it and paid."

"Sure, Phillip. Buddy, you sound as though you don't think . . . I mean . . ."

"I know what you mean. Don't come out here, Sam. Don't do it. See you, buddy." He hung up.

Phillip stood for a moment, collecting his thoughts, getting a firmer grip on his emotions, preparing himself for . . .

Death.

Phillip looked in on Jeanne. She was asleep. He went back to the guest room and looked in at Nora. She was wide awake and glaring hate at him.

And Phillip knew then that he had lost the battle.

171

"I don't know whether you're worth it," he told his daughter.

"You're a damn fool," she replied.

Nora was sitting up in the bed, the strips of sheets and leather belts torn loose, scattered about the room.

Suddenly the room turned very hot.

Phillip could hear Debeau's voice out in the hall. He understood the words. They were the last rites.

For Phillip.

"Well now, daddy," Nora said, in that hollow, evil man's voice. "Now what do you think you're going to do?"

Part Two

16

Fly down, Death; Call me:
I have become a lost name.
                    —Rukeyser

". . . and he made me take off all my clothes, mother," Nora's voice drifted to Phillip. "He hit me, two or three times. He . . . did things to me, mother. I have never been so humiliated in all my life."

"Poor baby," Jeanne's voice came to him. "I am so sorry."

Phillip sat up. Where was he? Jesus, his head ached. He tried to get to his feet. His legs wouldn't work. His eyes wouldn't focus. He thought he was in the hall.

"Daddy said such ugly, ugly things to me, mother," Nora said. "I will never forgive him for that, and for the way he touched me. He's crazy, mother. He's a crazy man. Look at my face where he hit me."

"I know, baby," Jeanne said. "And I'm so sorry."

Phillip managed to get his eyes to focus. The first thing he saw was a quart bottle of Scotch about a foot away from him. The bottle was empty. Good to the last drop, he thought.

I guess.

Something was nagging at his mind, but he couldn't bring it to the fore. Something about danger.

"Dad sure knocked the hell out of me," Phil said, his words reaching Phillip. "Nora, I don't know what brought all this on, but I'm on your side. We'd all better stick together in this."

With a groan, Phillip sat up. He looked around for Father Debeau. The priest was gone. He looked out a window at the end of the hallway. The sky was gray and sullen-looking. Even without the sun, Phillip could tell it was past noon.

He rose unsteadily to his feet and stood for a moment, swaying. He could not remember drinking the whiskey, he could not remember anything after going into the bedroom and seeing Nora free from her bonds.

He was blank from that moment on. He couldn't remember what it was. He remembered Debeau praying as he and Nora talked. But praying about what?

"You perverted beast!" Jeanne's sharp voice turned him around.

"What's happened to me?" Phillip asked, his words slurred. Christ! He was still drunk. "Where is Father Debeau?"

"Who?" Jeanne asked.

"Oh, come on, Jeanne. The priest. Father Joseph Debeau."

"I never heard of any priest named Debeau. Good God, Phillip, you're disgusting. You're still drunk."

"You're right about that. The question is: How did I get this way, and why?"

She shook her head. "You're a pitiful excuse for a

176

man and a worse excuse for a father. How *dare* you strike Nora! How *dare* you do those things to your own daughter?"

"You mean the exorcism?"

"The what?"

Phillip blinked his eyes and shook his head, trying in vain to make some sense out of what was happening. If he could just *remember*. "Don't you remember what happened to Else, Jeanne?"

"Well, of course I remember what happened to her. She *quit*!" Jeanne shouted. "After you cursed her while we were at church. I have her note."

"Quit?" Now Phillip was totally confused. "What day is this?"

"It's Monday afternoon. You've been drunk and abusive for twenty-four hours."

Her cursing him brought him closer to sobriety and filled him with anger. "Now look, Jeanne, I did what I thought was right and best for Nora. You have no right to curse me."

She stared at him. "Right and best?" she asked, incredulous. "You really have gone off the deep end. You need help, Phillip. Professional help. Can't you see that?"

That triggered a memory recall in Phillip's brain. Dr. Harte. Must call Sheela. "What was all that junk Nora was just telling you, Jeanne?"

She stared at him for what Phillip thought must be the longest moment of his life. "Junk," she said softly. "You really *don't* remember anything at all, do you?"

"Well, I remember the exorcism. I remember Father Debeau. I remember Sister Else . . ."

"Exorcism? *Sister* Else?" Fear touched her eyes.

177

"Phillip, I don't know and have never heard of anyone named Debeau or Sister Else. No one by that name or order has ever been in this house, not while I was present. Let me call Dr. Spalding and make an appointment for you. You need a rest; you need professional help."

"Me see the doctor?" He laughed grimly. "Jeanne, don't you remember the three of us talking in the den? You, me, and Father Debeau?"

She backed away from him. He could tell she was very nervous, and afraid of him.

Phil came out of Nora's room. The side of his face was bruised, his lips swollen. "What happened to you?" Phillip asked his son. "You and Alec have a fight?"

"Are you serious, dad?"

"Of course I'm serious!" Phillip snapped. "Can't I get a sensible reply out of anybody in this house?"

"You hit me, dad," Phil said. "Is that sensible enough for you?"

"When did I hit you?" Phillip asked, ignoring the sarcasm. "And why did I hit you?"

"Dad . . ."

"Tell him, son," Jeanne said. "He was so drunk he doesn't remember. Or claims he doesn't," she added.

"You hit me twice, dad. About seven o'clock this morning. I came back here to get some things for school. Mother was staggering around, all doped up on those pills you forced her to take. And Nora was half hysterical. Yelling and crying. You were sitting on the stairs, a nearly empty bottle of Scotch in your hand. I tried to get some sense out of your babblings . . ."

178

Phillip waved him silent. "What kind of babblings, son?"

"You were talking about the devil, about Nazis, about some sort of exorcism that failed. How you were going to die. You kept shoving me around. When I asked you to stop, you belted me."

"Phil, do you remember us going to the market . . . the other day"—he couldn't remember what day—"and talking about Nora?"

"Dad, I haven't been to the market with you in two or three years."

Manipulated, the word came to Phillip. Somehow Nora and . . . Satan—he mentally stumbled over the word—had erased from his family's minds all that had happened. For him to say any more would only make matters worse. But he knew he had to continue. And what had Phil said? That he was going to die?

Phillip glanced at his wife. "The attic. The attic door. My sister."

"Your . . . sister?" Jeanne questioned. "You don't have a sister, Phillip. Please, let's go into the den and sit down. Please? I'm sorry I yelled and swore at you. We've got to talk, Phillip, and you've got to see a doctor."

No, Phillip thought. I've got to see a priest. Especially one Father Joe Debeau. If I can find him. If he's real. If I'm not crazy.

"Very well," Phillip said. "But first I want to see the door leading to the attic."

"As you wish, Phillip." Jeanne stepped aside in the hall.

As he walked past her, carefully, Phillip thought: Nora doesn't know about Dr. Harte. I've got to keep

179

all thoughts of her out of my mind. And I've got to contact her.

That is, if she is real.

Phillip stopped at the short flight of steps leading to the attic. He looked at the door. It came as no surprise.

The door was intact. Not broken. Not splintered. Not temporarily patched.

"Are you satisfied, Phillip?" Jeanne asked.

"No. But for the time being, it will have to do. Let's go to the den."

"Are you sure you can make it without falling down?" she asked sarcastically.

"I've give the old college try," he said, an equal dose of sarcasm in his voice.

Weaver, he thought as he walked slowly down the stairs. Nora saw him last night too. Paul is in danger. I have to contact him.

That is, if any of this is real.

He knew it was all too real.

Got to call Sam too. Warn him of the danger. He had to get out of the house.

If he could.

And what had happened to Father Debeau?

In the den, he turned to face his wife. "I think I'll shower and change. Get something to eat. Then we'll talk. I think that would be best. I'll use the downstairs shower. Would you get me something to wear?"

She looked at him for a short moment. "All right, Phillip." She left the room.

Phillip checked his pockets for keys and wallet and grabbed his coat. He was a mile down the road before Jeanne realized he was gone.

She started to call the police, then pulled back her hand. No, not yet.

"He'll be back, mother," Nora said. "He's probably gone to get another bottle, since you hid all the liquor in the house."

"Yes," Jeanne said, smiling at the child. "I'm sure you're right, baby."

"I've got his pistol," Phil said. "I took it off the desk over there and put it in a drawer. It was loaded."

"He's insane, mother," Nora said. "Perhaps you'd better call the doctor and tell him what daddy has done."

"That is an excellent thought, Nora," Jeanne said. "Thank you for being so grownup."

"I'm just trying to help, Mother," Nora said. She fought to keep a victorious smile from her pretty little mouth.

Upstairs, in the closet, the jack-in-the-box chuckled gleefully.

Phillip pulled into a service station and used the pay phone to call Sheela's office. He caught her just as she was leaving. Tersely he told her what had happened.

"Where is Joe?" she asked, when Phillip broke for a breath.

"I don't know. He may well be dead for all I know. They're setting me up for the loony bin, Sheela."

"Nora is," she corrected. "Don't go back into that house, Phillip," she warned him. "Nora's taken over. She has full control of their minds. She can do anything she wishes now."

"Dammit, Sheela. I have to go back. Christ, I live there."

181

"It isn't safe."

"I sure know that."

"Do you have Sam's number?"

Phillip started to give it to her, then hesitated. "All you'll get is an answering machine," he lied, not really knowing why he was doing that. A tiny dot of suspicion had entered his mind. "Sam's out of town. Won't be back for several days."

"That's all right. It's you I'm worried about. Why don't you come into the city and check into a hotel?"

"OK. That's a good idea. I'll call you as soon as I'm checked in."

"I'll be waiting, Phillip."

He broke the connection and immediately dialed his office. He felt sure Sam would be working late, and he was right. "Don't talk, Sam. Just listen." he brought him up to date. "Get out of town, Sam. I think you're in danger."

"I'm not running, Phillip. Look, come on in and stay with me."

"No. I've got to go back to the house."

"Man, don't be a fool. If your suspicions are solid, everybody is against you. Weaver, Debeau, Dr. Harte—everybody."

"I know, Sam. But I have to try to get to the bottom of it. I've got to find out the why of it all. And I could be wrong about Weaver and the others. Jeanne and Phil are merely pawns in all this. Remember that, Sam, and take care of them. It isn't their fault."

"Phillip! Don't go back into that . . ."

Phillip hung up on his friend and walked slowly back to his car. He turned around and pointed the nose of his car north. Back toward his house. When

182

he pulled into the drive, the evil emanating from the huge old house struck him hard. He looked at his watch. Four-thirty. Be dark soon, he thought.

As he got out of the car, fat flakes of snow hit him in the face. Almost as if someone had opened a storm gate, the snow suddenly intensified, coming down in a blinding sheet of white.

He looked up toward the second floor. Nora was standing in her bedroom, gazing out the window. Even from that distance, Phillip could tell her face was swollen where he'd struck her. Nora was dressed all in black—at least from the waist up. It looked as though she was dressed in that Nazi getup again, he thought. Her blond hair was clean and shining. She smiled and waved to her father, motioning him to come to her.

"I remember now," Phillip said aloud, Debeau's words returning to him. His voice was flat against the falling snow. He remembered the Last Rites—*his* Last Rites. He stared at Nora. "One of us will not live through this night."

As if she could hear her father's words—and Phillip felt she probably could—Nora laughed.

Behind the girl, free from its confines, the jack-in-the-box swayed to the rhythm of the dirge.

Phillip walked toward the house.

17

"I was worried about you, Phillip," Jeanne said. "Where did you go?"

"Driving. To try to clear my head."

"I called Dr. Spalding. I made an appointment for you at ten tomorrow."

"That's fine. Now, Jeanne, I want you to tell me everything Nora claims I did to her. Bearing in mind the child has lied all her life."

Jeanne's eyes became filled with contempt. "You still insist upon blaming everything on that poor child, don't you?"

Phillip's eyes found something out of place in the den. He walked over to an end table to investigate. A pair of black leather gloves. He knew from looking at them they would be too small for him and too large for Phil. He picked up the gloves and held them out to Jeanne. "Not mine, Jeanne. Not Phil's, either. So who do they belong to?"

She looked at the unfamiliar gloves. Lifted her eyes to Phillip. "I . . . don't know."

"I do, honey. Father Joseph Debeau." He looked at the expensive gloves. Looked inside. *Fr J B* was stitched inside. He tossed the gloves to Jeanne. "I wonder who Father J B is?"

"You . . . ah, put them there," she said lamely, a wary look mixed with confusion entering her eyes.

"Grabbing at straws, aren't you, Jeanne?"

Music began drifting down from the second floor. "You know what that music is, Jeanne?" Phillip asked.

She looked up. "No."

"That's coming from Nora's little friend, Jeanne. The jack-in-the-box. Now do you remember?"

"I . . ." She paled, twisting her face as she struggled to remember. "Yes. In a way I do. How could I have forgotten that horrid thing?"

"Nora's using you again, Jeanne. The Vincincis, Jeanne. We talked about them—remember?"

"We . . . no, you can't know about that!"

"But I do, Jeanne. You and me and Father Debeau sat in this very den and talked it all out. The affair my mother had with the young priest. The Center up at Canaan. My sister Jane. Everything, Jeanne. We finally brought it all out into the open. Remember it, Jeanne. For God's sake, try!"

She put her hands to her temples. "My head, Phillip. God, it hurts!"

Jeanne was suddenly flung backward, hit by an invisible fist. She screamed as blood squirted from smashed lips. Sprawling on the floor, she sobbed in fear and pain and confusion. Glimpsing movement in the open den doors, Phillip looked up. Phil and Nora stood there. Nora had changed out of her black outfit.

"You horrible person!" Nora squalled at him, her words springing from her swollen mouth. She ran to

185

her mother's side.

"I didn't hit her, Phil," the father said. "I swear I didn't."

"You *liar*!" Nora screamed at her father. "Dirty, filthy liar! And I suppose you're going to say you didn't make me undress and sit naked in your lap last night, either, you dirty horrible pervert."

"You're sick, dad," Phil said. "I don't want to do this, but I have to do it. I'm calling the police."

Phillip's head once more suffered through that steel-band feeling, the excruciating pain that almost blinded him. He fought the sensation. When the pain had abated, he was filled with anger and frustration and helplessness. He glared at his son. "Listen to me, Phil. Please. Nora is using you, boy. Try to remember, son. Try to remember our talks about Nora. Think, son, *think*!"

The music began playing. The jack-in-the-box began laughing. Nora looked at her father, her eyes blazing with an evil light. Phillip felt his big hands curl into fists. He felt all control leaving him as he experienced a slight out-of-body sensation. Then another being or force took possession of him. He stepped toward Phil.

"Dad, don't hit me," Phil said.

Phillip raised his big fists. He tucked his chin into his shoulder and shuffled toward his son, his fists held in the classic boxer's position. He faked Phil out with a right and then busted the boy in the mouth with a left.

Phil's head snapped back as blood leaked from a cut lip. Phil stumbled, caught his balance, and darted into the hall, his father right behind him.

186

Phillip roared at the boy. "Come back here and fight, you goddamned little son of a bitch!"

"We've got to make better time," Father Debeau said to the three other priests in the car. "Damn this snow."

"Steady, Joe," the oldest priest, a bishop, said. "It won't do Mr. Baxter any good for us to be killed in a car crash."

"When he ordered me out of his house last night— this morning—and got his pistol, threatening me, I knew that Nora had grown stronger and had taken control," Debeau said. "It took me hours to get in touch with all of you. Nobody would answer the damn phone at the Baxter house."

The bishop looked disapprovingly at Debeau.

Each of the four priests had a small black leather bag, either on the seat beside him or on the floor-boards at his feet.

Picking up speed slightly, the rear end of the car slewed around sickeningly. Father Debeau regained control and drove on as fast as he dared. There wasn't enough snow to close the Merritt Parkway, but it did make driving hazardous.

"Where did you send the private detective?" the bishop asked, after offering up a small silent prayer for divine help in guiding Father Debeau's hands on the wheel. And his heavy foot.

"Bridgeport, to get the aunt. If she'll come," he added. "Damnit, it's a good ten miles off the Parkway to the house, and we haven't even reached the exit yet."

"Steady, Joe," the bishop said.

Phil circled around through the house and reentered the den through a side door. He had put his father's pistol in a small French desk.

The boy's eyes were savage as he thought about the .45. All reason had left him as Nora silently took control of his mind and actions. He dropped to his hands and knees and crawled silently and unseen by his mother toward the desk. He opened the drawer and found the big .45, his fingers closing around the butt. He knew what to do from watching TV and movies. Crouching by the desk, he pulled the slide back, jacking a round into the chamber. He eased the hammer down.

"There you are, you little sneak!" Phillip shouted, spotting his son. He ran toward the boy, knocking furniture aside as he charged.

Jeanne staggered to her feet, rushing between her son and her husband. "Stop it!" she screamed at Phillip.

Phillip backhanded her, knocking her spinning, stunning her, bloodying her mouth. She fell against a wall, pulling the drapes down with her.

A neighbor, outside getting firewood, stood staring, wondering what was going on.

"Jerry?" his wife called from the porch. "What's wrong?"

"Put your coat on, Linda. Come out here. Phillip Baxter is beating up on his wife."

"Are you serious? Let me get my coat."

"Goddamn you!" Phil yelled at his father. "You

188

leave mother alone!"

Phillip saw the gun in the boy's hand. He grinned. "You won't shoot me. You don't have the guts for it."

"Leave mother alone!" the boy shouted. He began backing up.

Phillip followed his son, his hands balled into fists. He lunged toward the boy, swinging a hard fist. The blow caught the boy on the side of the head, squarely on one ear. Phil's head rang as pain and shock momentarily deafened him. He reeled backward and fell out into the hall. Quickly he staggered to his feet, not losing the gun, and ran toward the stairs.

Phillip was lumbering and panting and cursing as he followed his son.

Nora and Jeanne crouched on the floor in front of the drapeless windows, in full view of the neighbors, screaming and crying.

"Jerry, do something," Linda urged.

"Do what? Phil's got a gun in his hand. Oh, to hell with it. You're right. I gotta do something."

"No, wait." She pulled him back. "You'll get yourself shot. Wait for a minute."

Phil turned as he reached the top of the stairs. He jacked back the hammer on the .45, pointing the weapon at his father. "I'll kill you!" he shouted. "Leave us alone, dad. Get out of this house or I'll kill you."

On both sides of the Baxter house, even though to each side lay a large vacant lot, neighbors were gathering, brought outside by the yelling and screaming. The men and women stood in the heavily falling snow, not knowing what to do or what was going on. This was definitely not like the Baxter family.

"Somebody should call the police."

"Yeah."

But no one did.

Yet.

Phillip started up the stairs, walking slowly toward his son.

The boy took aim. Blood leaked from his battered and bruised mouth and face. One ear was swelling; he could hear nothing but a roaring in that ear.

"I'm gonna take that gun away from you," Phillip said. "And then I'm going to jam it down your throat."

"Stay away, dad." Phil backed up slowly, the gun pointed at his father's chest.

Phillip continued his slow march up the stairs. "When I get through with you, boy, I'm gonna take a belt to your sister's butt. Then I'm gonna beat your mother and teach her who's boss around this place."

Phil began crying, the tears mixing with the blood from his mouth. "Don't force me to pull this trigger, dad. You're making me do it! You're crazy, dad! Insane. I mean it, dad. If you come any closer, I'll pull this trigger. God forgive me, but I swear I'll do it."

Phillip suddenly roared and charged the boy. Phil pulled the trigger, the report reverberating through the house. The big slug caught Phillip in the center of the chest, the force of the impact literally lifting him off his feet and hurling him backward. There was a shocked look on his face as he fumbled for the railing. Everything suddenly became clear to him, everything returned to him. He could hear the jack-in-the-box laughing as the music played.

"Forgive me," Phillip managed to say. "Forgive my son and guide him, God. I . . ."

He felt himself falling, falling, falling. The darkness took him.

Then there was nothing left to feel as his dead body slowly rolled down the stairs and came to rest crumpled and bloody on the floor.

The neighbors came on the run. They rushed into the house. They gathered in numb, shocked silence, staring at the bloody body on the floor.

One couple broke away from the group and went into the den. While his wife offered what comfort she could to Jeanne and Nora, the husband lifted the phone and punched the police emergency number.

A patrol car was in the vicinity and arrived at the Baxter house in less than five minutes.

The officer thought it strange that the child should be comforting the mother, whispering gentle words to her, calming her. He wondered about the woman's bloody face and the bruised and swollen face of the girl. Such a pretty little thing, too.

Phil sat on the landing, the .45 beside him. The boy was crying.

The quartet of priests saw the flashing lights long before they reached the Baxter house. To a man, they knew they were too late.

The bishop ordered Joe to pull over a block from the house. "We can't tip our hand now," he cautioned. "If the worst has happened, we have to find out how much control the girl now has."

"I can feel the evil from here," one of the priests in the back seat said. "Bishop, I have never experienced anything like it."

"Nor I," the bishop concurred. "Pull up a little closer, Joe."

A police officer stopped them as they slowly drew closer to the evil-emanating death house. Joe rolled down his window.

"Officer," he said. "Is there anything we can do to help?"

"I don't know, Father. I don't know if the family was Catholic."

"They aren't," a woman spoke from the snowy sidewalk. "They seldom attended any church. It's just awful. I don't understand why the boy killed his father." She walked back to the warmth of her house and closed the door.

"Good night, officer," Joe said.

"Good night, Father."

The priests drove slowly past the house. Through the open front door they could see the blanket-covered body of Phillip Baxter. They drove on.

"You must not blame yourself, Father Debeau," the Bishop said. "You did all that you could do. Had you not heeded the man's warning, he might have killed you last night."

"I know," Debeau said. "But that doesn't lessen the pain. I have Sam Sobel's number. I must call him, tell what has happened."

"He is in very grave danger," the fourth priest finally spoke. "We must warn him."

"I shall," Debeau said.

No one noticed the gaunt-looking woman in the shabby coat standing at the edge of the woods behind the Baxter house. She was smiling.

"It's over for poor Mr. Baxter," the younger of the

priests said.

"And just beginning for me," Joe said. "I hope I don't make any mistakes in dealing with this. A lot of innocent lives are hanging in the balance."

The bishop looked at him. "God will guide you, Father Debeau. And God does not make mistakes."

18

"Phillip thought you and Debeau and Detective Weaver were all against him," Sam told Sheela Harte. He was sitting in her office, both of them preparing to go to Connecticut. To view the body.

The law firm personnel had immediately closed the office, many of them not believing the tragedy had happened. The office would not reopen until after the first of the year.

"I sensed that from talking to him," she said. "The . . . last time I spoke with him. Phillip was under terrible pressure from Nora. He was a strong man—a very strong man, mentally and physically—but no one mortal is strong enough to fight Satan alone."

"If you had known Phillip as I did, you would have known he would try. There was no backup in the man. None at all."

"Yes. I saw that."

"All right, Sheela. We've cleared the air. Now would you please level with me?"

She sighed heavily and stared at him. "First I'll tell you what Joe said about it. He said to plead with you to leave the city. Get out for a time. You're in very grave danger here, Sam."

"The best friend I ever had in this world is dead," Sam said. "I'm not running. I'll see this through if it kills me."

"Nora might well kill us all, Sam. I'm . . . not at all certain you fully understand what we're up against. Nora's powers are awesome. I can't stress that enough."

"I'm staying."

She shrugged her shoulders. "All right, Sam. Well, there isn't that much more to tell. As far as I know, the coming together of Phillip, Joe, and Paul Weaver was pure coincidence. I know Paul because I've used his services before. Joe had met him several years back. Paul told me late last night he didn't want Phillip too deeply involved because Phillip was a lawyer."

Sam cocked his head. "What's that got to do with it?"

"I'm coming to that. I said coincidence. Perhaps it wasn't that at all. I'm wondering about that. Perhaps a . . . higher power brought us all together. I don't know."

"God?"

"Yes."

"You leaning toward that supposition?"

"Yes, I am."

"Perhaps you're right. How am I in danger, Sheela? Because I'm a Jew?"

"Yes. That's one of the reasons. The other is that to Nora, you're the enemy. Weaver is a Nazi hunter. He has devoted a lot of free work in searching down old Nazis and bringing them to justice. In a manner of

195

speaking."

Sam grunted. "Reading between the lines, I would have to say that Paul Weaver doesn't always operate within the limits of the law."

"That is correct. And that is the reason he wanted Phillip kept somewhat in the dark. Paul knows—as does any reasonably astute person who doesn't live in a cave in Tibet—about the resurgence of Nazism in this area over the past few years. He believes Otto Gunsche is here, directing the operation behind the scenes, so to speak."

When he heard that, Sam knew nothing could make him run away. Not now. "Including this . . . well, occult business?"

"Paul doesn't know if the two are directly connected. He thinks they may be."

"What do you think?"

"I think he's right."

"Debeau?"

"The same. But let me add this, Sam. I'm frightened."

"Join the club," Sam admitted.

Phillip looked so natural, so real, so alive. Sam expected him to sit right up in the casket and wisecrack, wearing that grin of his. Something like "Ha-ha, boys. I fooled you, didn't I?"

Sam mentally tossed that aside. He had to accept that his good and close friend was gone—forever.

This will not go unavenged, sarge, Sam told him. I promise you.

He shifted his eyes to what remained of the Baxter

196

family, sitting alone across the deeply carpeted and hushed room. The little she-devil Nora sat demurely, her gloved hands in her lap. A very faint trace of a smile on her lips.

Sam despised her with a passion that frightened him. He could scarcely contain his rage, his urge to kill. He fought the emotions back, back into the smoldering dark reaches of his mind.

Their eyes touched across the room; a silent battle raged. Each understood the other as Satan threw down an invisible gauntlet.

Silently and expressionlessly, Sam more than willingly, eagerly picked it up.

Nora very slightly nodded her head in understanding.

"Don't look up," Sheela warned in a low whisper. "But here comes Father Debeau and Weaver. Joe is wearing street clothes. Should be interesting to see how Nora handles this. And Jeanne. I'll bet she won't remember Joe."

"Does either Paul or Debeau have a stake in his hand?" Sam returned the whisper.

She looked at him. "I beg your pardon?"

"To drive through her black little heart," Sam whispered, the murmur failing to hide the harshness and hate within him.

"Steady, Sam," she said.

"Mrs. Baxter," Debeau said, extending his hand. "I am so sorry. I knew your husband only slightly. I was a . . . client of his. Please accept my condolences."

Nora abruptly excused herself, going to the ladies' room. Loathing filled her at the mere thought of touching the priest's hand. She felt like puking.

Seated across the room, Sheela whispered to Sam, "Jeanne doesn't recognize Joe. Now do you see how powerful Nora is?"

"She has a weakness," Sam said. "And I'll find it."

Jeanne took Debeau's hand. "Thank you very much, Mr. . . . ?"

"Debeau. Joseph Debeau."

Not one trace of recognition crossed Jeanne's face. She smiled and released his hand. Debeau and Weaver left her and walked to the open casket. Paul whispered, "The kid didn't want to touch you. Why?"

"Perhaps I left *my* mark on *her*," Debeau said. "In a manner of speaking."

Weaver grunted. "I still think we ought to shoot her. I know, I know," he said. "But now what . . . ?"

"We view the remains and leave."

In the ladies' room, Nora stared at her reflection in the mirror. Her eyes glowed with evil fire and hatred. They rolled side to side in her skull; they spun up and down. The room grew warm; a slight sulfuric odor drifted about. No doubt about it, the child thought. The filthy priest was a strong man. And somehow he had gained even more strength in the past thirty-six hours. The "how" of that troubled Nora, for she knew she had bested the priest the other night. Whipped him.

Now she knew she would have to kill him. Kill Debeau, and anyone else who stood in her way.

Especially Sam. She was going to enjoy doing that.

Weaver glanced at Sheela as he walked past her, out of the room, and jerked his head very slightly toward

198

the outside. Sheela had watched as Nora had left her chair. She had not returned. Sheela counted a slow sixty, then left the room, Sam with her.

"Sam," Debeau said. "Is it all right if we meet at your apartment in, say, two hours?"

"The sooner the better," Same replied.

"You know we're going to have to kill the kid," Paul said. "Let's accept that as fact, and do it."

"I've told you, Paul," Debeau said patiently. "We've been over all that. It's far too late for it. Nora can be destroyed, but she cannot be killed."

"That makes no sense to me, Joe," Sam said.

"No mortal can kill her," the priest explained. "It cannot be done without the help of God."

"You mean," Sam said, "just as in law, there is a procedure?"

"That is correct."

"And that's where you come in, right?"

"Yes. But even I, who have studied Satan all my life, cannot do it alone."

"Then that's where we come in," Sheela said.

"That is correct."

"All right. You want our help. Fine. But how can we help?"

"You can be strong. You can be my eyes and ears in detecting any weakness in the girl. And when the moment comes, all our faith combined can destroy the child. But you *must* keep your faith."

"I don't have any faith," Weaver said sourly.

"I don't believe that, Paul. Your work has disillusioned you, that's all. You have faith."

Weaver grunted, thinking: What a strange group of people. A lady shrink, a Jew, a Catholic priest, and a P.I. who doesn't much believe in anything. Be a damned miracle if we pull this off.

"No matter what we do," Sam said bitterly, "it won't bring Phillip back."

"Phillip does not have the slightest desire to return to this place," Debeau said. "Phillip is home."

"If you say so," Sam said.

Phillip Baxter was buried at ten o'clock Wednesday morning. The snow had stopped and the weather had warmed. The ground was mushy and muddy.

Sam endured the funeral in stoic silence, but he could not control his tears at the graveside services. He hated his lack of control; more than anything else, he felt Nora would take it as weakness on his part.

To hell with her, he finally concluded. He wiped his eyes and walked off.

Phil had been questioned by the police and released in his mother's custody. As yet, no formal charges had been filed. Sam was handling Phil's defense, and although it rankled him to do so, he knew the boy was not to blame. And he would fight as hard as he could to see him cleared.

Sam went to the Baxter house the day after the services. Jeanne had always liked and trusted Sam. Since she could remember absolutely nothing concerning what had brought about her husband's death—except what Nora had allowed her to remember—she had no reason to think of Sam as anything other than a good and trusted friend.

But Nora was silently seething with rage, knowing she had put herself into a closed box with Sam. She could not speak against Sam without arousing suspicion in her mother's mind. And if she attempted to implant subversive thoughts of him in her mind, Jeanne might well resist them.

Nora silently accepted the fact that for now, at least, she would have to tolerate him. Even if he knew about her. He couldn't prove a thing. Tolerate him until—she smiled—he had an unfortunate accident.

"No court date has been set for Phil," Sam told Jeanne. "So we don't have to discuss this right now."

"Now is as good a time as any," Jeanne said. Aunt Morgan was seated on the sectional beside her. The old woman was staying for a few days.

Sam looked at her. Phillip had told him, the last time he'd called—the very last time he would ever call—that Morgan knew about Nora.

Morgan smiled faintly and took Jeanne's hand.

"All right," Sam said, clicking on a small recorder he'd brought with him. "Tell me everything you remember about the events leading up to and including the evening Phillip was shot." Sam had detached himself personally, operating solely as a defense attorney. It was a draining experience for him, but he knew there was no other way to handle it. Not if he was to succeed.

As Jeanne talked, Sam knew the man she was describing was not Phillip Baxter. This was a perverted, crazed child molester, a wild man who beat her and the kids, who drank a whole quart of Scotch at one sitting and then beat up his son.

No way was that Phillip Baxter. But Sam knew

201

better than try to defend his friend's memory. Not at this time. There had to be a way to get through to Jeanne, but damned if he knew how.

When she had finished, Sam took Phil's statement, and finally Nora's. It was then, after the girl had finished, that Sam knew exactly what she was doing.

All three statements were the same. Identical. Word for word. The dumbest, most inexperienced prosecutor in the world would take those statements, tear them apart, and then Nora would—all carefully planned, of course—convict Phil with lies. Very convincing lies. No three people ever told the same story. Similar, sure. But never identical, word-for-word statements . . . not unless they were carefully rehearsed.

Nora was setting her brother up for prison. Being a minor, he wouldn't get the maximum . . . Sam let that drift off. Then it came to him. The Center Jeanne had spoken of. Sure. There must be criminally insane housed there. *That's* what Nora had in mind. Sam would bet on it. And once Phil was in there, he would never be released.

Sam looked at Nora. She was smiling sweetly at him. Sam would bet that she knew everything he had been thinking. "Nothing will happen to Phil, will it, Mr. Sobel?" she asked.

"No, Nora. No. I'd bet on it. As I told your mother, no formal charges have yet been filed, and I don't expect any will be."

"That's good," the child said.

Sam could not wait to get out of the house.

Nora's next words chilled him, stopping him cold in his chair.

202

"The other men came out here yesterday with a tape recorder," she said.

Sam sat back down. "What other men?"

"The men from the district attorney's office and the police. They talked to us all. Didn't they mother?"

"What?" Jeanne asked blankly. "Oh! Yes, dear. They certainly did. Didn't they, Phil?"

The boy looked at Sam through eyes that were numb, dead. "If you say so, mother."

Sam regained his composure and said, "And you told them what . . ."

"Why . . ." Jeanne hesitated and looked at her daughter.

"The same thing we told you, Mr. Sobel," Nora said.

Nora, Sam guessed accurately, was running the show. He lifted his eyes to Morgan. She winked at him.

Nora was going to run the show until the old woman stepped in, Sam again guessed accurately.

"Why wasn't I notified of this, Jeanne?" Sam asked. "Dammit, Jeanne, you're an attorney's wife. You knew better."

"We have nothing to hide, Mr. Sobel," Nora said. "It was self-defense. That's all. Mother waived our rights, as is her right to do so, and her own rights. We told the police anything they wanted to know."

I just bet you did, Sam thought. But this could be a godsend. He could charge that Jeanne was not in full emotional control; that the DA's investigators had taken advantage of her emotional state—there were a dozen ways he could go. Yeah. He hid his smile. Nora's little plan may well have backfired on her.

Nora sat by her mother and boiled in her own rage as Sam questioned Jeanne and Phil. She knew precisely what he was doing, and what he was about to do.

Sam packed his recorder away, closed his briefcase, and excused himself. Out on the snow-free sidewalk, as he was walking to his car, he suddenly felt giddy, control leaving him. Sensing his feet going out from under him, he fell as he had been taught in jump school in the army. He came up rolling, still holding onto his briefcase. Feeling foolish, he looked around him. He saw Nora, standing alone in the front door, behind the storm door. She smiled and stepped out onto the small porch.

"Oh, Mr. Sobel," she said innocently. "Did you hurt yourself?"

"No, Nora. I'm just fine."

"That's good, Mr. Sobel. I wouldn't want anything to happen to you. We're depending on you to take care of Phil, you know." She gushed sweetness. It was sickening.

Sam had taken about all of Nora he could endure for one day. "Cut the crap, Nora!" he said, the anger bursting out of his mouth. "I know what you are, remember?"

"Yeah," the pretty little blond-haired, dark-eyed girl said. "I know you do. But you can't prove a thing, and you know it." She laughed softly. The sound was tinged with evil. "You wanna come play with my jack-in-the-box, Sammy boy?"

Before Sam could reply, Jeanne stuck her head out the door.

Nora suddenly sobered. "Mr. Sobel slipped and

fell, mother. I came out to inquire about him."

"That's so considerate of you, baby," Jeanne said. She looked at Sam. "Are you OK, Sam?"

"Oh yes, Jeanne," Sam snickered. "I'm absolutely fine." He waved and got into his rented car, backing out of the drive.

"Whatever in the world is so funny?" Jeanne asked.

"I have no idea, mother," the child said. "But we'll see who has the last laugh . . ."

19

"You know as well as I do they're all hiding something," the county DA said to Sam. He tossed a folder containing the typewritten statements on the desk. "Word for word, Mr. Sobel. Identical statements. On the tape, every voice inflection was the same. Now let's don't, please, insult each other's intelligence. The kid is guilty as hell, and you know it. It's a cover-up."

"I don't know any such thing," Sam countered. "I do know the entire family has suffered a severe emotional blow. Your eager beavers went out to the Baxter house and stuck a microphone into the faces of, one: a badly rattled child; two: a boy who had just had the hell beat out of him by an ex-boxer"—the DA could not hide his shock upon hearing that—"three: a woman who has a Valium habit. The kids had just that day buried their father, the woman her husband. Your people went out there the very day of the goddamned funeral, Mr. Ellis. The girl is emotionally disturbed," Sam told a small lie, feeling sure if it came to it, Sheela would back him up. Once again, the DA looked mildly shocked. "Now would you like to bet I can't get those statements tossed out?"

The DA drummed his fingertips on his desk. "Ex-boxer, huh?"

"Yeah. And an ex-Army combat Ranger as well. I know. I was in the same outfit."

"Emotionally disturbed child?" There was a definite note of despair in the young man's voice.

"You got it."

"Damn!" the DA said. He struggled to regain his composure. "Well . . . all of that still adds up to zero."

"Bull, Ellis! Now it's my turn to say, and you know it."

"Aw, come on, Mr. Sobel. I'm not pushing for the max on this. Jesus. I'm not an ogre, for Christ sake. The most the kid's gonna serve is a couple of years."

"He isn't going to serve any time, Ellis."

The DA sighed.

Sam knew he had the prosecution on the defense. Dean Ellis was a young DA, just a few short years out of law school. In his second year in office he had surrounded himself with other young hotshots. And this was not the first case they had bungled in their eagerness and inexperience.

"All right, Mr. Ellis, let's talk it out. I'd be willing to have Phil undergo counseling for a specified period of time," Sam conceded.

"*Counseling!* The kid just blew his father away with a handgun!"

Sam did not share his counterpart's horror at handguns. Sam was too worldly for that. "Only after the father, an ex-heavyweight boxer, had beat up the kid's sister and sexually molested her"—Forgive me,

Phillip—"beat up the mother, and then beat hell out of the boy. I'm looking forward to this going to jury, Mr. Ellis. Ed Weiskopf is champing at the bit to help on this one."

The DA paled. Ed was right up there with F. Lee and Melvin and Camille. "Look, Mr. Sobel, give me a break, huh? Besides," he grabbed at his last straw, "the mother waived rights in giving those statements."

"While popped to the eyes with sedatives," Sam pointed out. "And I can prove it," he lied.

The DA sighed. "My people might have made a mistake in going to the house the day of the funeral," he conceded.

"*Might* have made a mistake?"

"We made a mistake."

"Fine. We're getting someplace. It was self-defense, Mr. Ellis. Pure and simple. If you want to charge otherwise. I'll throw my entire law firm at you, and public opinion is on my side. And *you* know *that*. I'll have these statements," he said, tapping the folder, "tossed out as inadmissible. That's going to make you look very foolish."

The young DA sighed. "Counseling?"

"Counseling. Dr. Sheela Harte will be fine."

"All right, Mr. Sobel." The DA shrugged his shoulders. "Well, it looked good for a time."

Sam started to tell the young man his case had never looked anything but lousy. He checked his words. He had won, no point in rubbing the guy's face in it. But what had he won?

Would Phil have been safer in prison? No, he thought. No. It was no place for a young, well-brought-up kid. Besides, Nora's powers were proba-

208

bly strong enough to reach behind the walls of Gray Rock College.

Sam closed his briefcase, shook hands with the DA, and left the building. Phil was off one hook, but left dangling on another. The boy was in danger. How to free him?

Sam didn't know.

He went back to the Baxter house. As he pulled into the driveway, the evil from the house touched him almost physically. The touch felt clammy. Fighting back his revulsion, Sam walked up to the door and punched the doorbell button, hoping Nora would not be the one answering the door. He had seen quite enough of her for one day.

Mrs. Morgan Vincinci opened the door. "Please come in, Mr. Sobel. I rather hoped it was you. We need to talk. Jeanne and the children are resting."

"I would rather not speak in the house, Mrs. Vincinci," Sam said. "The day is not unpleasant. Could we talk out here? In the car?"

She smiled knowingly. "Of course. Just let me get my coat."

Sitting with her in his rented car, Sam said, "I believe I've cleaned up most of the legal matters concerning Phil. Of course, the boy will have to make a court appearance; probably in the judge's chambers. Certainly in a closed courtroom. I'll be notified as to the date. Next month, probably."

"That is splendid news, Mr. Sobel. I thank you."

Sam expelled a breath of air. He didn't know where or how to start. He didn't know how much the old woman knew or suspected.

"The detective, Weaver, came to see me," Morgan

said.

"Yes. Father Debeau said he would." Sam decided to let her carry the ball the distance.

"I don't want this family's personal . . . problems opened up like a crate of stinking fish for the entire world to see, Mr. Sobel."

"I have no intention of doing that, Mrs. Vincinci. If it can be avoided."

"It can. Now about Nora . . ." She left it hanging, waiting for Sam to pick it up.

"Yes, Nora. Mrs. Vincinci, may I be terribly blunt?"

"I suppose it's time for that."

Sam's short bark of laughter held not one note of humor. "I would say it's about two hundred years too late."

"You're probably correct in that. But without being able to prove anything."

"Is that the way this matter is going to be handled?"

"This family will take care of its own problems, Mr. Sobel. It always has, and we shall continue doing so."

Sam cut angry dark eyes at the old woman. "A very fine man is dead, Mrs. Vincinci. A nun was murdered. A little girl horribly burned to death. And you're telling me, in your high-born, genteel way, to stay out of it? I got a news flash for you, lady. Too many people now know about Nora. Oh, you're correct, as far as you took it. I—*we*—can't prove anything. But don't you think for a moment we're going to just sit back and do nothing. We're not going to allow that . . . that little spawn of hell to spew her venom all over everybody she comes in contact with.

She's poisonous, Mrs. Vincinci, and you know it. She's dangerous, and you know that too. Aren't you afraid of her, lady?"

"No," Morgan said quietly. "She can't harm me. She isn't, as yet, strong enough. Quite the opposite. Nora is afraid of me."

"I don't understand." The unthinkable popped into Sam's mind. He pushed it back. "Why should she be afraid of you?"

The elderly woman was silent for a moment. "It's a long story, Mr. Sobel."

"Call me Sam. And I have nothing but time, lady."

"My name is Morgan. All right, Sam. Let's be brutally frank."

That reminded Sam of the old joke about the two old maids. He didn't think Morgan would appreciate it.

"I'm waiting, Morgan."

"We have had an entire generation of children born to . . . various members of the family, Sam. All sides. Only Nora was born with the curse on her. That is the first generation in a very long time to have only one . . . marked child."

"Congratulations," Sam said drily. "But that still leaves Nora to be dealt with. And how do you know it wasn't a fluke?"

"Nora being the only one?"

"Yes."

"Well, of course we don't know. But it certainly is a good sign."

"A . . . good sign? That still doesn't tell me why Nora should be afraid of you." He paused for a few seconds, that pushed-back thought coming once more into the light of consciousness. No. The whole concept was insane. "Oh. Yeah. I get it. I think. Lady, are you trying to tell me that you're the . . . how do I put this? The chief witch?" He suppressed laughter.

Morgan's chuckle was genuine. "What do you know about witches, Sam?"

"I married one."

Morgan smiled. "Perhaps she was a princess."

"That too."

"Are you aware that there are good witches and bad witches?"

Sam twisted in the seat. "Morgan, are you *serious*?"

"Quite."

"And you're a . . . good witch? Is that what you're trying to tell me?"

"In a manner of speaking, yes."

"I don't believe I'm hearing this! I don't believe I'm sitting here listening to this!"

"Ask your Father Debeau about it."

"He isn't my Father anything. Look, Morgan. What I'd really like to do is go off on a week's drunk and try to forget all that's happened."

"You and Phillip were very close, weren't you, Sam?"

"Closer than most brothers, Morgan." He stared into her eyes. "I'm going to kill that little she-devil in that house, lady. Do it, or die trying."

"Oh, don't be a fool, Sam! You can't kill her. The priest can inflict some damage to her powers, but even he cannot kill her. In the end she would defeat him. No, Sam. Only one person—other than God—can destroy Nora."

212

"Let me guess. You."

"That is correct." I hope, she silently added.

"And what else did she say, Sam?" Debeau asked.

"To back off and let her handle it. She is taking Nora up to her house this weekend. I guess then she is going to do . . . whatever the hell it is she has planned. I don't know."

Father Debeau, Sheela Harte, and Paul Weaver sat in Sam's apartment, drinking coffee and talking. Debeau rose from his chair to pace the room, a worried look on his face.

"You have doubts, Joe?" Sheela asked.

"Many of them. Even if Mrs. Vincinci is what she claims to be—and I have no reason to doubt it—she is still an old woman. Her powers are probably not as strong as she thinks."

"And Nora could kill her?" Sam asked.

"Yes. It would like an accident, I'm sure," the priest replied. "And there is this: Nora knows she must be careful. She can't have many more sudden unexplained deaths in her presence. She can't draw much more attention to herself. So anything now will have to look natural." He shrugged. "Well, all we can hope for is the best."

"Let's talk about the unthinkable," Sheela said. "What happens if Nora cannot be stopped?"

"A coven," Debeau said softly. "A devil's coven would then be formed."

Paul stirred in his seat. He didn't know if he really believed in all this stuff or not.

"And what does a coven do?" Sam asked.

"Worship Satan. Work black magic. Spawn more evil."

Paul folded his arms across his chest. The expression on his face could have filled volumes.

"How about Phil?" Sheela asked.

"I think he's clear of any serious charges. The DA wasn't thinking when he sent his people out there. I'll probably be able to get him referred to Dr. Harte for counseling. Anyway, Phil is a juvenile. Even if he's convicted of manslaughter, he would only serve a couple of years."

"That law stinks!" Paul said, considerable heat in his voice. "Not in Phil's case, but generally."

"I agree with you," Sam said. "I believe if a person commits an adult crime, he or she should be tried as an adult."

"Gentlemen!" Sheela said. "Time, please. We're getting away from the issue."

"No," Sam said, drawling out the word. "I don't think so. Something just occurred to me. Nora cannot be permitted to live. Even if she does slip up and the law catches her, she'll be sent to the Center—and she knows that too. Once there, she'll be safe."

"Yes," Debeau agreed.

"Well, what can we do?" Sheela asked.

"We must wait," Debeau said. "Even if Mrs. Vincinci is successful, there is still the matter of Phillip's sister."

"And his mother," Sam reminded them.

"Now wait just a minute," Paul said. "I gotta say something. Get something straight in my mind." He looked at Debeau. "Are you telling me that if I stood, say, oh, a hundred and fifty meters back with a seven-

214

millimeter magnum and put a slug through that kid's head, nothing would happen to her? Do any of you know what a seven-millimeter mag can do? Father, I just don't believe that. I think you're wrong."

"Paul, her master would never permit that to happen. Satan would never allow you to harm her. He would stop you. Probably kill you. No, Paul. You just don't understand what we're dealing with here."

"I'm willing to take that chance," the P.I. said.

"Meeting violence with violence," Sheela mused aloud, "is not the answer, is it, Joe?"

"We never know with Satan," the priest admitted. "We're not dealing with a human person. We're dealing with a force. But as of this minute, I would say, no, violence is not the answer. That doesn't mean we won't have to resort to it. You see—all of you— Satan is cunning, devious, cruel, violent. He finds a person's weaknesses and plays upon them. Satan likes hatred and violence. It is gentleness and love that he cannot tolerate or understand. He is not gentle, and he cannot love. Those emotions are alien to him. You see, he has his weaknesses too."

Sam looked out his apartment window. It was snowing again, a white blanket gently covering the dirty city streets, hiding the crud beneath a clean shroud. He turned to face the others, waving a hand toward the outside. "There is a monster out there. Something—some*one* that I can't really comprehend. But she has a name, and Nora is evil. We can no longer afford the luxury of viewing her as a child. She has to be thought of and treated as a monster, a rabid dog, a poisonous serpent, a despicable, dangerous, vile creature. And she must be destroyed—at all costs.

No, Joe, I don't feel very lovable toward her. Now, I haven't practiced my faith for a good many years. Just stating a fact."

He chuckled softly. "I got this mental picture of going back to my old neighborhood and telling Rabbi Birnbaum. 'Look, Bernie, I got this little problem. A good friend of mine—he's dead—has this kid who is possessed by the devil. She killed her father? Eh? How? Well, she took control of her brother, and the brother killed the father. I have *not* been drinking, Bernie. Come on! Anyway, the kid has strange powers. She can fix broken doors just by looking at them. She can look at people and knock them down. And she's got this Nazi jack-in-the-box, see? And if we don't kill her, she's going to start up a coven. A *coven*, Bernie! Don't you ever go to the movies? How old is this monster? Ah . . . ten, I think.'

"I don't even like to *think* what his reaction would be. He'd ask me was I getting enough rest? Eating properly? Had I seen a doctor lately? Maybe I should go see his son-in-law who is a shrink over in Yonkers?" Sam shook his head. "The point is, people—we're alone. Just the four of us. We can't fail. And we can't bring anybody else into this thing. Who would believe us? Love, Joe? No. I don't go with that at all. Love won't defeat Nora. But strength will."

"Love is strength," Debeau said. "It takes great strength to love. Love almost never dies, Sam, not if people work at it. Usually love is murdered. But you're wrong if you think love doesn't require great strength to endure."

"Then why is an exorcism so violent?" Sam asked.

"Because Satan is testing the exorcist's love of God,

216

is one way of putting it. I said, Sam, we may have to resort to violence. Don't rule it out. But for now, strength is our best weapon."

"Give me a three fifty-seven any time," Paul said, then smiled grimly.

Sheela looked at the men. "I think you're all right, in varying degrees. But for now, Joe—what do we do?"

"The only thing we can do. Wait."

20

Nora sat silently brooding on the trip up to Morgan's home in Bridgeport. She could feel the power rolling from the old woman in invisible waves, and she did not like what she was experiencing.

Nora knew that soon, very soon, there would be a test of wills. She was not afraid. She knew her powers were much stronger than the old woman's. But she also knew they should not be fighting each other. They should instead be joining forces.

She knew too that would never come to pass. Morgan was going to try to destroy her.

"You're awfully quiet, darling," Jeanne said, glancing into the back seat.

Nora almost told her mother to shut her stupid mouth, catching the words at the last moment and swallowing them. "Oh, I'm just enjoying the trip, mother," she replied. "It's nice to be away from the house."

Morgan looked back at the child. Evil, she thought. Evil secretly personified. And strong too. Very strong. She knew the Old Evil One was near the child; that, or one of the Dark One's minions. Morgan hoped it was the latter. She had dealt with them before, and had always bested them.

But the Old One . . . that was quite another matter.

The young child of Hell and the elderly woman touched eyes across the short distance between them in the car.

They understood each other very well. And both knew that one or the other would not live through the upcoming weekend.

"I don't want to leave Phil alone for any length of time," Jeanne had explained. The boy was spending the day with Judy Gipson, just long enough for Jeanne to drive Morgan and Nora to Bridgeport, turn right around, and return home.

Nora and Morgan stood on the huge front porch of the old home and watched as Jeanne headed back south.

The day had turned cold, and was getting colder as the afternoon waned. The sky was a dirty, sullen gray, spitting snow. From off in the distance the faint sounds of "Come All Ye Faithful" drifted from loudspeakers at a shopping mall.

Nora looked up at the old woman. "Now what?" she asked.

"You shouldn't have done it, Nora."

"I only did what I was put here to do, Aunt Morgan. And you know it."

"And you think what you did was right?"

"It wasn't wrong."

"Don't answer me with riddles, child!"

"And don't raise your voice to me!" Nora popped back, standing her ground. "You're just like me. I'm a part of you and you're a part of me. Try to deny that."

"I can't. And won't. Where is Jane?"

A sly look crept into the girl's dark eyes. "Jane? Why, I don't know. The only Jane I know is Jane Berman. She's in my class. She . . ."

Morgan slapped the girl, open-handed, almost knocking her off the porch. Nora recovered and lunged at the woman. Morgan held up her hand. Nora stopped as if running into an invisible wall. She stood stunned, shaking her head. Clearing her head, she stood glaring hate at the woman.

"Jane." Morgan repeated. "Your Aunt Jane. Where is she?"

"You'll pay dearly for striking me, you stinking old bitch!" Nora said.

Morgan popped her again, the force of the blow spinning Nora halfway around on the porch. "Watch your mouth, child," Morgan warned. "Answer my question."

Nora stood trembling with hate and rage. She glared at Morgan. But no matter how hard she glared, nothing happened. Nora summoned all her strength. She willed fire. No fire came. She willed disaster. Nothing. She willed pain. The only pain appeared on her own head. Her shoulders slumped. She dropped her eyes.

"I don't know where she is," Nora mumbled. "I think she's living in that old house a couple of blocks behind us."

"You haven't seen her since your father discovered her in the attic?"

"That puke was not my father! And you know it."

"How long had she been living there?"

Nora mumbled her reply. *"Das macht nichts."*

"Yes, it does matter. Where is Otto Gunsche?"

Nora smiled. *"Meinst du es ernst?"*

"Yes, I'm serious. Where is that evil creature?"

Nora shook her head.

"You're an evil little girl, Nora. Your mother and I made a very bad mistake in thinking we could change what you were born to be. We should have destroyed you years ago. Now it's up to me. Get in the house, girl."

"Old woman," Nora warned. "I was put here for a purpose—and you know what that purpose is. Don't push me. I mean it. Don't push me."

Morgan raised her hand to slap the girl. Nora's eyes glowed. Morgan's hand was stopped in mid-air. The woman fought to free her hand from the invisible chains. She hissed at Nora as the girl smiled sweetly at her. Although the air was cold, sweat beaded Morgan's face. Very slowly Morgan brought her hand down, breaking Nora's will. Nora was panting from her exertions.

Nora growled like an animal as the old woman bested her. Now it was the girl who could not raise her hands.

"Where are the servants?" Nora gasped.

"Gone. I dismissed them for the weekend."

Nora's eyes spun around in her head. When she spoke, it was in that hollow man's voice. "You're a goddamned fool, old woman."

Morgan opened the storm door and the door leading into the home. "Get in the house, Nora."

Nora spat in the woman's face, that stinking, muddy, bloody brown glob. "One of us won't leave here alive, you hag!" Nora hissed at her, venomous hate spewing from her mouth. Spittle oozed down her chin.

"I know that far better than you, girl," Morgan said. "Get in the house.

"I wonder what's happening in Bridgeport?" Sam asked.

"One witch confronting another," Debeau replied. "Good and evil at war."

The three men sat in Sam's office. A few floors away, Sheela was seeing patients. The law offices were silent and deserted. No quick buzz of computer printouts, no telephones jangling.

"There has to be a motive for everything," Sam said. "So what is Nora's?"

"Money," Paul said.

"What need does someone like that have for money?" Sam asked.

"To aid Otto Gunsche, perhaps," Debeau said.

"If he's alive," Sam said.

"He's alive," Paul said. "That is one Nazi who sold his soul to the devil—literally."

"Didn't they all?" Sam's question was laced with bitterness.

"Not like Gunsche. No, it's all tied in," Paul said. "It has to be. I did some quiet snooping. Morgan Vincinci's money—all of it, and it's considerable—goes to Jeanne. If Nora has control of her mother's mind, she could dictate where the monies are to be spent."

"And the money could be used to assist Gunsche in

setting up more Nazi cells around the city," Sam stated.

"That would be my guess."

"Wonderful," Sam said. "That's just what this city needs."

Father Debeau glanced at his watch. "It's getting late, gentlemen. Are you sure it's all right for us to stay at your place, Sam?"

"Certainly. I have lots of room. And I think it best we stay together. When do you think we'll hear something from Bridgeport?"

"I should say Nora and Morgan are testing wills about this time," the priest said. "Late tomorrow, I would think. Nothing is going to happen on Sunday."

"What if Nora wins?" Paul asked.

"We're in trouble."

The elderly woman and the girl sat in the drawing room, staring at each other. The house was silent except for the unusually loud ticking of a grandfather clock in the hall.

Morgan tried to stare the child down. She could not. Nora had the ability to see into Morgan's thoughts. And the child knew the old woman would not kill her.

"You can't do it, can you?" Nora said with a smile.

"I haven't tried," Morgan admitted. "I want to help you, Nora. Save you. Not kill you."

Nora laughed, an ugly bark. "You're an idiot." Her voice had once more changed from that of a young girl to a man. "I have absolutely no desire to change."

"You might not have a choice, girl."

Nora spat on the floor at Morgan's feet, some of the spittle landing on the woman's shoe.

"Wipe it off," Morgan commanded.

"No!"

Morgan looked at a box of tissues on a table. Several tissues pulled out of the box and drifted to Nora's lap, settling gently.

Nora balled them up and tossed them to the floor.

Morgan rose gracefully from her chair and poured a cup of tea from a service. The tea had steeped aromatically while Morgan and Nora sat and glared at each other. "Care for a cup?" she asked Nora.

"Stick it up your ass, you old bat!" the girl told her.

Morgan's sudden move belied her age. She spun, hurling the cup of hot tea at the girl. Nora ducked and squalled as most of the hot liquid missed her face. She hissed at Morgan, her breath fouling the heated air in the house.

Nora leaped from her chair and rushed toward the woman. Morgan stuck out one foot and tripped the girl, sending her sprawling on the carpet. Nora screamed her outrage.

Nora jumped to her feet, balling her small hands into fists. She started toward the elderly woman, intending to hit her. She paused, a faint smile on her lips.

"No, not this way," Nora said. "Oh yes, auntie dear. I see. You thought you could trick me, didn't you, you silly old fool?"

Morgan knew it was futile, but she plunged ahead. She looked at a vase across the room. The child followed her eyes. The vase lifted from its stand and floated through the air, to dangle before Nora's face.

Nora laughed in that odd hollow man's voice. She stared at the vase. The expensive antique vase exploded in mid-air, pieces of it falling about the room.

"Tricks, old woman?" Nora said. "Tricks are supposed to impress *me*?" Her smile broadened. "Oh yes," she said in her own girl's voice. "Now I see. Now I know. You *can't* do so-called bad things, can you?"

Morgan did not reply. But she could not continue meeting the child's eyes.

"You're dead, old woman," Nora said grimly. "Dead, dead, dead."

"You haven't won yet, child."

"I think I have."

Nora's feet flew out from under her, depositing her butt first on the floor. She tried to rise and found she could not.

Nora's eyes spoke her silent hate and rage. She felt she could easily kill the old woman, but she knew it must not appear to be in any way connected with herself. There must not be any evidence that she had any part in the death.

Morgan bowed her gray head. Nora felt the force leave her. She crawled to her feet to stand smiling at Morgan.

Morgan looked at her. "You find this amusing, child?"

"I find you pathetic, old woman." Her voice was once again not her own. "And I find you confusing.

"Confusing?" Morgan knew she must not let the child know she was stalling, regaining her strength. She had guessed, and guessed accurately, that she was not strong enough to best the little devil-child. She could only hope to hurt her, numb the girl's powers.

"I don't know what you mean by that, Nora."

"You gave up eternal life and all the power you could ever hope for," the girl said, in that hollow, evil-sounding man's voice. "Turned your ass to the Master. In return for what?"

"The love of God," Morgan stated quietly.

Nora cringed at the mention of God's name. Spittle leaked from one corner of the girl's mouth, falling on her shirt. "That prissy, pukey faith!" she hissed the words. "How stupid of you!"

"God will not forget that remark," Morgan warned her.

Nora shrugged her shoulders. "So who gives a big rat's ass? What can He do to me? I won't suffer. Even if I should die, I would just go home to live forever."

"In exchange for ten thousand innocent lives," Morgan reminded her. "I believe that is the current rate of exchange."

"Twenty," the girl corrected. "The Master's choice."

"When was it doubled?"

"That's my option," the girl giggled. "And so what?" she shrugged that away. "You pays your money, you takes your chances." She giggled obscenely and brazenly hunched her slender hips at the woman.

"You are beyond redemption!" Morgan said, disgust in her voice. "You are no more than offal on a slaughterhouse floor."

"Happy days are here again!" the girl sang, spinning around and around on the floor. As she spun madly, her eyes caught movement outside the huge old home. A car was being parked across the street.

Nora stopped her spinning. Her body was facing Morgan, but her head remained grotesquely, impossibly twisted, the back of her head toward the woman. Nora's eyes watched a man get out of the car. He walked across the street, carrying a briefcase.

Her head turned slowly, her dark eyes staring once more at Morgan. "Your time is here, old Christian woman," she said. "How does it feel knowing you are about to die?"

"I don't know any such thing, girl." But Morgan did know. Fear touched her. But also hope; not for herself, but hope nevertheless. She had found Nora's weakness at last. One of them. The girl was too sure of herself. Too much in love with self. She must get that information to Sam. Armed with that, he might have a fighting chance. A slim one at best, with Otto's people after him, but still a chance.

"You are an arrogant little slut, aren't you?" Morgan asked.

"Slut? My, what an apt choice of words. Yes. That is what I am about to become, auntie dear. And you are going to play a very active part in your own demise. Isn't that amusing, you old hag?"

Morgan was confused. She could no longer read the child's mind. A fog seemed to cover Nora's thoughts. A sick feeling centered itself in the pit of Morgan's stomach. Her fear became stronger.

Nora sensed it, and laughed. The girl spun around, racing toward the front door, skipping happily along.

"Wait!" Morgan cried. "Where are you going? What are you doing?"

"I'm about to get raped, auntie hag. Isn't that delightful?"

"You're not only evil—you're going *mad*!"

"No, auntie baby," the girl called over her shoulder. "You heard me. I'm going to get *raped*!" Nora paused long enough to freeze Morgan with one glance. Her powers were growing stronger with every passing moment; she rooted the woman to the carpet. Morgan could move only her eyes.

Nora flung open the door, startling the man standing on the cold, windy porch.

"Hi!" she said. "My name is Nora. What's your name?"

"Uh . . . Herb Peery. I'm looking for the Carson house. Could you help me?"

"No. But you can certainly help *me*, Mr. Peery." She opened the door wider. "Won't you please come in?"

Weird kid, Herb thought. He could see an elderly woman standing in the room off to his right. The woman stood motionless. Rock-still.

Nora followed his eyes. "Oh, that's my auntie," she said. "She lives here. I'm just visiting. She can tell you where the Carson house is, I'm sure. Please come in."

"Well," Herb said. "Sure. Why not?"

And Herb stepped into his own private little hell.

21

Herb followed the pretty little girl toward the elderly woman. He couldn't figure out what was the matter with the old gal. She just stood there like a piece of carved granite.

It was her eyes that held Herb's attention. The woman seemed to be trying to say something through her eyes.

Then Herb stopped. Not of his own volition. He tried to move. He could not. He could not move any part of his body. He was paralyzed. Herb panicked, his heart rate quickening and his blood pressure soaring. He tried to speak. No words would form on his tongue. His eyes followed the pretty little girl. They widened in disbelief as she smiled at him.

"Enjoying yourself, Mr. Peery?" she asked.

Herb grunted in fear.

"Not very articulate today, huh, Mr. Peery?"

Herb grunted.

Nora ripped open her shirt, the buttons popping and flying about the room.

Herb tried to scream at her to stop. All he could do was grunt and gurgle, the words a mass of incomprehensible noises.

Nora tugged and jerked at her expensive jeans,

breaking the button and ripping apart the zipper.

Herb started sweating. He grunted in panic. Spittle oozed from his mouth to dribble down his chin.

Nora stepped out of her jeans and walked toward him.

Herb wanted desperately to twist away from the child, but he could not move. He knew what she was going to do. But the why of it baffled him.

He raised his eyes and looked over at the old woman. Her eyes shifted, touching his from across the room. She seemed to be struggling. But against what? Herb wondered.

A small patch of fire erupted from the girl's shoulder, the bare flesh burning. She screamed in pain and whirled around, her eyes darkening in fury. She slapped out the tiny blaze. Her hair started to smoke. Then her eyes glowed, and the old woman dropped her hard gaze. The smoke ceased. Nora turned around once more to face the man.

Clad only in panties, she unbuckled Herb's belt and unzipped his trousers. His pants fell around his ankles.

Nora's hands ripped open his boxer shorts, tossing them aside. He heard her laugh—a strange-sounding laugh, more like a man's—as her fingers touched his nakedness.

Herb experienced a few seconds of weightlessness as his body was lifted off the floor and laid stretched out on the carpet on his back.

Nora knelt beside him, her fingers touching and stroking him. Herb mentally fought away the touch of her fingers. He tried to think of everything he could except the touch of this crazy little girl, but despite himself, Herb found himself responding. Something was wrong with his mind. Nothing seemed to be right or logical. He felt all will to control his actions leave him. He lay on his back on the floor, helpless to do anything.

Morgan watched in disgust as the girl impaled herself on the helpless man's stiffness. Nora fought back a scream as blood stained her inner thighs. She worked herself up and down until she felt the man involuntarily ejaculate. She pulled away from him and ran upstairs to her aunt's bedroom. She jerked open a drawer and took out a little pearl-handled stainless steel .25-caliber pistol. She jacked a round into the chamber and ran back downstairs.

Calmly and systematically she turned over a chair, a small writing desk, a lamp. She mussed a throw rug in the hall. Then she coolly stood over the man and shot him twice in the face. The second slug entered his right eye and penetrated the brain. The sound of gunshots did not leave the confines of the house.

Nora wiped the pistol free of her fingerprints and put it in Morgan's hand. She closed the fingers around the butt and pointed the gun at a wall. She pulled the trigger twice, the slugs banging into the dark paneling of the room.

"Drop it," Nora commanded.

The gun fell to the floor and went off with a cracking, spiteful sound.

"Run in place," Nora commanded.

Morgan's feet began moving up and down. "Faster, faster!" Nora said.

Morgan had no choice but to comply. She no longer had any will left to fight. She was flushed and her chest heaved for breath.

Nora knew the old woman had already had two heart attacks. This shouldn't take too long. To hasten matters, Nora began prodding her with a poker, jabbing at her buttocks, but not hard enough to leave any bruises.

Morgan ran in place for five minutes, much longer than Nora had anticipated. "Die, you old bag!" Nora said. "Hurry up and drop dead."

Morgan ran in place. Even when the phone rang, she continued running. Nora picked up the phone, standing naked, dried blood staining her thighs. It was her mother.

"Yes, mother," Nora said. "Everything is fine. Aunt Morgan is asleep. Yes, I'm fine. Oh, I have to go now, mother. There is a man at the door. Oh, mother! I'm sure it's just a salesman or someone like that. Yes. I'll see you soon. Goodbye, mummy."

Nora hung up and laughed and laughed.

She looked at Morgan. "You old bitch. Die, goddammit."

Morgan began staggering in place. She clutched at her chest and cried out once. She fell to the floor and was still.

Nora bent over her, checking her pulse. The goddammed old bag was still alive!

Then the girl smiled as Morgan attempted to speak. Her words were a babbled mass of nothing. She had suffered a stroke. Nora smiled and picked up the poker she had been tormenting the old woman with. She turned the woman over on her face and savagely struck her on the back of the head with the poker.

Wiping the poker clean of her prints, Nora fitted the poker into Herb's hand and tossed it to one side. She straightened up and looked around her. She smiled in satisfaction. Then she forced herself to cry, the tears running in tiny silver rivers down her face. She became hysterical. She walked to the phone and dialed the police emergency number.

"Please help me!" she told the person answering the call. "I've just been *raped*!"

Sam slowly replaced the receiver and turned to the others. "That was Jeanne. It seems a man came into the Vincinci home in Bridgeport and knocked Morgan out. He then raped Nora and was killed by Morgan. She shot him, then suffered a stroke. She is completed paralyzed and unable to speak."

"Everybody present who believes that will please stand up and whistle Dixie," Weaver said drily.

Nobody jumped up and started whistling.

Weaver sighed and stood up. "I'll get on up to Bridgeport and do some snooping on the dead man's background."

"No need to," Sam said. "We all know Nora set him up."

"Let's be sure." Paul started for the door.

"Paul?" Sam stopped him. "When Nora is released from the hospital, I'd like a couple of your men to tail her. I'd also like to know everyone Nora and Jeanne and Phil talk with."

"Good idea," Paul agreed. "I'll get on it." Then he was gone into the gathering dusk of approaching night.

Early Sunday morning, Paul called in.

"Herb Peery was a solid, straight, no-nonsense guy. Big church worker. Very, very happily married. Four kids. Never been in trouble in his life. Married his college sweetheart twenty-two years ago. As far as I can find out, the guy's never even looked at another woman."

"How are the police handling this?" Sam asked.

"Rape and attempted murder. Nothing there to point anywhere else."

"Morgan?"

"Not good. The doctors say she's just barely hanging on. They say it was a quote-unquote 'miracle' she managed to get to her pistol after being struck on the head."

"Yeah. I'll just bet it was. OK, Paul. Thanks."

"I'll be in town all day." He gave Sam a phone number. "That's my mobile number. Call if you need me."

Sam had just hung up and turned around to speak to Debeau when the phone rang again.

"My son is dead," a woman's voice rasped. "And you are in extreme danger. You are being watched by those who worship Satan. You must be very careful."

Sam clicked on his phone-side cassette recorder. "Would you repeat that, please." She repeated her warning. "Who is this?" Sam asked.

Silence came mutely down the line.

"Mrs. Baxter. Is that you?"

Debeau stood quietly.

Sam heard the woman catch her breath. She remained silent.

"Mrs. Baxter?"

"Burn the house," she finally spoke. She sounded as if she had a very bad cold. Sam heard her cough for a full fifteen seconds. He heard her painfully spit out phlegm and fight for breath.

"Mrs. Baxter, have you seen a doctor?"

"No time for that." She did not deny her name. "I don't have long left me. Nora has a weakness. She has a fatal flaw. She is too cocky, too sure of herself, and too much in love with herself. Use those imperfections against her, and you might have a chance of defeating her. Please . . . I stress *might have a chance*."

"I understand, Mrs. Baxter. Do you know where your daughter is hiding?"

"Jane will not be far from Nora. Jane is more mad than evil. But she is nevertheless very dangerous."

Sam recalled Phillip telling him how Jane had tried to kill her mother with a knife. "The Gunther family, Mrs. Baxter—tell me, is their real name Gunsche?"

"A very long time ago. But they have no connection with Otto. Other than to despise the evil creature."

"Then Otto is alive?"

"Oh yes. Spewing his evil philosophy to anyone who will listen. He is living in the city under an assumed name. I don't know what it is. But he has a large following. I say large; several hundred men and women. They are responsible for the bombing of several synagogues and the kidnapping, torture, and rape of several young Jewish girls. The girls were eventually sacrificed to Satan. Otto is quite insane, and is in league with the devil. He is attempting a Nazi comeback."

Sam felt sick to his stomach. Would the madness never stop? "Why have you remained in hiding all these years, Mrs. Baxter?"

"I . . . had my reasons. I have told you all I know. Now I must go. Good luck, and goodbye." She broke the connection.

"Phillip's mother?" Debeau asked.

"I'm sure of it." Sam rewound the tape and played it for Debeau.

The priest listened to the tape. "The woman sounds as though she has pneumonia."

"She's very sick, that's for sure. We'll want to play this for Paul." He paused. "I think the woman knows more than she's admitting."

"Yes. And obviously she is very frightened. And the house keeps coming to the fore. My initial impression was correct."

Sam walked across the large living room of the apartment and looked out the window to the street below. The snow had stopped about dawn and traffic had been very light. The scene below was picture-perfect: winter holiday time in the city. He shifted his gaze, his eyes finding the man leaning against a street lamp post. The man's eyes were raised upward, looking straight at Sam's apartment.

Arrogantly he gave the Nazi straight-arm salute.

"Son of a bitch!" Sam cursed him. He jerked the drapes closed, paused, and then opened them again.

The man was gone. But in the snow by the post, he had marked his position by dragging the toe of his shoe in the snow, leaving behind a large swastika.

Sam cursed again.

"Calm yourself, Sam," Debeau said. "That's what

they want, for you to go off half-cocked. You'd be much easier prey then."

Sam took several deep breaths. He said, "I've got to get things straight in my mind. All the ducks in a row, so to speak. Who comes first, Nora or Otto?"

"Nora," the priest quickly replied.

"That's what I think. For the time being, Otto must be shelved." It was a hard thing for Sam to say. He had lost family in Hitler's concentration camps. He would very much like to see any remaining war criminals brought to justice, put to death. But Otto was not the head of this particular snake. Nora was. And that damnable jack-in-the-box. Destroy them, and the snake might die.

"I've got to go to Phillip's house," Sam said.

"I thought you would."

"Joe, how could a *house* possibly hurt me? It's just a . . . a thing. Wood and brick and concrete and tile. It isn't alive."

"Don't bet on that," the priest said.

"All right. You're going to stay here?"

"Yes. Take your time. I'll monitor your answering machine and intercept any calls I feel might be important. You're driving up?"

"Yes. I rented a car for a month." Sam pointed toward a small radio. "They said the roads were clear."

"Be careful, Sam."

Sam smiled grimly and reached into his attaché case. There was a pistol in his hand. A big nine-mm Colt Commander. Two extra clips lay in the briefcase.

"Nice pistol," Joe said. "But I prefer a forty-five. When was the last time you fired that, Sam?"

237

Sam laughed. "Last month. I belong to a shooting club."

A note of warning leaped into Joe's brain. "Just to be on the safe side, Sam, why not take my car? I'll have Paul check yours out when he gets back."

"You think Otto's people . . . ?"

"I wouldn't be at all surprised. Now that I know for certain you—we—are being watched."

There was very little traffic and the roads and parkways were almost totally clear of snow. Before leaving, Sam had called Morgan's house. Jeanne and Phil were there. Sam had told her he was going to their home to collect all of Phillip's casework. That would be fine, Jeanne said. Yes, Sam still had a key. Sure, he'd see them all very soon.

He headed for the Baxter house, all senses working overtime. As a Ranger-trained LRRP, Sam had spent a lot of time working with the enemy all around him. Under the most dangerous conditions possible for a combat soldier. That hones the senses fine. Blocks before he had left the city, Sam knew he had picked up a tail.

Four men in a dark Ford.

Sam opened the attaché case and touched the Pachmayred grips of the Colt. He hoped the men following him were members of Otto Gunsche's slimy little group. For if they were, he would take one alive and find out where Otto was hiding.

He would take one alive.

If they were members of the Nazi Party, he planned to kill the others.

22

The dark Ford stayed well behind Sam, but remained persistently on his tail. As he drove, Sam reviewed matters in his mind, worrying them like a dog with a bone.

He reached the conclusion that the whole thing was mind-boggling. His entire organized, structured life had suddenly turned topsy-turvy, and when it stopped whirling about like a top out of control, he had found himself face to face with unreality. The supernatural. The devil. "Unreality" sure sums it all up, he thought.

A month ago everything was sailing along on smooth seas. Now I've lost my best friend, his daughter turns out to be a little monster—literally—and I'm up to my neck in Nazis.

And outside of my own little group, not one goddamned soul would believe me if I went to them with the story.

Not one.

Hell, my best friends would have me committed.

He glanced in his rearview and cursed. He pulled

on a pair of unlined leather gloves and turned off the Merritt Parkway, heading north. Sam knew there were stretches along this section of the road that were lonely and uninhabited. He remembered an old dead-end road where he had stopped one night to piss. It had been most embarrassing. The cops had come along and caught him in their headlights with his dick in his hand. They had reminded him, in typical solemn cop fashion, that as a well-known attorney he should know better.

Suddenly, catching the rear car by surprise, Sam floorboarded the pedal and roared out of sight, the rear end fishtailing for a few seconds before he could bring it under control and straighten it out on the wet pavement.

It had begun to sprinkle rain, more like a light mist. The temperature had warmed considerably, leaving pockets of ground fog where earlier snow had brightened the land.

Sam slid around a wet, slippery curve, fighting the wheel, knowing he was overcorrecting, and almost lost the car. Nobody had to tell Sam he was a lousy driver.

He pulled into an overgrown old road, the blacktop crumbling and filled with dead weeds. Trees and brush lay all around him. He jumped out, the Colt in his hand. He squatted down beside Debeau's car and waited, the Colt Commander cocked and locked.

"Forgive me, poppa," he murmured. "I know you wanted me to be a peaceful man, like you. But it just ain't in me. You and mother just relax down in Miami, and let me kill some Nazis."

He shook away his father's face and directed all his thoughts toward the job at hand. Sam had never admitted this to anyone other than Phillip, but he had liked combat. He had enjoyed testing his skills against the enemy. If his future had not been laid out in front of him like some interstate highway, and he hadn't known for certain that his father would have gone into Mt. Sinai with a heart attack and his mother taken to her bed forever, Sam would have stayed in the Rangers.

He thumbed off the lock and waited.

He could practically hear his mother saying, "Now, Samuel . . ."

"Ma, forgive me, but shut up," he muttered.

He heard a car stop and the clunking of doors being slammed.

Sam could almost hear his favorite great-uncle saying, "Give them a kick in the nuts for me, Sam."

"Yeah," Sam muttered.

Laughter drifted through the drizzle, reaching Sam's ears.

The laughter enraged him. Real sure of themselves, he thought. Must have all been reading Der Führer's bullshit that all Jews are cowards. Won't fight. Come a little bit closer, and I'll stuff that screwball paperhanger's words up your asses—after I blow your heads off.

"Where's the bastard go?" a man said.

"I told you. He turned off the road right there! See his tire tracks? Goddamn, they're right in front of you."

"And he's liable to be waiting right around the bend with a gun in his hand, too," a voice said quietly.

"Naw. Shit, Dave!"

"All right," Dave said. "Let's fan out and take him

241

slow and easy."

"Piss on you! I ain't gettin' all wet and nasty in there. Hell, Dave. What's the matter with you? You scared of him?"

"The bastard was a Ranger in Nam. They don't give them Ranger tabs to anybody who walks in the room. Yeah, he'll be tough."

"Bullshit!" another voice spat the words. "There ain't none of them guys tough. Bunch of lousy little Christ-killers!"

"Then you take the lead, Benny," Dave said.

"Be glad to. We'll take him back to the colonel and torture him. Listen to him squall."

"Come on," Dave said. "Lets move on out."

"Ain't it about time for us to . . . you know. You never did tell us, Dave—do you all really offer them up to . . . *him*?"

"You'll find out soon enough. Get off the road! A car's coming!"

The car roared past. Once more the day became sullen in its silence.

The sky darkened further, as if the gods were angry. The rain picked up.

"Move out!" Dave called. "Take the bastard alive."

Sam chanced a quick look around the rear of the car. The men were just approaching the turnoff. They were all armed with pistols.

Sam ducked back down.

A cold, hard rain began falling, hushing and deadening any sound.

"There's his car! The son of a bitch took off runnin.' I bet you he's so scared he's shittin' in his drawers."

242

Sam let the others laugh. For a very brief time. He abruptly stood up and emptied the Colt into the knot of men who had, fortunately for Sam, forgotten to fan out. The slugs knocked them spinning. The men screamed as the slugs tore into flesh, shattering bone. One slug hit a man in the throat, the hollow point expanding, almost tearing the man's head off. His blood gushed upward in a crimson river. His legs jerked and kicked, then were still.

Sam fought the bucking nine-mm, holding it in a two-handed grip, trying to keep the muzzle chest-high. His gloved hands were slick from the driving rain. Quickly he ejected the empty clip and popped in a full one. He ran to the fallen men. Their blood was running off the broken blacktop, urged on by the rain. Two of the Nazis were dead, he could see, and one was very close to death, with two holes in his chest, his spittle pink from a shot in the lung. The fourth man was hit in the side and arm. He glared hate at Sam.

Sam kicked him in the mouth, forgetting he had on only loafers. "Hurt me about as bad as it did you," he muttered. But the man was unconscious.

Sam dragged the least hard-hit man to the car and opened the trunk, silently praying no car would drive by until he was finished. Centuries-old rage and hate filled him with unexpected strength. He dumped the man into the trunk cavity and slammed the lid shut. Then he ran back down the broken blacktop to the fallen men. He dragged them off the road and shoved them into the bushes. He backed Debeau's car out and pulled the gunmen's car as far up the weed-grown road as he could, then gunned it. The car nose-dived into the bushes, hidden from view. Maybe the police

243

would think this a gangland hit. Sam hoped. He opened the glove box and removed all the papers, sticking them in his jacket pocket. Outside, he picked up his empty brass, ran back to his car, and roared away.

His heart was hammering. He fought for breath. He could smell his nervous sweat drying on his body. OK, you mighty warrior, he thought. Now what? You really stepped in it this time, Sam.

He pulled into the first service station he came to, which was closed—fortunately, for the Nazi in the trunk was hammering and yelling—and called Father Debeau.

"Turn off the recorder," Sam said.

"Done," Debeau replied.

He told him what he had done.

The priest remained steady as a rock, not flying off into a tantrum or an admonition or starting to pray. This was one hard-nosed priest.

"Change locations and call me back in ten minutes," Debeau said. "I'll call Paul and arrange a meeting place. Paul can take my car and you can take his. Don't get any further involved in this Nazi thing, Sam. Not if you can help it. If the man knows where Otto is hiding, Paul will get it out of him."

Sam didn't ask how the P.I. might accomplish that. As an officer of the court, he didn't want to know. "Right. Ten minutes."

Ten minutes later, he called back.

"Where are you, Sam?"

"Highway 106. Just south of the Norwalk Reservoir."

"Paul will meet you at the Westport exit on the

244

Parkway. Drive slowly, give him time to get there. Sam, be careful in the Baxter house. Be very careful. The house is evil."

"I know that, Joe. I just don't know *how* it could be evil. Joe? What kind of a priest are you, anyway? I mean . . ."

"I know what you mean," Debeau said. "While I fully believe that love will conquer all, I believe that at times one must carry a big club to get the message across. Some people are hardheaded."

Sam chuckled. "Yeah, we had a policy something like that in Nam."

"Oh? I didn't know that."

"Yeah. It read: Give us your hearts and minds, or we'll burn your damn hut down."

The priest laughed, not taking offense at Sam's remark. "Take care, Samuel," he said. He broke the connection.

"I had you pegged wrong, buddy," Paul Weaver said. "All wrong. You'll do to ride the river with."

"I have this thing about Nazis," Sam said. "I just don't like them."

An odd look sprang into the P.I.'s eyes. "My grandmother was Jewish, Sam. She died in Dachau. I don't have much use for them myself."

The men exchanged cars after Paul opened the trunk and looked at the wounded Nazi. The Nazi's eyes glowed hatred at the two men standing outside in the light rain. He spat at Paul.

Paul laughed at the man. "You sure as hell don't look very superior to me," he said.

The Nazi began cursing them both. Filth rolled from his mouth in loud waves of racist hate.

"You may have a difficult time getting any information out of him," Sam said.

Paul's smile was not pleasant. "I'll get it out of him." He slammed the trunk lid shut. A howl of pain came muffled from the trunk cavity. "Caught his fingers," Paul said matter-of-factly. "Gee, I sure am sorry about that."

Sam drove through the steady rain back toward the Baxter house, some miles away. He wished he had brought a change of clothing. He was soaked and his feet were cold. Then he remembered he had left a change of clothes at Phillip's—he corrected that. At the Baxter house. Used to spend a lot of time out there, he recalled with a sharp pang of emotional hurt. Funny-sad, he thought, you never know how deeply you feel about a person until you lose them.

Sam sighed, knowing he was driving toward the unknown.

But his memories would not fade—rather, they became more illuminated.

He remembered how, as silly freshmen in college, the four of them had been inseparable. One night they all,—Phillip, Sam, Ed, and Bob—had, after quaffing about a dozen quarts of beer, solemnly sworn to be brothers forever. Whatever one did, the others would do. And they had. Army basic training, jump school, Ranger school, LRRP training, Vietnam. Then a solid partnership.

Sam realized with a mental jolt that he and Phillip had been fools. There had been no valid reason for them to have excluded Ed and Bob. Two more brains might have been able to combat Nora more effectively.

He would talk it over with . . .

Sam sighed. No, he wouldn't. 'cause Phillip was dead. Forever. Accept it, Sam. Face it. All right then, he would talk it over with Debeau and Sheela and Paul, see what they thought about bringing in Ed and Bob.

He could depend on those two at least to listen before calling the nut ward and making reservations for him.

He drove automatically, deep in thought. He wriggled his toes in his wet socks and grimaced. Then he saw he had turned up the street before he realized it. From the driveway, the house loomed up like an evil monument before him.

He pulled into the drive and sat for a moment, staring at the house. Despite himself, Sam felt the goddamned house was actually staring *back* at him. The upstairs windows seemed alive, unblinking and watching him.

He started to put his Colt behind his belt, then dropped it back into the attaché case and closed the lid. Hell! he thought. What am I going to do? Shoot a house?

Where would I shoot it? In the furnace?

Then he thought of the men he had just killed. He was cold, emotionless, unfeeling. No, that was not true. He did feel that justice had been served.

"Hell with them," he muttered.

He got out of the car and waved at a neighbor he knew slightly. The man was picking up a broken tree limb from his yard.

"Any word about Nora?" Sam called, walking toward the vacant lot separating the properties.

"Nothing since last night, when Jeanne called from

the hospital. Nora will be there for a couple of days. Damn shame. That family's really having a rough time of it."

"Yes," Sam agreed, the word sour in his mouth. "I'll be gathering up and going over Phillip's cases most of the day," he told the neighbor. He couldn't remember the man's name. "Might as well work here where it's quiet."

"You need anything, you come on over," the man said.

"Thanks."

Using the key he'd had for years, Sam opened the front door and stepped inside. The silence greeted him. Heavy and tomblike. Oppressive, was the word that came to his mind.

And evil.

The evil was almost tangible. Sam's flesh felt as though something slimy were crawling on it.

He shuddered and fought the feeling away.

He looked at the bottom of the staircase. The police chalk marks that had crudely traced where Phillip's body had been could still be faintly seen. Sam sighed, lifting his eyes from that awful spot. He looked around the house.

All the good memories came rushing back, flooding him. The parties here. The laughter. The closeness and camaraderie that had spanned more than two decades. Gone. Never to return. And all the while the little devil-child had watched and waited.

Then Sam heard the music.

He clenched his hands into fists and stared at the stairs leading to the second floor. The deadly tone of the music chilled him.

He put his briefcase on the floor and listened. The music stopped. Laughter took its place. Taunting laughter, evil laughter. Voices suddenly filled the house. Crying voices, pain-filled voices.

Sam had heard them before. In this very house, during his . . . whatever it had been, that awful night when he and Phillip had discovered the terrible truth about Nora.

"Stop it!" Sam shouted.

The voices faded into nothing. The big house was silent.

Sam walked toward the stairs, his wet shoes squeaking. At the base he stopped for a moment. He despised his fear of climbing those stairs. He knew he had to go up those steps.

"Come on up, Sammy boy," a heavy voice called to him. *"Ich warte auf Sie hier."*

"Yeah, you do that, you bastard," Sam said. He put one foot on the step.

The storm outside broke open, intensifying. The heavy rain drummed on the roof.

"Come on, pork-face," the voice called.

Sam slowly began the climb upward.

23

The haunting music cut the silence into ragged, morbid slices as Sam climbed the stairs. He lifted his eyes to the landing above him. He stopped as vision registered the human horror awaiting him in tattered silence.

Sam closed his eyes, wishing and willing the sight to go away. He opened his eyes. The scene was the same.

Men and women and children stood there, all of them dressed in filthy uniforms, all of them with the Star of David sewn on their jackets. They were so thin, so emaciated-looking, so drained and pale, Sam could not believe they would have the strength to stand. But there they were, standing on the landing, hands outstretched toward him. Their faces were gaunt, their eyes sunk deep into their sockets. Sam could smell the odor of death on them, starvation, as they died from within.

Sam stood for a moment, his shoulders slumped. Then he straightened, facing the living proof of man's inhumanity to man. "You're dead," he said. "And you're not really real. Not here, not at this time. I'm sorry; I feel your pain. I lost family too. But you're dead. Now leave me. I know, somehow, you don't have to stay. Please. Go."

The pitiful band of men and women and children faded from view, leaving the landing empty. But the odor of them remained. How could that be? Sam wondered.

He didn't know.

He wondered if it had all been real?

Real once. But now it was only meant to torment him. No, he corrected himself. It was still real in gulags.

Sam walked on, into the unknown.

He stopped for a moment on the empty landing. Then he turned up the hall, toward the guest room where he had always stayed. The music became louder. He did his best to ignore it. Stepping into the room, he closed the door and quickly changed clothes. Clean, dry underwear, jeans, heavy shirt, dry socks, and tennis shoes. Dressed, his feet finally warm, he walked to the window and looked out. He caught his breath while his head seemed to swim for an unsteady moment than seemed more like an eternity.

He was looking out at a bleak winter landscape. More than that, he was looking at a concentration camp. Dark, sooty smoke pumped into the cold air from the chimneys. He smelled the stench; he knew what it was.

He stared in horror for a moment, then jerked the curtains closed. He stood trembling. "It's a trick, Sam," he said aloud. "A damned trick, and you'd better wake up to that fact real quick." He opened the

251

curtains. Everything had returned to normal—whatever normal meant in this crazy place, he mentally corrected.

He turned around to look at the closed door. The music changed. A harsh, guttural voice sang, "The worms crawl in and the worms crawl out. The worms play pinochle on your snout."

Hysterical laughter echoed throughout the house.

Sam stood very still, listening, leaving the next move up to . . . whatever in the hell was in the house.

Pitiful cries reached Sam's ears. He remembered the sound from the living nightmare he had experienced with Phillip.

He did his best to ignore the nerve-wrenching cries. The house fell silent.

"Can't find me, can't find me!" the voice chanted.

"What do you want?" Sam shouted, more than anything else just to relieve the tension building within him.

"Come on, pork-bait. Let's play hide-and-seek. Can't find me, can't find me!"

Sam opened the door and stepped out into the hall. The voice fell silent. The house actually seemed to sigh.

Impossible, Sam thought.

An odd chuckle reverberated through the silence.

Sam started walking toward the stairs.

"Wait!" the guttural voice yelled. "Where are you going?"

"None of your business," Sam returned the shout, feeling just a bit foolish at speaking to a bodiless voice.

"You can't leave. I won't permit it!"

"Oh, I'll be back. Just shut up and be patient."

Dear God, Sam thought. I'm losing my mind. I'm actually holding a conversation with a jack-in-the-box.

Sam went downstairs and found a heavy flashlight. He checked it. The beam was strong. In the kitchen he picked up a heavy butcher knife and carefully slid the blade between belt and jeans. He walked to his attaché case and opened it, taking out and checking his Colt. He jacked a round into the chamber and eased the hammer down, putting the automatic into his belt. He slowly walked back up the stairs.

He went straight to Nora's room and opened the door, stepping inside. There he could actually *feel* the evil, stronger than he'd ever experienced it. It was here. He felt he had found the source.

Wonderful, Sam thought. So I've found it. Now what in hell do I do with it?

That silent question was answered as soon as the thought entered Sam's mind.

"Can't find me, can't find me!" the voice taunted him.

Sam slowly turned, his eyes finding a closed closet door.

He walked across the carpet, his footsteps silent, and jerked open the door.

The long, dirty neck uncoiled and the jack-in-the-box lunged at him, yellow teeth snapping, the powerful jaws just missing Sam's arm. Sam ducked back, pulling the butcher knife from his belt. The heavy blade came down on the wooden neck, knocking off paint and chips of wood.

The jack-in-the-box howled and shrieked in pain

and fury. It lunged at Sam again, its mouth open. A foulness hissed from the cruel mouth, almost sickening him. He swung the heavy blade, missing the clown head. The closed door began swinging, smashing against him, knocking him to one side, numbing his arm.

Sam stepped away from the swinging closet door and dropped the knife, picking up a chair from Nora's vanity. He smashed the chair against the door, tearing it off one hinge.

Sam drew back to hit the door again.

He checked his swing, fear and abhorrence flashing across his face at the sight before him.

Phillip was standing there, his face streaked with dirt, his hair mussed. His eyes were solid white. He held out his arms, the fingers working, reaching and beckoning for Sam to come closer. Phillip's mouth worked up and down, a grunt passing the lips. The grave-stench was foul.

Suppressing a scream of fear and anger, Sam swung the chair. Phillip disappeared as the chair struck the door. The door broke loose from the bottom hinge and fell to the floor. Sam turned toward the yawning darkness of the closet.

The jack-in-the-box was gone.

"How . . .?" Sam said.

He dropped the chair and picked up the butcher knife. He prowled the room, his breathing ragged, his heart pounding. He was momentarily confused as something clouded his mind.

"Can't find me!" the voice taunted.

Sam spun at the sound. "You're right," he said. He walked out of the bedroom to stand in the hall, listening.

Then the thought came to him: I can't win in this house. Not alone. If I continue fighting that *thing* alone, it will eventually kill me.

"Awww!" the voice sprang out of the air. "Don't you want to play with me anymore?"

Sam tucked the blade behind his belt. "No," he said. "I don't."

"Coward, coward!" the voice shouted. "*Feigling!*"

Sam walked back into Nora's bedroom to repair the door.

But the door was in place, its hinges intact. He looked on the floor for the chips of paint and wood he'd knocked from the clown's head. He could find no traces of them. Confusion nearly overpowered reason in his mind. He steadied himself and retained control.

He turned off the lights in the room and walked back downstairs.

"Where are you going, puke-face?" the voice called after him.

When Sam did not reply, the voice began cursing him. The house rang with ethnic slurs and profanity. The voice cursed and reviled Sam in several languages. Sam ignored it until he reached the bottom of the stairs. There he turned around and looked up toward the empty landing.

"If Nora were here," he said, "I think you could hurt me. But without her, you are nothing. You can only make me hurt myself. So to hell with you."

"You think you're so smart, don't you?" the voice said. The big house once more echoed with profanity.

"I don't have to be afraid of you," Sam said. "So go sit in the dark and stick your ugly head up your ass!"

No laughter, no music, no taunting voice came after that. Sam smiled. He had won a small victory. He went into the study and gathered up what work of Phillip's he could find. He put the folders and briefs in his attaché case and then forced himself to sit in the den for an hour, reading several magazines. He didn't delude himself about the house. He knew it was evil; he also guessed accurately that by itself the house could do nothing except play with his mind. The catalyst was Nora.

Then he thought of something. The basement. Had Phillip ever mentioned anything odd about the basement? Yes, Sam thought he had. But he couldn't remember what it had been. He tried to recall what Phillip had said. It would not come to him. Sam knew the Baxters never used the basement for anything. When they had purchased the old house, they had had it completely renovated with central air and heating, the furnace unit disconnected.

"Oh yes," That harsh voice spoke for the first time in more than an hour. "By all means, puke-face, go down into the basement."

Sam did not dwell on how that . . . *thing* had known what he was thinking. He was accepting a great many things that only a few days back he would have laughed at.

"Screw you, Karl," Sam muttered. He went in search of the basement door.

It took him ten minutes just to find the damned door. He knew there had to be a basement entrance somewhere, but what had Phillip and Jeanne *done* with it?

Then he discovered it. When Jeanne had had the

kitchen remodeled, she had redone the pantry, and it was there he found the door leading to the basement.

Naturally, it was locked.

Sam rambled around looking for the keys, finally finding them in a drawer in the kitchen. He couldn't imagine why Phillip had put such a massive lock on the basement door. The door squeaked open on rusty protesting hinges. Sam guessed that no one had been down in the basement for years. He fumbled around for the light switch. It didn't work. With a sigh, he went back into the kitchen looking for a flashlight. Jeanne had one of those rechargeable home lanterns hanging on the wall. Sam pulled it from the base and tested it. The beam was very powerful. He looked toward the blackness that was the basement. Taking a deep breath, he stepped into the dusty murkiness.

As he cautiously went down the steps, a smell drifted up to him that he could not immediately identify. Suddenly he knew what it was. The smell of death. It was very faint, but very real. He thought. Sam wondered if his imagination was overcoming reality?

He stood on the basement floor, casting the beam of light all around him. He wondered how, if Phillip had never used this place, the pest control people did whatever in the hell it was they did?

Then he remembered what he had been struggling to recall. Phillip had shown him the house just after they'd moved in, and the tiny holes all the way around the base. That was where the termite people had stuck their . . . whatever in the hell it was they stuck in there to zap the little critters.

It all came back to him. The day Phillip had shown

off the house. He and Phillip had walked around the yard, Phillip pointing out the outside entrance to the basement. Phillip's words returned to Sam.

"Funny how Jeanne wanted this so securely blocked," he'd said. "She has this thing about basements. Don't ask me why. I think she had a bad experience with a basement as a kid. She told the carpenters in no uncertain terms that this entrance was to have the biggest, strongest, steel—reinforced door they could find. And then they were to chain it shut. Look," he'd said, pointing. "The eyebolts are set in concrete. And that's the biggest damn lock I've ever seen in my life."

Sam had agreed. The lock was huge. "What's down in the basement, Phillip?"

"Nothing. Not a damn thing. I prowled all over the place. Nothing but . . . well, kind of a peculiar smell. I guess it was all the new materials they'd used."

"What new materials?"

"Somebody remodeled the basement. Put a new floor down there. Concrete must be two or three feet thick. Maybe thicker. Smooth as glass. I wanted to make a game room out of it, but Jeanne threw a fit. I pointed out all the new paneling, all the money someone had put into the place. But she said, Hell, no."

Why? Sam wondered. Why would she so strongly object?

He shone the strong halogen beam around the basement. The place was dusty. And very empty. Just one great big room. Very few cobwebs hanging about. He cast the beam upward. Jeanne—or somebody; he guessed Jeanne—had even had the carpenters close up the little windows of the basement.

"Odd," Sam muttered. "Very odd."

He shone the beam over the smooth floor. It was as Phillip had told him. A very professional job. Smooth as glass. Now why, he wondered, would somebody go to the expense of putting a new concrete floor down, and new paneling up—good paneling too—and not use the room for anything?

Sam's mind ran wild. Maybe the floor was put down to cover bodies? Oh, come on, Sam! Or—his next musing chilled him—to keep something down there that wanted to get out.

"Jesus, Sam!" he said aloud, the words echoing around the barren stillness. "Now cool it, will you?"

The old floor was probably cracked, he surmised. So to increase the value of the property, a new floor was put down.

OK. But why the expensive paneling? Well, one way to find out.

Using the blade of the butcher knife, Sam began prying loose the paneling, section by section. Under the third piece of paneling Sam found some printed words. Using his handerchief, Sam rubbed the years of dirt and crud from the words and put the beam of light on the wall.

Help me . . .

Help me . . . *what*? Sam couldn't make out the last word. He spat on his handkerchief and rubbed a little bit harder, the damp linen clearing away the caked-on dirt enough for Sam to make out the word.

It took Sam a couple of moments for the word to register on him.

It wasn't *just* a word. Not by any means. It was the

Tetragrammation. The four letters, *yod*, *he*, *vav*, *he*—the Hebrew word for God. *YHWH*. Sam put his fingertips on the word, tracing the letters of the ineffable word; that never-spoken word. It was to be only uttered inaudibly by the high priest on Yom Kippur until the destruction of the Second Temple.

Sam pulled his fingers away in . . . fear? Maybe, he silently admitted, as his faith returned to him, stronger than he had experienced in years. Yeah, fear. So what?

But why had someone scrawled YHWH and not *Adonai* or *Elohim?* Or even *Yahweh?*

Unanswered questions.

Disturbing questions.

Puzzling.

Help me, *YHWH*.

Help me, *God*.

Help me . . . *why?*

And had the man—if it was a man—spoken that word as he wrote it? What terrible moment of desperation or agony or . . . whatever had prompted the words? And had his plea been answered?

Six million pleas weren't, Sam thought, his thoughts tainted with bitterness.

So why should this *one* have been?

Sam studied the brick wall more closely He found where some sort of steel or iron bolts, thick ones, had been cut off flush with the bricks before the paneling was put up. Why would thick bolts be here? He allowed his mind to race. To hold somebody prisoner, perhaps? In chains, perhaps?

"Come on, Sam," he said aloud. "Don't let it get away from you."

But in this dark place, full of hidden secrets and cryptic pleas to God, that was quite easy to do.

Sam went back upstairs and searched for a box of candles. He found them in a drawer in the kitchen. He went back to the basement, placed the candles around the huge room, and lighted them. Then he began ripping down the paneling. The more he ripped, the more his suspicions became solidified into reality. He discovered a number of cut-off bolts, sunk deep into the walls. He became convinced the basement had once been used as some sort of prison.

Or torture chamber.

Then he tore off another piece of paneling and found that concrete had been spread over . . . something. About four feet square, the concrete seemed to be covering something.

What, he didn't know.

But he intended to find out.

Sam went back upstairs and found a hammer and thick screwdriver that would serve as a chisel. It didn't take him long to find the rhythm and the path to follow in what was not concrete but mortar. The mortar had been poorly and probably hurriedly mixed. It was crumbly, almost soft, easy to knock out of the wall.

With a sigh, Sam knew what it was long before he knocked out the last bit of mortar. He quietly cursed under his breath. The profanity fit the occasion.

Sam stepped back and let the candlelight flicker over the large, grotesque, and hated symbol.

He had uncovered a swastika. Red and black and ugly.

Help me, God.

The words written in pain and humiliation and despair. Sam felt sure of that. Sudden, hot, wild anger filled him.

He turned around at a noise.

The door to the basement slammed shut, the sudden withdrawal of air blowing out the candles, plunging the basement into darkness.

24

"She's such a brave little girl," a nurse told Nora's doctor. "And so sweet and pretty. She never complains."

"Uh-huh," the doctor said noncommittally. He had discovered something odd about this rape patient. It had bothered him from the outset, until finally he figured out what it was. There were no bruises on the girl. No marks left by strong male fingers, clutching at child flesh in hurried, perverted passion. There was not a mark on the girl. Dr. Terhune found that most odd. And for a child of Nora's age, rape is often quite painful, yet Nora did not behave as though she were in any pain, had not asked for any painkiller. Odd. It was just odd.

The nurse walked away, leaving Terhune with his thoughts. The doctor finished his rounds and started back to his office. He abruptly changed his mind and went to the hospital's morgue, to look once again at Herb Peery. Something about the dead man bothered the doctor too. He pulled out the sliding drawer and flipped back the sheet that covered the remains. There it was. No bruise marks on Peery, either. He had been shot with the old lady's own gun, so he had to have entered the house unarmed. He had parked his car right across the street, in plain view of anyone who

wanted to look at it, and then had walked to the house
. . . and what? Broken in? No, said the police. Been
invited in? Had to be that.

Terhune turned at a slight noise behind him. One of
the detectives stood looking at him.

"May I help you?" the doctor asked.

The detective shrugged. "Maybe. This is your third
trip down here, doc. You discover something fishy?"

"I should imagine you're already mulled that over
in your mind, detective."

"Yeah, I have, doc. No marks on the girl, the old
lady, or the dead man. What do you think about
that?"

"You tell me."

"Weird," the cop said. He sighed and removed his
hat, running fingers through his hair. "Doc, I got a
telephone call from a buddy of mine. He's a P.I. down
in the city. Private investigator. Military intelligence
for years. ASA, CID, CIA. And others. One sharp
guy. Steady, prodding, cool as hell. What I'm trying
to say is this: he's not going to go off the deep end.
Doc, he says the rape victim, Nora, is possessed by
the devil. That she manipulated her brother into
killing the father, after manipulating her father to go
wild. He told me all kinds of weird stuff, Doc."

Dr. Terhune did not change expression. "And what
do you think, detective?"

The cop smiled, but there was very little humor in
it. "Between us, doc?"

"There is no one else present except the dead man."

The detective's eyes flicked to the body of Herb
Peery, back to Terhune. "I don't think the kid was
raped. Look, doc, the girl was wearing kid boots at

264

the house. The old lady had on shoes. Look at that guy's shins. No kick marks. No scratches on his face or neck or arms. And Herb Peery wasn't armed. He was a totally nonviolent guy. Didn't even own a gun. Didn't carry a pocket knife. There is not one black mark against him—anywhere. Now, anybody can be a child molester, doc. I probably know that better than you. But once you discover a child molester, you begin to uncover patterns. Herb Peery just doesn't fit."

"All right. Go on."

"You going to go inside his head and look for tumors that might have caused the guy to go off his nut?"

Dr. Terhune was accustomed to a layperson's mangling of medical terminology and procedures. "That is not up to me. But if the police request it, we certainly will."

"We'll request it, doc. 'Cause I think this thing stinks. Now you tell me, if you will, what you think about it, doc."

Terhune met the man's steady gaze. "I am not a religious man, detective." In her bed, Nora listened and smiled at that. This one would be easy. "So I absolutely reject the concept of devil possession." Nora had to fight back wild laughter. Easy, easy, easy. "But I don't believe the girl was raped. And you didn't hear that from me."

"Then what was her motive for doing this, doc? Ten-, eleven-year-old kid. What's behind it?"

Terhune shook his head. Damn, he suddenly felt . . . well, *funny*. "That's your job to find out, not mine."

Nora listened intently, alone in her hospital room.

Jeanne had left the room, believing Nora to be asleep. Phil was staying at Morgan's house, with several of Morgan's friends with him.

"Herb Peery was set up," the cop said. "Why, I don't know. It's crazy. But I damn sure intend to find out the why of it."

"Good luck," Terhune said.

The cop nodded. "You believe in God, doc?"

"No, I don't, detective. Never have."

"I do," the cop said softly. He walked out of the morgue, leaving Terhune alone with his thoughts and the body of Herb Peery.

Terhune put out a hand to steady himself as that odd sensation once more filled his head. He bent down to pull the sheet back over Peery's body. He looked up as an attendant entered the room.

"I'll do that, doctor," the man said.

"OK, Bobby. Thanks." He stepped away. "Have you seen Dr. Morrison?"

"I think he's gone home, doctor. But he has the autopsy scheduled for first thing in the morning."

"Fine. I want to be present for it. Well, see you in the morning, Bobby."

"Good night, doctor."

As Terhune walked back to his office, he felt that odd sensation once more fill him. He stopped in the hall and shook his head several times. The sensation would not go away. It seemed to be growing stronger. Terhune started laughing softly.

"All right," he said aloud. Several nurses passed him, looking at him oddly. "Yes," Terhune said. "That sounds like fun. Fine."

Dr. Terhune walked to the elevator and took it to the

top floor of the hospital. He walked to the door leading to the roof and stepped out into the cold, windy late afternoon. He walked to the edge of the roof and looked down. He smiled. He removed his jacket, folded it neatly, and laid it aside. He stepped up on the edge of the roof and beat his chest like Tarzan. Several people in the parking lot looked up.

"I can *fly*!" Terhune yelled.

The people below watched in horror as the doctor went off the ledge head-first. He landed in the parking lot, on his chest and stomach. He died about three minutes later, from massive internal injuries.

Nora lay in her bed on the crisp white sheets, and smiled.

She just loved to play jokes on people. It was such fun.

Sam instinctively dropped to the concrete floor the instant the candles were blown out. He lay very still, all senses working hard. When he could hear nothing, he began very quietly easing his way across the floor, toward the wall opposite the wall containing the swastika. He pulled the nine-mm from his belt and placed his left hand over the hammer, his right thumb cocking the pistol, the left hand muffling the metallic click. He waited, crouched in the cool darkness of what Sam believed to be an old torture chamber. Or a meeting place for Nazis. Same thing.

Footsteps thudded on the overhead. Sam gripped the Colt tightly, then relaxed his hold so his fingers would not cramp. He followed the footsteps with his ears as they made their way from the den up the hall and into the kitchen. One person.

The footsteps stopped in the kitchen.

Sam then remembered he had forgotten to lock the front door before he came down to the basement.

"Mike Hammer I ain't," he muttered. What am I doing here? he silently asked himself. Jesus, I'm in this thing so deep it would take a crane to pull me out.

He heard the footsteps enter the pantry. The door was slowly opening. Sam leveled the Colt in a two-handed grip, silently vowing that he would not go into that long sleep quietly, or alone. He would take as many of *them* with him as possible.

"Make every round count, Sam," he softly murmured.

The door suddenly opened with a bang as it struck the wall. Sam's nerves were stretched so tightly he almost pulled the trigger at the noise. He heard a gasp from above him. Lights from the kitchen flooded the basement. Sam could see the person standing at the top of the stairs. He exhaled slowly as his jangled nerves began to quiet. He slowly lowered the nine-mm, easing the hammer down.

Dr. Sheela Harte stood framed in the bright light. "Sam?" she called. "Sam, are you down there?"

"Yeah." Sam stood up. "Down here, Sheela. Dammit, I almost wasted you." He had slipped back into the slang of Nam combat. "You almost got your shit blown away, lady. Stay where you are until I can light these candles."

The candles lighted and flickering, Sheela stepped down the stairs.

"How did you know I was in the basement?" Sam asked.

"I didn't. But I looked everywhere else. Then I saw

268

the door in the pantry and the keys in the lock. I didn't know where else to look."

She stepped onto the basement floor and hissed her revulsion at the sight of the huge swastika.

"Yeah," Sam agreed. "In spades. Sheela, what are you doing here?"

"I called Joe. He told me you were out here." Her eyes touched his in the semigloom of the basement. "I'm being watched, Sam. I was followed partway out here, but I lost them."

"You're sure?"

"Positive. Sam? Joe told me to tell you that your car was wired to explode. Paul disarmed the device." She looked around her. "What is this place?"

"I don't know. Not for sure. A part of Hell, I think." He showed her the heavy, cut-off bolts and told her his theory behind them. "I believe I'm right," he concluded.

She shuddered. "Let's get out of this place, Sam. It gives me the creeps."

"Very professional summation of your feelings," Sam kidded her.

"Right now I don't feel very professional," she replied.

The candles blown out and gathered up, Sam and Sheela climbed the stairs into the bright lights of the kitchen. Both of them experienced the eerie sensation of wanting to look back over their shoulder as they climbed the steps. Both were relieved as the door was closed. Sam locked it and put the keys back where he'd found them, storing the candles away.

Sheela looked at the locked door and sighed.

"Me too," he said.

She knew exactly what he meant.

"Now what?" she asked.

Sam leaned against the sink and looked at the woman. "Joe tell you everything that happened to me this day?"

"Your gunfight?"

Sam neither changed expression nor acknowledged her question.

"Joe told me you killed three Nazis and wounded another," Sheela said. "You and Paul switched cars and Paul is now attempting to get information from the wounded man."

"You know if you don't go to the police you could be charged and jailed?"

"I'm aware of that."

"And?"

"My interest in this is personal. I don't care what happens to any damned Nazi."

"When did you change your name?" Sam guessed at that.

"I didn't. My father did. Before I was born."

"And your father was from . . ."

"Poland. He fought in the Warsaw uprising. My uncles and aunts and cousins were all killed there. Or starved to death. Most of them. Those that were found alive were taken to Treblinka. They were never heard from again."

Sam nodded. "And you aren't in the least appalled by my violence?"

"It has been my experience—admittedly limited— in dealing with Vietnam veterans that you all are capable of violence. Especially those who were in special units."

Sam laughed aloud. The laughter felt good after the oppressiveness of the basement room. His laughter was not at Sheela, but at her remarks. Someday, Sam hoped, the shrinks would get it all together and discover that what was normal as described within the dry pages of textbooks was not normal in a stressful situation. And "normal" was a multifaceted word, not meaning the same from person to person. And there sure as hell was no thing as a fair fight. There was a winner and a loser. Period.

Sam remembered the day his father and mother had watched as an older boy picked on Sam on the sidewalk outside their apartment building. The boy told Sam he'd make a mark on the sidewalk with the sole of his shoe. He dared Sam to step over it. While the boy was marking the spot, his head down, Sam knocked the hell out of him.

When you're right, you're right. There was no such thing as a so-called fair fight.

"Why are you laughing and what are you thinking?" Sheela asked.

Sam told her. And told her about his early decision to win if pushed.

"What did your father do about that?" she asked.

"He said he would pray for me. I told him I'd rather be paid for some karate lessons."

It was Sheela's turn to laugh. "And that didn't sit well with him?"

"You got that right."

As they walked toward the den, Sheela asked, "You consider it normal to kill three human beings?"

"If they were trying to do harm to me, yes. Besides, Nazis aren't human beings. They're monsters. Surely

271

you would agree with that?"

She studied his face and vocally played devil's advocate, flip-flopping. "You don't appear to be overcome with remorse."

Sam elected not to play her game.

After seeing he was not going to reply, Sheela said, "I have some news that . . . probably concerns Nora. I heard it on the radio coming over here. A Dr. Terhune—I missed his first name—jumped off the roof of the hospital about an hour ago. Witnesses said he wasn't pushed, so it is listed as a suicide. I'll bet you he was Nora's doctor. And I'll bet you he was suspicious about the rape."

"You'll get no bet out of me. Sheela, I—we—keep getting deeper and deeper in this quagmire, and I can't see any end in sight."

"We all warned you to stay clear of this, Sam. It's going to get a lot worse before it gets any better."

"Yeah." Sam checked his watch and was surprised to see it was almost five o'clock. He looked outside. Dark. "Come on. I'll buy you an early dinner."

"You're *hungry*?"

"Hell, yes. Phillip . . . used to kid me about it. I even enjoyed C-rats."

"Rats!"

"No, no." He laughed at her expression. "C-rations. Military field food."

"That's a relief."

The morbid, haunting music began, drifting from the upstairs.

Sheela paled. "What in God's name is that?"

"The jack-in-the-box. Lovely, isn't it?"

25

Both Sam and Sheela were relieved to close the door of the Baxter house, leaving the laughter and the music confined in the house. Sam followed Sheela back to the Parkway. Back in New York State, they pulled over at a restaurant they both were familiar with and went in. As soon as Sheela smelled the aroma of food, she realized she was ravenous. They ordered drinks and studied the menu. After ordering, with Sheela in awe at the amount of food Sam ordered, she said, "May I make a guess concerning your childhood?"

"Sure. But why would you want to?"

"Based solely on the amount of food you just ordered. Sam, one person can't eat that much."

"Oh yeah? Wait until you see me sometime when I'm really hungry."

"Nobody eats *two* Cornish hens."

"Wait until the dessert cart comes around. I'll really show you something. Now what revelations do you have about my childhood?"

"Well, I'm just guessing. It's a game I like to play. Your family was very poor, right?"

He looked at her to see if she was serious. She was dead serious. "Poor? *Me?* Sheela, my old man retired a millionaire several times over. That's just the money I personally know about. I really don't know what's he's worth." He grinned. "Pop uses another attorney for that. He thinks I still got a noodle for a brain." Again he grinned. "I gave him plenty of reason to think that, I suppose. I drove a new Corvette to college my freshman year. After I wrecked that, pop bought me a new Thunderbird. I totaled that one— me and Phillip—and the state police jerked my license. I'm really not a very good driver," he admitted. "I will always believe pop had something to do with pulling my license. He shipped a bicycle up to me. And he was a lot happier after I stopped driving."

Sheela laughed at him and at her own hasty and totally inaccurate assessment of Sam's childhood. "Well, you can't win 'em all. Where are your parents now?

"Down in Florida, living it up. They earned it, raising me."

Sheela watched in undisguised amazement as Sam devoured everything on his plate and then ordered and consumed a huge ice cream with chocolate charlotte.

"And you never gain a pound, right?" she asked, a slight note of jealousy in the question.

"That's right. I can still wear the clothes I had in college. I've got a lot of nervous energy to burn up. I guess that takes care of the calories."

"I'd hate to have to cook for you."

"It would be a relief to keep company with someone who *could* cook," he said drily.

And that little imp with the bow and arrows slipped up behind them and conked them both on the noggin.

"The wounded man is no longer wounded," Paul Weaver said. "He's dead. The Connecticut police are having fits about the bodies, but you're in the clear, Sam. We all are. Now, about Nora. I spoke with a buddy of mine on the Bridgeport P.D. He doesn't believe it was rape. And you were right, Sheela. The doctor who took a header off the roof of the hospital onto the parking lot was Nora's physician."

"Otto Gunsche?" Sam asked.

"No luck there. I dead-ended on finding out where he lives. The Nazi lived long enough to convince me he didn't know. The four dead goons were minor figures in Otto's Nazi cells. Otto and his nasties do dabble in devil worship, but I don't know to what extent. Not as much as I had first thought. And I'll tell you something that might come as a surprise to you, Sam: I'm beginning to believe Nora and Otto have no direct connection. I think it's coincidence. But," he said, holding up a warning finger, "the two could come together."

"Then would you please explain why those creeps were after me?" Sam asked.

"I wondered about that. Just before he died, the Nazi told me. Ernest von Meter."

Sam sank back into his chair. He slowly nodded his head. "The Nazi I helped deport almost ten years ago."

"You got it. He's out of prison and believed to be back in this country. Somewhere in the Midwest. Nebraska, the guy thought. But he's still got a hard grudge against you, Sam."

"Von Meter has to be at least sixty years old," Sam said.

"Around that," Paul said. "But he's more dangerous than ever. With a strong neo-Nazi group of cells to back him up. And getting stronger."

"Well, to hell with him. How about the basement of the Baxter house?"

"You're probably correct in your assessment. But we'll probably never know for sure. The man who owned the house in the forties, during the war, is dead. But he was antisemitic. Anyway," Paul said with a sigh, "I've ordered your car sent back to the rent people. From now on, you wanna go somewhere, one of my people will take you. Same goes for Debeau and Dr. Harte. Now give me that nine-mm of yours, Sam."

Sam reluctantly handed over his Colt.

Paul said, "I'll dispose of this. If you are questioned about it, and I don't believe you will be, just tell them you gave it to Phillip Baxter a couple of years ago." He handed Sam another Colt Commander. "That one is legal and registered. To me. I loaned it to you for protection."

Sam hefted the nine-mm. "We sure are dumping a lot on Phillip."

"He won't mind," Paul said.

Father Debeau returned to his own residence several days later. There was no reason for him to remain at Sam's. The autopsy on Herb Peery found nothing that would have caused him to behave as he did. Paul posted a twenty-four-hour guard around Debeau, Sam, and Sheela—off-duty NYPD personnel Paul used occasionally. People he knew could keep their mouths shut. Christmas came and went with nothing happening. Nora returned home and stayed there quietly. Dr. Terhune's death was ruled a suicide. Sam and Sheela decided to bring in the New Year together.

New Year's Eve, and at the Baxter house Jeanne was preparing to step back into society, her first time since Phillip's death. At the quiet mental insistence of Nora. She was going to spend New Year's Eve with Judy and Matthew Gipson.

And Nora had something special planned for her precious brother.

"You are both sure you don't want me to have someone come over and stay with you?" Jeanne asked the kids.

"Don't be silly, mother," Nora said. "We'll be fine. We'll probably go to bed early." She yawned. "I am rather tired."

Jeanne looked at Phil. "That OK with you, Phil?"

"Sure, mom. We'll be fine," the boy assured her. "You go on and have a good time. You need some relaxation."

She kissed them both just as a car honked outside in the drive. Jeanne was gone a few moments later.

Nora looked at her brother with a smile on her lips. "I think I'll go upstairs and take a bath, Phil. Get into bed and read for a while."

"Yeah, OK, sis. I'm going to sit in the den and

watch TV."

"Goodnight, Phil."

"Goodnight, Nora."

She watched as Phil moved zombie-like to the den, switching on the TV and sitting down. He had no idea what was on the screen. Nora left him and took her bath, then dressed in her Nazi uniform, complete with polished, high boots. She fitted the death's-head insignia on the collars and took a four-by-four-foot Nazi flag from a trunk in her closet. She hung it carefully, lovingly on the wall, where the red flag with a black swastika set in a white circle seemed to dominate the room, casting an evil aura over everything.

She took the jack-in-the-box from the closet and placed it on the floor, opening the lid. The jack-in-the-box slowly, almost shyly, wearing its foolish, evil grin, came wavering and jiggling out of the wooden case. It bobbed and grinned and clicked its yellow teeth in front of Nora. Nora pointed to the Nazi flag on the wall. The eyes of the clown head shifted, staring at the flag.

"Softly now," Nora instructed.

The music began to play.

In the den, Phil shifted restlessly in his chair. He could not concentrate on the program. His thoughts kept returning to his father's gun cabinet, in the study. His father owned only two long guns: a rifle and a shotgun. Since the moment of the shooting, Phil had thought about his father's shotgun, his thoughts urged on by strange voices in the boy's head. The voices spoke to him several times a day, urging him to do awful things. At first the suggestions seemed awful. Now they seemed to be the right thing to do.

The voices had justified the killing of his father. And they had convinced the boy there was more killing to do.

"I would, Phil," the now-familiar voice entered Phil's head.

The boy sat in the chair and listened.

"There is no need to just sit and think about it. Do it!"

Phil nodded his head in agreement.

"And it would be fun, too. You know all those who professed to be your friends are now having fun and laughing at you."

"Laughing at me?"

"Yes. Laughing at you."

"The bastards!"

"And bitches."

"Yes."

"Go on, Phil," the voice urged, speaking silently and soothingly. "Just get the shotgun, look at it, touch it. It might help you to make up your mind."

"Yeah," Phil said. "You're right." He rose from the chair to walk into his father's study. He found the key to the cabinet and unlocked it. Had he turned his head at just that moment, he would have seen a hideous face looking at him through a window. The lips were drawn back in what the woman felt to be a smile. The tangled, matted hair resembled a modern-day Medusa. The woman's eyes glowed with evil and madness.

Phil touched the lightly oiled barrel of his father's twelve-gauge pump shotgun. His father had accepted the rifle and shotgun as gifts from a man he had successfully defended in a case. Phillip had never used them to hunt, only to skeet shoot several times a year at a club.

Phil had asked his father to show him how to operate the rifle and shotgun, and his dad had.

Phil took out the twelve-gauge and hefted it, feeling the balance of the expensive weapon. He removed the plug as his father had shown him, and loaded the shotgun full with three-inch magnums. He stuffed his pockets full of shells and then found his jacket, slipped it on, and filled the jacket pockets with shells too. There was a strange smile on the boy's face. He took a hunting knife from the cabinet and fitted the sheath onto his belt.

"That's good, Phil," the voice spoke to him. "That is very good. You know what you have to do, so do it."

"Yes," the boy whispered. "Yes, I know. All right. I'll do it."

"Fine. You're doing the right thing, Phil. They're laughing at you right now. You know they are."

"Yes, I know."

"They should be punished for that. It isn't right for them to make fun of you. And that's what they are doing."

Phil's eyes changed, turning hard and bright and mean. His fingers gripped the shotgun. "Yes, You're right."

Phil walked out into the hall, carrying the shotgun, his pockets bulging with shells. He looked up toward the second floor landing. He was not surprised to see his sister there. He had been expecting her.

Nora stood slim and pretty, dressed all in black,

Silver death's-heads on her collars. Her blond hair was clean and brushed and shining. She raised her right arm, the fingers straight and stiffened. "All praise the Dark One," she said. "Power to those who worship the Prince of Darkness. Long may the Third Reich reign. One people, one Reich, one leader: the Prince of Darkness."

"Yes," Phil whispered. "Do I get a pretty uniform like yours?"

"All in time. Listen to me, Phil. Do you renounce all faith and belief in God?"

"Yes," Phil replied, mesmerized by the sight and sound of his sister. He felt a strange power take control of him.

"Good, Phil. That's good. Now, do you loathe and despise all things pertaining to Christianity?"

"Yes."

"Do you renounce mother and father and pledge total allegiance to Satan?"

"Yes."

"Do you renounce all ties to things of this earth?"

"Yes."

"Do you believe in the superiority and purity of the Aryan race?"

"Yes."

"Now go and do what you know you must."

Phil turned and walked through the house, exiting out the back door.

The jack-in-the-box began laughing. Nora's girlish laughter joined in. The house rang with evil laughter. The girl waved her hand and the laughter ceased. Nora returned to her bedroom. She closed the jack-in-the-box and placed it in the rear of the closet. She saluted the Nazi flag and removed it from the wall, folded it carefully, lovingly, and placed it in a drawer. She removed her SS uniform and put it back in the trunk. She changed into pajamas and slipped into bed.

Everything was going well. Right on schedule. This night should prove very interesting. Oh yes. Most interesting.

The jack-in-the-box laughed, muffled by the closed container.

A mist materialized in the room, red-tinted and foul-smelling. A misshapen and horrible figure rose out of the mist to hover over Nora's bed. The child slipped out of her pajamas and spread her legs, allowing the creature to enter her.

Nora moaned as she physically became one with the creature.

The woman dressed in tattered rags had watched Phil leave the house. She waited in envy as the marriage was consummated between the child and Satan. She slipped silently onto the back porch and softly made her way up the stairs. She paused on the landing, averting her eyes as the mist leaked from under the closed door to Nora's bedroom. She waited until the mist was gone.

"Go to your place, Jane," Nora called. "And don't come out again until you are instructed to do so."

"Yes," Phillip's sister said. "At once. I only live to serve you, little princess."

"Stop babbling and let me rest!"

"Yes, missy."

Jane climbed the short flight of steps to the attic. She found her place in the darkness. She curled up like the evil animal she was born to be and went to sleep.

Phil was ready to begin his bloody night's work. He smiled at the thought.

Happy New Year, everybody!

26

Phil walked the alleys and dark backyards toward Alec's house. He knew Carl and Betty would be at the club this New Year's Eve for the big bash. He also knew that Alec was having a party at his house that night, and he had not been invited. That pissed him off. All of them were probably sitting around making out and drinking beer and laughing at him. The dirty bastards. Some of them were probably screwing too. Phil was still a virgin. But that was about to change. Soon.

He approached the house from the rear, after checking all the houses close by. He heard the music playing and the laughter of young people having their noisy fun.

Phil would show them some fun. He gripped the shotgun and touched the hunting knife. Yeah. He'd turn this party into a real sharp blast.

He laughed softly at that.

Phil pulled on thin leather gloves and jacked a shell into the chamber, feeding another shell into the magazine. He stepped up onto the porch, knowing the back door would be open. The Tremains never locked their back door.

He looked in through a window and saw Linda Greene in the kitchen. She was alone, pouring beer from the can into a glass. Phil licked his lips.

Phil laid the shotgun aside and tapped on the window. Linda looked up, a frown on her face. When she saw who it was, she smiled and walked to the back door, opening it.

"Hi, Phil!" she said. "I didn't know whether you were coming or not."

"I'm planning on coming," Phil said. "Come on out here, Linda. I want to talk to you."

She hesitated, then shrugged her shoulders. "Sure, Phil."

Linda stepped out onto the porch and Phil hit her on the jaw, knocking her to the floor, stunned. He tore at her clothing, ripping her jeans off, stripping her naked from the waist down. He dropped his jeans and underwear to his ankles and forced the girl's legs apart.

Linda groaned and bit at her lips, fighting back a scream. She endured the rape in silence as Phil hunched on her.

When he was finished, he jerked up his shorts and jeans. Linda curled into a soft ball of hurt and glared at him.

"I hate you, Phil Baxter!" she cried.

Filled with rage, he reached down and cut her throat, the sharp blade ripping her. He kicked her body off the porch. It hit the ground with a soft, lifeless thump. He slipped into the house, past the kitchen, and into a room where he waited.

"Hey, where's Linda?" the voice rose over the

throbbing of music.

Phil recognized the voice as George Miller's. Big jock type. Phil realized he had always hated George.

"In the kitchen," Susan Ward said.

"I'll get her," George said.

But when he went in she wasn't to be found. He saw the back door open and went to look outside.

The sight that awaited him shocked and sickened him.

George's mouth worked up and down, his Adam's apple bobbing, no sound coming out. He walked around the body, not believing what he was seeing.

Phil appeared out of the darkness and drove the blade of the knife into George's back, all the way up to the hilt. It wasn't as easy as it looked in the movies. George made all sorts of disgusting sounds. He cried out and moaned and jerked his body. Phil grunted as he pulled the blade out. That wasn't as easy as the movies made it seem either.

Phil dragged the still-jerking and crying George into the dark room off the kitchen and began whacking at the boy's throat with the bloody hunting knife. He stopped his gory work and wiped his blade clean on George's shirt. He stepped into the kitchen and found a long butcher knife with a thick, heavy, very sharp blade. Then he resumed his whacking. Blood sprayed the walls and the floor; blood covered Phil.

"Hey, what are you two doing in there?" someone yelled.

The red-tinted mist gathered on the back porch. Eyes appeared from out of the mist, unblinking and staring in satisfaction at the scene.

Phil locked the dead bolt of the kitchen door and

put the key in his pocket. He slipped through the house, walking into a bedroom, his silent movements not disturbing a boy and a girl making love in a spare downstairs bedroom. Phil stood and watched.

What did disturb the coupling pair was when Phil picked up a heavy iron bookend and beat their heads in with it. He knocked them both unconscious and then hammered their heads into a messy, unrecognizable, bloody mass of bone and blood and brains.

Phil slipped into the foyer and locked the front door, again using the dead-bolt lock and again pocketing the key. Moving quietly, with the butcher knife tucked behind his belt and carrying the shotgun, Phil locked as many of the windows in the house as he could. The noise of the rock-punk music, turned up very loud, covered his silent, shadowy movements.

Then he bumped into a warm, soft, breathing body.

Carrie Dewese. She jumped back in fright then laughed nervously as she recognized Phil.

"What are you doing sneaking around, Phil?" she asked. "Why . . . that's a *gun*!" She looked at him in the gloom of the bedroom. "God, Phil, you're covered with *blood*!"

"How very astute of you, Carrie," Phil said. He butt-stroked her with the shotgun, the butt breaking her jaw and dropping her unconscious on the floor. Then he sawed and hacked at her throat with the butcher knife.

Her screams brought other kids running. It took about ten seconds for the crowd to react. Pandemonium took over. Some of the girls began screaming; some of the boys began puking. Everybody began running around in a wild panic, not knowing what to do.

Phil knew what to do, even without the voice telling him.

He stepped under the archway and began pulling the trigger of the shotgun. Phil knew the very loud music would cover much of the shotgun's blast. The houses on both sides of the street had been dark and empty; all the adult residents of the very affluent neighborhood were at the country club for the big party. And a cold rain had begun falling, deadening the bloody night.

Brains splattered the walls as slugs tore the life from the knotted-up young people in the den. Blood dripped from the walls, the drapes, the pictures hanging in the den. Great jagged, smoking holes appeared in the expensive paneling. Pictures were torn loose, smashing on the floor.

Phil ducked back into the darkness and quickly reloaded. He ran through the house and once more appeared in the door leading to the kitchen. Several young people were at the back door, struggling and screaming, trying to open the locked door, trying to escape the carnage. Phil leveled the shotgun and pumped five rounds into them, knocking them spinning, great bloody holes in their bodies. Blood splashed around the kitchen.

Phil reloaded and turned the muzzle of the shotgun toward the hall, pulling the trigger. Pieces of teenagers bounced wetly around the hallway, smearing the walls and ceiling and floor with a deep crimson.

Phil stepped over the crying, moaning kids and walked through the house. Everybody was down. No, there was one huddled in a corner. Phil blew the boy's head off. He caught movement to his right. A closet door closing. Grinning Phil reloaded as he walked. Pausing, he turned the stereo up, the rock-and-roll music blasting the quiet. Phil thought it blended in quite well with all the crying and moaning.

He jerked open the door and found Susan Ward huddled on the closet floor. She was shaking and weeping uncontrollably. Her terrified eyes lifted. "Oh God, Phil!" she wailed. "Don't kill me! Please, God, don't let him kill me."

Susan began slobbering. She banged her head against the closet wall, her eyes wild with sudden madness. Phil poked at her with the muzzle of the shotgun. There was no response. Susan was totally bonkers. Flipped out into zonkoville.

Then Phil remembered something: Where were Alec and Jennifer? He walked through the house, pausing to cut the throat of each boy and girl as he searched. Alec and Jennifer were not in the house. The moaning and crying had ceased. The house knew only the throb of rock and roll as hearts labored and stopped beating. Stepping over the sprawled bodies, Phil looked outside just as headlights of a car flashed, pulling into the driveway.

"Ah-hah!" Phil said, grinning through the blood splattered on his face. He unlocked the front door and turned off most of the lights in the den. He crouched down in the foyer, waiting. The door opened and Jennifer stepped inside. Phil drove the butcher knife into her soft belly and jerked up, the blade tearing through stomach and nicking the heart. Jennifer fell to her knees, dying in a vaguely prayer-like position. He drove the butt of the shotgun into Alec's belly and then kicked his friend in the face, knocking him out.

Phil stripped Alec down to his underwear and then stripped off his own gory clothing. He dressed Alec in his clothing and put on Alec's clothes. He put the shotgun in Alec's hands, several times pressing the unconscious boy's fingers all over the blood-splattered barrel of the weapon. He put the butcher knife in Alec's hand, pressing the fingertips onto the blade several times. He very carefully tossed the knife across the room. He found stashes of grass on several of the kids and put them in Alec's pocket. He found some blues and greens and stuck the pills in Alec's mouth, rubbing his throat until the boy swallowed them.

Very carefully, he made his way back to the kitchen. He picked up the phone and dialed the police emergency number. "Please help me," he said. "It's just awful." He made his voice gruff and hoarse. "There's blood everywhere. Everybody is dead. I'm at 1006 Maplewood Drive. No, no! God! Don't!" he screamed. "Please, Alec, don't kill me. God, Alec, you're crazy! Don't . . .!" he screamed, letting the phone fall against the wall.

He pressed the fingers of a dead boy onto the receiver and let it dangle. He left the house by the back door. Carefully, keeping to the shadows, he walked through the rain to his house. He was home long before the wailing and moaning of sirens cut through the wet night. Quickly he showered and changed into pajamas and robe. He put Alec's clothing into the clothes hamper, at the very bottom. He would wash clothes tomorrow. He'd been doing that since his dad had . . . gone. Helping out his mother. She would think nothing of it. He went into the study

290

and broke the lock on the gun cabinet. He replaced the few shells he had left, and closed the door. He settled down in the den, watching TV.

Like his sister, whom he now loved very much, even worshipped, Phil was beginning to appreciate the value of a good joke. And the events of this night had been funny. The way they all jerked when the slugs hit them. Like cute little dance steps. Might call it the Hot Lead Boogie. Phil laughed at that.

But upstairs, in her bed, Nora was furious. Her brother had botched it all up. Phil was supposed to have been *caught*.

Goddammit!

The red mist materialized, soothing Nora. Telling her it was all right. Everything would work out. Just be patient.

In the closet, the music began playing, lulling Nora into sleep.

In the den, Phil chuckled.

27

"Turn loose of your cock and grab your socks, buddy," Paul Weaver quoted the old military wake-up call.

"Wh . . . what?" Sam mumbled. Sheela opened her eyes and looked at him. They were in Sam's apartment, in Sam's bed. They had chosen to celebrate the New Year in their own fleshy way, and then had fallen into a deep sleep. Sam looked at the bedside clock-radio. They had not been asleep long. "What's up, Paul?"

"There's been a goddamn massacre at the Tremain house. That's just up the street from the Baxter house. Eighteen kids shotgunned and stabbed to death. One girl totally flipped out, and the Tremain boy, Alec, is going to be charged with eighteen counts of Murder One."

Sam sat up straight in bed, now wide awake, the adrenaline pumping. "Paul, I don't believe the Tremain boy had anything to do with it."

"Neither do I. But what do we tell the police? That the devil made Phil or Nora do it?"

"Damn!"

"I concur. But that doesn't bring us any closer to putting a stop to this madness, does it?"

"What next, Paul?"

"Kill Nora."

"But Father Debeau said . . ."

Paul cut him off. "I know what Joe said. Listen, Sam, Joe is a very fine, decent man, a very honorable man. But he is basically a peaceful man. Naturally. It's his profession. I'm not. Now I've got you all covered with my people and personnel from the NYPD. You might not hear from me for several days. You may never hear from me again. If you don't, you'll know I failed."

"Paul!" Sam shouted. "Don't try this alone. One person can't do it. But together . . ." He checked his words, realizing he was speaking to a broken connection.

He told Sheela what had happened. "I got to call Father Debeau." He punched out the numbers and heard a sleepy voice say hello. "Father Debeau?"

"Yes."

"Sam Sobel." He briefed the priest and told him what Paul was planning.

Debeau sighed heavily. "The brave fool. And that poor Tremain boy."

"Joe, we've got to move, and we've got to move now."

"Don't go off half-cocked, Sam. You'd be playing right into Satan's hands."

"Do we have a choice, Joe?"

"No."

After hanging up from Debeau, Sam called Jeanne. The phone was answered on the first ring. "Jeanne? I just heard. What is happening at your place now?"

"The police are here, Sam. Oh God, Sam. It's just terrible. Those poor kids."

"Put the officer in charge on the phone, Jeanne."

"Lieutenant Blassingham, Mr. Sobel."

When Sam donned his attorney's clothes—in this case, his skivvies—he did not mince words. "Why are you there and what have you asked Phil?"

"Relax, counselor," the cop said. "Phil's in the clear. We just wanted to ask him about Alec Tremain. We found where his father's gun cabinet had been broken into. The kid was as surprised as anyone; showed us where his dad kept the key. Hell, Mr. Sobel, Phil was in his pajamas and sound asleep in front of the TV when the first team got here."

"I'm going to ask you honestly, lieutenant: Is it essential that I come out right now?"

"No, sir. We're clean on this end. We're leaving right now."

"Will you be at work in the . . . this morning?"

The cop grunted. "With eighteen dead kids, one kid stark raving insane, and the community up in arms—what do you think?"

"Then I'll see you in a few hours, lieutenant."

Lieutenant Steve Blassingham sat for a silent moment, staring at Sam. He cleared his throat and said, "Would you mind repeating that, Mr. Sobel?"

"You heard me, lieutenant. It wouldn't be any different the second time around."

"Ah . . . *yeah!*" the detective blurted. He rubbed a hand across a tired face. "Mr. Sobel, I really don't appreciate your humor."

"I'm not joking, lieutenant."

Blassingham took a sip of cold coffee, grimaced, and tossed the paper cup into the wastebasket. "Devil possession? Evil jack-in-the-boxes? Haunted houses? Come on, Mr. Sobel!"

"Call Detective Archie Fremont of the Bridgeport P.D. Ask him his opinion, off the record, of Nora's rape. Go ahead." He gestured toward the phone.

"I been knowin' Archie for years. But what'll it prove?"

"It might prove to you that Nora is vicious and cunning and ruthless."

"Maybe that's true. But that don't prove she's possessed by the devil."

"It's a starting place for you. I already know the truth."

Blassingham hesitated, then grabbed the phone. Bridgeport P.D. on, he asked to speak to Fremont. He chatted for a moment, swapping good-natured insults with the other cop as old friends will, and then asked about the rape case. Blassingham listened, grunting every now and then, said he'd be back in touch, and hung up.

Blassingham looked at Sam. "That's one for you, counselor. From what Archie said, I'd say the kid molested the guy and then started hollering rape. But it doesn't prove devil possession."

"What faith are you, lieutenant?"

"Catholic."

"Would you believe a priest?"

The cop's eyes grew wary. "Well, I'd sure listen to what he had to say."

"Nora killed a nun."

"Why wasn't it reported? Never mind! I'm sure it's got something to do with the devil."

"You want to talk with the priest here?"

"No," Blassingham said quickly. "Café just up the road. The priest with you?"

"Sitting out in the waiting room. But I'd rather not meet in public. I want you to hear some tapes Phillip and I recorded."

"We can use the back room of the café. I've used it before. Guy who owns it is a retired cop. It's very private."

"Half an hour?"

"I'll call ahead and tell him the two of you are on the way."

"Three. I have Dr. Sheela Harte with me. She's a child psychologist."

"Naturally," the cop said drily. "Why didn't I guess?"

Blassingham listened to what Debeau had to say, what Sheela had to say—beginning from when Phillip first entered her office—and then listened to all the tapes.

He leaned back in his chair, his face suddenly sweaty. "Jesus!" he said. "Holy Mother of God!"

"I gather we can no longer compare you with Thomas?" Debeau asked.

"I get the point, Father," the cop said. "All right, let me play the doubter for a moment. Not that I'm fully convinced, mind you. Who killed all those kids at the Tremain house?"

"Phil, probably," Sam said. "But I doubt if he remembers doing it."

"That would depend entirely upon whether the boy

has renounced all faith in God," Debeau said. "If he's now willingly in league with Satan, he knows exactly what he did, and will kill again if commanded."

Blassingham crossed himself. He looked at Father Debeau. "Can you . . . uh . . . you know, exorcise the kid?"

"I doubt it," Debeau said. "Priests are not magicians, lieutenant. Several weeks ago, on the night of Phillip's death to be precise, four of us were coming to the Baxter house to do just that. When we saw what had happened, we all agreed it was too late. To be perfectly honest, I don't know what to do about the situation."

"I can work on the Baxter kid and maybe come up with enough to shake his story," Blassingham said.

"Nora would probably help you," Sheela said. "In her sly little way."

"That would be cutting off just the tip of the tail of the snake," Debeau said. "We want to crush the whole monster."

Blassingham shook his head. "Wait a minute, people. Just hold on. Jesus. I can't go to my boss with this stuff. Any of it! He'd toss me out on my ear."

"There is a private detective name of Paul Weaver," Sam said. "He's been working on this with us. He's going to try to fight Nora alone. Probably within the next day. Maybe today. He's not going to make it alone."

"Now what are you trying to tell me?" Blassingham asked.

"That Nora will kill him."

Blassingham nodded. "As I said, you know I can't go to my boss with this. He'd have me committed.

297

But OK, I'll agree that wherever this kid, Nora, goes, something terrible happens. But," he lifted his eyes, taking in the trio, "I get the feeling there is a lot more that you're not telling me."

Debeau, Sam, and Sheela sat quietly. Debeau finally said, "What do you mean, lieutenant?"

"Like those three neo-Nazis we found, shot to death with a nine-mm. I don't suppose you'd own a nine-mm, Mr. Sobel?"

"Sure do. I loaned it to Phillip Baxter." Forgive me, Phillip.

"Sure you did, Mr. Sobel." Blassingham expelled a long breath of air. "This county just set a record for murders. That Tremain house looks like a slaughter-house. I never seen *anything* like it. There's maybe a couple of guys, three at the most, that I could convince to help me—us—on this thing. Maybe four guys; I forgot Shawn Cosgrave. Big, wild Irishman. He'd help, for sure. Christ, I must be nuts for doing this."

"Then you'll help?" Debeau asked.

"Yeah," the cop said wearily. "Why not?"

The car pulled up behind Paul Weaver's car, parked just up the block from the Baxter house. Two men got out. Paul knew they were cops the instant he spotted them. He watched them in the rearview as they walked up to his car.

Paul rolled down the window. "Something, boys?"

"I'm Shawn Cosgrove, this is Burt Riley. We'll be working with Father Debeau and Mr. Sobel on this . . . thing, Paul, don't try this alone."

"You boys going to stop me officially?"

"No, Paul."

"You boys get in out of the cold. We'll talk. I got a big thermos of coffee."

Seated in the warmth of the car, the off-duty cops accepted paper cups of coffee. Shawn said, "Anything going on at the Baxter house?"

"That little she-devil knows I'm out here watching her and the house." Paul said. He handed Shawn high-powered binoculars. "Top floor, last window on the front."

Shawn lifted the field glasses and sighted them in. "Yeah. I got her. Pretty little kid. But what is that thing she's holding?"

"Antique jack-in-the-box. It's alive," Paul tossed that at the cops.

"*Alive?*" Burt said.

Shawn dropped the binoculars and let out a yelp of pain as the glasses grew too hot to hold, burning his hands. "What the hell!"

Paul chuckled grimly. "She's been playing tricks on me for a couple of hours. Rocking the car, turning on the lights, the wipers, the radio. Turning off the heater, the ignition. She's having a fine old time."

The engine suddenly died. The windshield wipers began working. The radio came on. But it was no local station. The funeral march began playing through the speakers. Burt Riley was suddenly bounced up and down on the back seat, spilling his coffee and banging his head on the roof of the car.

The engine came back on. The wipers stopped working. The radio became silent. The cop in the back seat settled down.

Paul never took his eyes off the faint figure of Nora,

299

a half block away. "You boys see what I mean?"

"Holy shit!" Burt said, squirming around in the back seat, trying to avoid the coffee spill.

Shawn's arm suddenly shot up, the hand held against the roof of the car by some immensely powerful invisible force. He tried to pull his hand down. He could not.

"Relax," Paul said. "Think of God. Of a worship service. That will free you. Or it should."

Shawn closed his eyes and thought of the past Sunday's Mass. He recalled the priest's sermon. His arm dropped free.

"I'm not believing this," Burt said. "I see it, but I'm not believing it."

Burt suddenly began rocking back and forth, his head whipping to and fro as his torso jerked uncontrollably.

The cop's movements were abruptly halted, the suddenness of it tossing him to the floorboards.

"You boys sure you want in on this piece of action?" Paul asked.

Burt crawled back onto the seat. His voice was shaky. "Could we back off if we wanted to? Not that I want to," he quickly added.

"I don't think so," Paul said. "That is just a hunch on my part. No, I think we're closer to death than any of us have ever been. Another hunch on my part. I've had a lot of time to think about . . . spiritual matters sitting here today. Let's just say I've gotten closer to God than I've been since I was a little boy."

The cops sat quietly and listened.

The radio began playing a dismal dirge, the music draggy and off key.

The music stopped.

"I thought about making some sort of deal with God," Paul said. "Then I recalled something a preacher said one time about God not making deals. So I rejected that idea. I think. But," he sighed, "one thing I know for sure. And that is, that little monster in that house has to die. That's the bottom line, boys."

"And you are . . . ?" Shawn left the question openended.

"I'm going in that house after her," Paul said. He pulled a Smith & Wesson model 57 from a shoulder holster. He hefted the big .41 magnum. "And I'm going to shoot her right between the eyes."

28

Jeanne sat alone in the den—alone except for her thoughts. What she didn't know was that the words in her head were not her own. She had known all along, as she had admitted to Phillip and Debeau, that Nora was an evil child. She had known all along her daughter had manipulative powers. She just didn't know to what extent. Now she knew, but it was too late. She had no more control over her own thoughts, her own life, her own destiny. There had been a complete reversal of roles between mother and daughter.

Nora was now in total control.

But some very tiny part of Jeanne's mind was fighting the new suggestions being silently forced into her brain. They were disgusting suggestions. Jeanne would absolutely, positively refuse to obey.

The thought-thrusts became stronger.

Jeanne would absolutely, positively refuse. Jeanne would absolutely, positively . . . Jeanne would absolutely . . .

Jeanne would.

She rose from her chair and picked up her purse.

She looked up as Nora and Phil entered the room. "I'll be driving up to Bridgeport to see about Aunt Morgan. I'll be back late this evening."

"Do your duty, mother," Phil said.

"Yes, mother," Nora said. "You will kill her, won't you?"

"Of course, darling," Jeanne said.

Jeanne slipped into her coat and left the house.

Nora looked at her brother just as the haunting music began. Brother and sister began laughing.

"Sam," Bob Turner said, "I know you and Phillip were more like brothers than friends and partners, but do you realize what you're saying? Good God, Sam! We could put this down on paper and sell it to a scriptwriter."

Sam had expected this. If Bob or Ed had accepted the story straight out, he would have worried about their mental state. He shifted his gaze to Ed. "There are about ten members of the NYPD, one entire private detective agency—the ones we use—five or six members of a Connecticut police department, a child psychologist, and a priest working on this thing, boys. Just listen to these and then make up your mind."

He played them all the tapes.

"Jesus Christ!" Bob blurted.

Sam didn't let up. He told his friends and partners everything. Those awful hours in the hall of the Baxter house. The hideous images. He and Phillip perhaps seeing the vague outline of Satan. He told him about Nora's so-called rape. He told them everything.

Ed slumped back in his chair in the firm's conference room. "But there is still more you haven't told us, right, Sam?"

"I've told you everything that is pertinent to this matter," Sam said shortly.

"All right, Sam," Ed said. "As you wish. Just what is it you want us to do about . . . Nora?"

"I don't know," Sam admitted. "Other than keep it to yourselves, of course."

"I'm gonna run right home and tell my wife," Bob said sarcastically. "And I'm sure Ed's going to do the same thing. I can just imagine her reaction."

"Pointless thing for me to say," Sam said. "Forget I said it."

"What *can* we do?" Bob asked.

Sam stood up, pushing his chair back. "I'll be out of pocket for . . . , I don't know how long. Until this matter is resolved. I hate to dump my case load on you guys . . ."

Ed and Bob both waved that off. Ed asked, "What else can we do, Sam?"

Sam's eyes were bleak. "Pray for me."

The P.I. and the two off-duty cops watched Jeanne leave the house and drive away. As she drove past them, they all commented on the odd expression on her face.

"Tail her," Paul said. "If she heads for Bridgeport, get to the hospital ahead of her. I think she's going to pull something."

"The old lady?" Shawn asked.

"Yeah."

Shawn left, taking the unmarked car. Burt and

Paul sat in the car and watched as Phil left the house, carrying something in a paper sack.

"Now what?" Burt asked.

"I don't know. But you take the car and follow him. I'm going in that house and do what should have been done a long time ago."

He was out of the car and gone before the off-duty cop could protest.

Burt lost Phil for a minute, then picked him up again as the boy cut through back yards. He seemed to be angling toward the old water tower, about a mile and a half from the Baxter house.

But what would he be going there for? the cop thought. And what would he be carrying in that sack?

Unanswered questions.

Burt parked the car and continued following Phil on foot. He stayed well behind the boy and didn't think he had been spotted—yet.

"Yeah," he muttered. "No doubt about it. The kid is heading for the water tower."

But why?

That question was soon answered as Phil pulled something out of the bag and discarded the bag. He was holding a long length of rope.

Then it hit Burt. The kid was going to hang himself!

Burt was still a good three hundred yards away when Phil started to climb the old tower. The cop began running and yelling.

"Don't do it, boy! Come on, now. Let's talk about this."

Phil climbed faster. Burt slipped in the mud and fell heavily. Jerking himself up, he ran toward the tower.

"Phil! Phil Baxter! Stop, Phil. Talk to me, boy!"
Phil climbed faster and higher.

"I ain't gonna make it." Burt panted. "I ain't gonna make it!"

Paul pushed open the door to the Baxter house and stepped inside. The house was very warm. *Warm*—it was plain hot. And what was that sickly smelling odor? It smelled like . . . death and disease and rotting meat and bloated maggots and . . . Paul didn't know what else.

"*Guten Tag*, Herr Weaver." The voice came from above Paul.

He looked up. Nora stood by the railing on the second floor. She was dressed in an SS uniform. She smiled at him and snapped him a Nazi stiff-arm salute. "I salute you, you who are about to die."

"One of us is, girl. That's for sure."

"*Ja*, Herr Weaver. That is correct. One of us is about to die."

Paul jerked the .41 magnum from leather and jacked back the hammer.

Nora laughed at him.

"You find the most powerful handgun in the world amusing, girl?" Paul asked.

"I find it amusing that you should think you, and that weapon, could inflict any harm on me."

Paul lifted his arm, aiming the .41 at Nora. His arm and hand began trembling. Slowly, despite all his efforts, the muzzle of the pistol began twisting in his hand. No, not in his hand. His entire hand and wrist was turning.

"Jesus help me!" Paul shouted. "Help me, Michael. Help me destroy this devil-child!"

Nora laughed at him.

"God!" Paul screamed, unable to control his hand and wrist movements. "I'm willing to die, but let me kill this creature in doing so."

The music began to play.

Halfway up the water tower, Burt saw Phil scurrying down the other side, on the other ladder. "Goddammit, boy!" he shouted. "What in the hell are you trying to pull?"

Phil scampered down the steel ladder, on the ground long before the older and out-of-shape Burt. Still wearing the rope looped around his shoulders, Phil ran back toward his house.

Burt cursed and panted his way back down the ladder. On the ground he began jogging on trembly legs after the boy. "Foot pursuit," he said. "At my age. Wonderful."

Burt he wasn't about to give up.

His heart hammering, his head swimming, Burt followed the boy back to his house.

Paul had ceased his struggling. He now stood with his arms at his side, the .41 pointed at the floor. He seemed to be waiting for someone. He was. He heard the front door open, but only his eyes moved. He watched Phil enter the house and go straight into the den. The boy did not seem to notice Paul standing at the base of the stairs.

Burt staggered into the house, nearly exhausted. He leaned against the foyer wall, gasping for breath. He heard Paul say, in a strange, hollow-sounding voice, "Watch out for the boy. He's got a gun."

"What?" Burt panted the word.

"He's going to kill you," Paul said.

Burt looked all around him. He could not see anyone else in the house. The cop pulled his snub-nose .38. "Where is he?"

Phil suddenly jumped out of the den, screaming. He had a gun in his hand. As he screamed, he hit the floor.

Burt fired, the bullet tearing a hole in the paneling. Paul lifted his .41 and shot the cop in the stomach. The slug knocked Burt backward, against the wall.

"You son of a bitch!" Burt said.

Paul shot him again, the slug hitting the cop in the leg, knocking his feet from under him. As he was falling, Burt raised his .38 and shot the P.I. in the center of the chest, the slug tearing into the heart. Paul staggered, righted himself, and stared at the dying cop through dead eyes. He slowly fell to the floor, landing on his face, smashing his nose and mouth. The .41 slid from dead fingers.

Burt heard laughter coming from above him to the right. He looked up. Nora stood on the landing, the jack-in-the-box in her hands. The ugly clown head was swaying back and forth as some dismal piece of music played. The cop shifted his gaze. He was having a difficult time making his eyes focus; his vision seemed to be cloudy. He could just make out Phil, standing in the archway of the den entrance.

Oh no! Burt thought. That's a toy gun in the kid's hand. A friggin' cap pistol.

Phil laughed at the cop. Burt watched him go to a cabinet and place the toy pistol in a drawer. He turned and said, "Fooled you, didn't we?"

"Why?" Burt managed to gasp, the pain in his stomach almost blinding him.

"Call the police, Phil," Nora said.

"Hell, I am the police," Burt said. Somehow he didn't think that would impress the kids very much.

"Not anymore," he heard Nora said, as the darkness began to wrap its cold cloak around him.

"What do you mean?" Burt uttered his last statement.

"You're just dead," Nora said.

29

"Damn!" Shawn said. "Lost her."

Jeanne had cut off the Parkway and shot the juice to the BMW as she headed south. Shawn didn't know how she'd lost him, but she sure had.

"Maybe I can beat her to the hospital," he said, turning around and heading back toward the Parkway. As he drove, he thought: Wonder what's happening back at the Baxter house?

"Just what I need!" Shawn mumbled as his eyes caught the flashing lights coming up fast behind him. "A highway cop."

He pulled over and got out of his car.

Shawn showed his I.D. and explained that he was on a tail. The highway cop nodded.

"You know a Burt Riley?" he asked.

"Sure, he's my partner."

"Not anymore, sergeant. It just came over our Tach frequency. He and some P.I. name of Paul Weaver just shot it out in a private residence outside of New Canaan. Both men are dead."

Shawn slumped back against the highway cruiser.

"But they were working *together*."

"Sorry," the highway cop said. "This have to do with that mass murder the other evening?"

"Yeah," Shawn said, his voice just a whisper. "It sure does."

Jeanne looked at the old woman lying pale and motionless on the bed. Morgan was awake and staring at her. The left side of her face was paralyzed, that eye permanently open and staring. The eye blazed with fury at the younger woman.

Morgan opened her mouth and tried to speak. Grunting sounds were all she could manage. She gurgled and slobbered on herself.

Jeanne stood over the old woman and smiled down at her. "You knew it had to end this way, Morgan. The Prince is impatient."

Morgan snorted more incomprehensible words and tried to pull away from the evil smile.

Jeanne took a pillow from the bed and covered Morgan's face with it, holding it firmly. The old woman jerked on the bed as air was cut off.

It did not take long for the woman to die. When her heart monitor began straight-lining, Jeanne put the pillow back on the bed and rushed out the door, waving frantically at the nurses who were running up the hallway toward the room.

"Help me, please!" Jeanne said. "She's . . . she's having trouble breathing."

Jeanne was escorted down the hall to the waiting room. A few moments later, a doctor came to her and told her the old woman had died.

Jeanne sobbed on the doctor's shoulder for a moment, and then straightened up, wiping her eyes. "It was just a matter of time, I suppose?"

"Yes, Mrs. Baxter," the doctor said. "Frankly, we were all amazed she lived this long. She was a very strong woman."

"I'll . . . make the arrangements," Jeanne said.

"Mrs. Baxter?" a man spoke from the corridor.

Jeanne shifted her eyes to the man. "Yes?"

"I'm sorry to have to tell you this; it's a lousy time. But there has been some trouble at your house. Your kids are both OK; not a scratch on them. But there's been a shooting. Two men dead. I'm to escort you back to your home."

Jeanne's hand flew to her throat. "Nora and Phil?"

"They're just fine, Mrs. Baxter. I assure you of that. Is there someone you could call to help out with . . . this?" He waved his hand, indicating the hospital.

"My brother. I'll call him. Then you'll drive me home, Mr . . . ?"

The man's eyes were very cold. "Fremont, Ma'am. Detective Sergeant Archie Fremont."

"All right, Sam," Ed Weiskopf said, standing in front of the small group but looking at Sam. "I have no more reservations. I believe there is some sort of . . . supernatural happening behind all of this."

The group, sitting in the conference room of the law offices of Baxter, Sobel, Turner, and Weiskopf, included Sam, Father Debeau, Sheela, Steve Blassingham, three cops who were working with

Steve—Shawn Cosgrave, Mark Hopper, and Charles Brewer—Bob Turner and Ed Weiskopf, Archie Fremont, and the DA of the county, Dean Ellis.

The young DA's face reflected a mixture of inner emotions: fear, disbelief, shock, and horror.

But after listening to all the tapes and hearing all the conversation, young Ellis was beginning to believe. He was really ready to believe just about anything. He had eighteen murders to cope with in his county. Twenty-one, if he counted the three dead Nazis.

If anybody really gives a damn whether a Nazi is killed.

"Devil possession?" Archie asked. "I mean, are you all really taking this *seriously*?"

They were, and all said as much.

"OK," Archie said. "I'll play along."

"Jenny Wright," Sam said.

"I beg your pardon?" Archie asked.

"Jenny Wright. She's the kid I told you all about. The one institutionalized at the Center. If she could speak, even write out a statement, telling us that Nora killed Carla Donna, we could put so much heat on Nora she might be forced to reveal her true self." He looked at Dean Ellis.

"It happened in my county," the young DA said. "All right. You want me to send someone up there?"

"I'll go myself," Sam said. "And I'm not taking anything away from you or your people. OK?"

"Fine with me, Mr. Sobel."

Sam nodded. "How about the Tremain boy?"

"Being kept in isolation," the DA replied. "What few friends of his were left alive have told the police

313

and my investigators there is no way Alec could have done it. He had never fired a gun in his life. Did not use dope—of any kind—and he had not been drinking the night of the massacre. There are glove prints all over the lower floor of the house. Lots of them. And Alec was not wearing gloves. Furthermore, tests indicate he did not fire the weapon. And that is ironclad. Lastly, there is not a bruise anywhere on the boy's body. That was a twelve-gauge shotgun, firing three-inch magnum rounds. At least twenty-five rounds were fired. The recoil of that weapon is fierce. It would have left marks of some sort on the boy's shoulder—his side, even, if he'd fired it from the hip. Fibers from the shirt were found on the butt pad, and a thread from the shirt was caught in the weapon. But the boy's mother said those were not her son's clothes. The giveaway is the shoes. Virtually blood-free. Unlike the shirt and pants, which were blood-splattered Alec Tremain did not kill those boys and girls."

Going to be a fine lawyer, Sam thought, revising his earlier opinion of the young man.

"And now . . . ?" Ed asked the DA.

"Alec?"

Ed nodded.

"We're going to keep him in lockup, but in a very safe area."

"Mr. and Mrs. Tremain?" Bob asked.

"I have given them my opinion," Ellis said. "And told them we'd like to keep Alec in lockup—very safe lockup—for a few more days, to give us more time to work this thing out. They agreed—reluctantly. But their attorney told me, bluntly, that if something isn't resolved within seventy-two hours, all this information will be leaked to the press and he'll demand Alec's freedom."

"That would drive Nora further underground," Father Debeau stated.

"Yes," Ellis said with a sigh. "I'm afraid that is correct."

Sam looked at Sheela. "Want to take a trip up to the Center?"

"Sure. Right now?"

"Right now."

"She hasn't spoken a word in years," the doctor told them. "She eats her food properly. Her body functions are handled normally. She makes her bed and cleans herself and brushes her hair. But she will not speak. And she is utterly terrified when we take her out of her room."

"Where is Monsignor Vincinci?" Sam asked.

The doctor's expression became wary. "I thought you were here to discuss the Wright girl?"

"The two are connected," Sam told him. "And you know why and how."

"Don't get pushy, Mr. Sobel," the doctor warned. "I am under no obligation to discuss *anything* with you. I can terminate this conversation any time I desire."

Sam smiled and opened his briefcase, taking out a folder and opening it. "Dr. Walter Kent. You have an interesting background, doctor. As do most of the resident doctors at this institution. Very strange, doctor, that you are all highly schooled in religion first, and *then* in psychology, psychoanalysis, et cetera, et cetera. It's also odd that almost all of the nurses here have such an extensive religious background. I've been in several mental institutions at one time or another, and I have never been in one that openly displays so much religious paraphernalia. Especially since this is a private institution, and not funded— that I can discover—by any church."

Dr. Kent smiled at that.

"Parapsychology, doctor. You believe in that?"

"What is it, specifically, that you want, Mr. Sobel?" the doctor asked.

"I want your opinion of what is really wrong with Jenny Wright."

The doctor drummed his fingertips on his desk. He sighed. "I have been keeping up with what has been happening with the Baxter family, Mr Sobel. Morgan kept me informed. A very strong, very fine woman. She shall be missed."

Sam remained silent, letting the doctor ramble, finding his own way to the crux of the matter.

"What would you do if I refused to cooperate with you, Mr. Sobel?"

"I honestly don't know, doctor. But I do know that Nora must be stopped. I will—I think—go to any lengths to accomplish that. That answer your question?"

"Vaguely, and containing all sorts of veiled threats, yes. You're wrong on one point, Mr. Sobel . . ."

"Call me Sam."

"Very well, Sam. Various churches *do* give us contributions from time to time. But this is a privately owned *hospital*. Not an institution. People of all ages are sent here, Sam. After everyone else has given up

316

on them. Tell me, both of you, what did you feel upon entering this place?"

Sam looked at Sheela. He had felt . . . *something*. Sheela said, "A strong spiritual sensation."

"Very good, doctor. Most people can't readily identify it. We call it a tranquilizer of faith. If all the evil contained within the confines of the Center could be gathered, it would destroy the world. Believe it."

Sam looked pained. "Doctor, what is this place?"

"A repository for living evil."

30

Nora sat in her bedroom and turned her gaze toward the outside. She flung her commands across miles. She was getting stronger with each passing hour; soon she would be unstoppable.

She laughed softly.

At the home of the counselor and the coach, Rich stirred in his chair, looking at his wife, Bette. He averted his eyes, afraid his wife might be able to see inside his head, read his thoughts. He couldn't allow that to happen.

He was thinking about that cute kid in his P.E. class. The one built like a beauty queen—Mary Bennett. Hard to believe she was only twelve years old. Or was she eleven? Didn't make any difference, Mary knew what she was doing. Rich was certain of that, the way she batted her eyes and flirted with him. He got aroused just thinking about it. Tomorrow would be the day he'd call her bet; tomorrow would be the day he'd make some excuse to keep her after school, and then he'd take what she was so blatantly offering. He'd bet he wouldn't be the first one. She just had that look about her.

Tomorrow. Yeah!

Bette was feeling very odd. She didn't think she had ever been this depressed. And she didn't know why she should be. But she was. She looked at her husband, and felt nothing for him. Nothing. Just a great big empty void where she had once felt love. Or had she? Maybe she had never loved him. Yes, that was it. She hated the big sloppy pig. And she hated his boring football games too. And what was the slob doing just sitting over there with that stupid damned expression on his face?

She said, "You know, Rich, you're a real slob, you know that?"

"Huh?" Rich said, jerking his head around, glaring at her.

In her room, Nora laughed softly as she manipulated the couple.

In the closet, the music played dirge-like.

"I said, you're a big, fat, stupid slob!" Bette told him.

Rich rose from his chair and walked over to his wife. He belted her, knocking her out of the chair. She lay on the floor, glaring up at him.

"Asshole!" she said.

He kicked her on the leg. She screamed in pain and kicked back, catching him on the knee. Rich grabbed his knee and hollered, one-legging it as he hopped around the room.

"That's my bad knee!" he yelled at her. "That's the one I hurt in our homecoming game."

"Really?" she said sarcastically. She got to her feet and banged him on the head with a glass ashtray, nearly knocking him out. She opened the door and shoved him out onto the small porch, throwing his coat out after him. "I'll see you in the lawyer's office, you fat pig!" She slammed the door.

Nora laughed and laughed, clapping her small hands in glee. Tomorrow was going to be such fun, she thought. She couldn't remember ever having so much fun.

"What are you saying, doctor?" Sam asked. "A repository for living evil?"

"They're all here," Dr. Kent said. "All that the church cannot help are sent here. And here they live until the day they die."

"They?" Sheela said.

"The epitome of evil, Dr. Harte. The very essence of evil. The damned, the marked, the possessed, the believers and worshippers of the Prince of Darkness. The prison system is full of them, but the juries don't know that when they sentence them. Some of the prosecuting attorneys know, or at least suspect, but can you imagine some DA getting up and telling the jury that the person they are about to convict of whatever crime is actually a witch or warlock or demon, or a possessed person? Not likely. So we have them. Here, and in . . . other places."

"That's why the open display of so much religious paraphernalia," Sam said.

"Yes. And that is why the Church keeps several priests here at all time. Satan cannot stay long in such an atmosphere." He held up a warning finger. "But make no mistake about one thing: Most of the people we house here are evil. They are the children of Satan, and they know it! If we were to drop our guard for one

320

instant, they would sense it and destroy us."

"Gee, I never even *suspected* the existence of such a place!" Sam said.

"We don't exactly advertise," Dr. Kent said drily.

"Father Debeau could have told us about this," Sheela said accusingly.

"He told me he would have, in time," said Dr. Kent. "He knew that soon you would have to come up here. He felt it would leave a more . . . lasting impact if you witnessed it personally."

"Could I—we—see the patients?" Sheela asked.

"If you wish. I have to warn you both, it is not a pretty sight."

Understatement of the decade, Sam thought, as they walked the corridors of the hospital. He—and he was sure Sheela was experiencing it as well—could literally feel the evil all around them. Behind heavy locked doors, Sam could see dark and malevolent eyes staring at them through the steel-reinforced slits in the doors. The human demons, the possessed, the lovers of Satan hissed and cursed them as they walked.

"Ignore them," Dr. Kent said. "Keep your faith strong and to the fore."

"That didn't help Paul Weaver and Burt Riley," Sam told him.

"They tried to combat Satan with human instruments. Those are useless. Worse than useless. The demon-child turned the weapons against them. A favorite trick of Satan."

Sam and Sheela kept their eyes to the front as they walked. They both had seen and felt enough. Their skin felt as though slugs and leeches were crawling on the flesh, leaving an invisible trail of slime.

321

Suddenly the aura of evil ceased. Sheela commented on that.

"We changed wards," Dr. Kent explained. He stopped at a huge steel door, manned by an armed guard—armed not with a gun, but with a Bible.

"I'm not believing this," Sam muttered. "A *Bible* can stop these people?"

"Most of the time," Kent said, once they were on the other side of the huge door. It slammed hollowly behind them. "Sometimes we have to use physical force. But we would rather not."

"Doctor, how can you get away with this?" Sam asked. "Government and state inspectors, I mean."

"We are registered as a home for the criminally insane, among other things. This place is a country club compared to some. Ah! Here's little Jenny's room."

Dr. Kent opened the door. "Jenny," he said. "You have some people here to see you, darling."

Jenny looked up at Sam. "Get out of here, Jewboy!" she said in a strange hollow voice. A man's voice.

Then she leaped at Sam, screaming and shrieking and clawing at his face.

Bette went into the kitchen, ignoring the pounding on the front door. Finally she heard Rich's car start up and drive off. She felt sure he'd go to the gym and spend the night in his office. He had a cot there, and several changes of clothing.

Not that she cared where he went. Hell with him.

She fixed a drink and downed it standing by the table. Then she fixed another. That tasted even better

322

than the first one. She had several more. Maybe she'd take a bath, fix her hair, and go out. Look for some fun. That seemed like a great idea.

She loved this new and very different change in herself. She felt . . . well, *free*. "Oh, baby," she sang. "Free at last."

She had another drink while she bathed. She looked down at the bathwater. It had changed color. It was red. *Red?* And it didn't smell very nice. Matter of fact, it stank. As she watched, something like a mist began to rise from the steaming waters. She had never seen anything like it. It fascinated her.

The mist drifted around her face, and she breathed deeply. Strange, savage thoughts entered her head. She mentally fought, feebly, against the suggestions, finally succumbing to them.

"All right," she said. She climbed from the tub and dried. She dressed and put on a warm coat. She turned off the lights and locked up the house, walking to her car. She drove off into the cold late afternoon.

Oh yes, Nora thought, sitting by the window of her bedroom. Things were definitely looking up. The next forty-eight to seventy-two hours promised to be fun.

Dr. Kent reacted immediately and decisively, jerking Jenny off the startled Sam and flinging the girl to her bed. Within ten seconds attendants were at the scene, subduing the girl, giving her a shot, and strapping her down.

Dr. Kent did not seem at all surprised at the girl's behavior. "Nora's powers reached her," he explained. "Ever since Morgan called me a few months ago, I've been waiting and watching for something like this to happen." He looked at Sam. "Come on, I'll see to those scratches on your face."

After tending to Sam's face—the scratches were not serious—Dr. Kent walked Sam and Sheela out to the parking lot.

"What happens now?" Sam asked. He was still shaken by the suddenness of the girl's attack.

"Nora must be stopped," the doctor said.

"Well, I *know* that!" Sam said. "But how?"

"I don't know the how of it," the doctor admitted. "But I think it's going to be up to you, Sam."

Somehow that did not come as any surprise to Sam. He had been experiencing an uneasy feeling about that very thing for the past several days. But he had to ask, "Why me?"

The doctor stood in the cold, windy parking lot with Sam and Sheela and shook his head. "You were her father's closest friend. You stepped in and took up the fight after she killed her father. Therefore that makes you the enemy."

"You've known about Nora for how many years?" Sheela asked.

"We have quite an extensive file on people who are known to be candidates for possession. There are hundreds scattered throughout the United States and Canada. We try to monitor them as closely as we possibly can."

"I won't profess to understand all of this," Sam said, waving his hand at the hospital complex. "And I won't ask you how many of these places you have around the country. I'm not sure I want to know. It's amazing to me that you have managed to keep these places a secret from the press. Some muckrakers would love to blow this out of the water."

"One rather obnoxious press type did manage to penetrate us several years ago," Kent said. "I believe that man was the most thoroughly irritating person I have ever had the misfortune to encounter. He didn't seem to care at all about the safety of others; he just wanted to expose us for his own personal gain. One night he broke into the complex and managed to hide until night. Then he slipped past the guards and worked his way into the maximum security area." The doctor paused to light his pipe.

"What happened to him?" Sheela asked.

"We found him the next morning, sitting in the corridor, his back to a wall. He had suffered a breakdown. You know the evil you both felt inside?" Sam and Sheela nodded. "It drove him insane. It is my opinion that he was not a very nice person initially. Rather weak, morally."

"Where is he?" Sam asked.

"Confined here. A babbling idiot, if I may be permitted to use an unprofessional description." The doctor held out his hand and Sam shook it. "Good luck, Mr. Sobel. God be with you."

31

Rich slept fitfully on the cot in his office just off the
gym. He dreamed of Mary Bennett. He slobbered on
himself as he dreamed

Bette drove aimlessly throughout the evening. She
didn't know what to do or where to go. Her mind was
a jumble of confusion. Finally she pulled into a rest
area and managed to sleep, waking up every fifteen
minutes to look around her at the unfamiliar darkness.

Jeanne lay wide awake in her bed. She could not
sleep at all. She could understand that what she had
done to Morgan was wrong, but she didn't care.
She didn't care what happened to herself, or to
anybody else—not anymore. Nothing mattered. Finally she rolled over on her side and closed her eyes.

Father Debeau rose early, long before dawn, and
carefully packed a few things in a leather bag. He
dressed and left the house. He pointed the nose of his

car toward Connecticut.

Sam awakened and lay beside Sheela. From her breathing, he knew she was awake. "It's today," Sam said.

"I know. And I'll be with you."

"No."

"Yes,"

Sam sighed impatiently. "Sheela . . ."

"I'm going with you. And that is that. You ready to get up?"

"Yeah. Might as well."

"You want some breakfast?"

He grinned. "Not even the devil could keep me from eating."

Steve Blassingham opened the front door. He was not surprised to see Archie Fremont standing on the porch. He waved his friend inside.

"I got a hunch," Archie said.

"Yeah. Me too. Whatever is going to happen, is going to go down today or tonight."

"That's what I think. You call the rest of your boys?"

"Just about to do that."

Dean Ellis tossed and turned until five o'clock. With a curse he threw back the covers and got out of bed. He dressed in jeans and boots and a heavy flannel shirt. He slipped into a leather jacket and left the warmth of the apartment. He drove to a café and drank coffee until dawn.

The young DA had never been so confused in all his life. He could defend or prosecute a living human being, but how in the hell does one go about fighting the devil?

An elderly woman stepped off the train and began slowly walking through the early morning light. "Taxi, lady?" a man called.

"No," she said in a soft voice. "I want to enjoy my last day. I prefer to walk. But thank you."

With the cab driver looking at her very oddly, the old woman slowly walked away.

Bob Turner called Ed Weiskopf at dawn. Ed answered the phone before the first ring had stopped.

"Bob here, Ed. What are you doing?"

"Waiting for you to call. Don't ask me why. I'd probably give you a totally stupid answer."

"Yeah. I understand. You want take a drive up to Connecticut?"

"I thought you'd never ask. Pick me up in about an hour?"

"I'll be there."

In the Baxter house, Jane sat up on the rags she called a bed. She waited.

The house uttered a long, shivering, evil sigh.

Just inside the Connecticut line, Sam pulled over and he and Sheela drank coffee for an hour. They both knew they were waiting, but neither one could say exactly why, or for what.

"Sam?" He looked up. "How are you—we—going to handle this? We can't just burst into the house."

"Yeah. But there is nothing to prevent us from going calling. Paying our respects, so to speak."

"Concerning this Morgan person."

"Yeah."

She glanced at a tiny wristwatch. "It's far too early for that."

Before Sam could answer, his eyes caught a familiar figure walking through the café door. Father Joseph Debeau. Sam waved him over.

Joe sat down and said, "And the forces of good gather to fight the good fight, eh?"

Sam said, "I've never considered myself an exceptionally good person, Joe."

"Oh, but you're not to be the judge of that, Sam. Nor I. But I can detect a great deal of good in you."

Tactfully, deliberately, Sam changed the subject. "I get this feeling that we three are not alone in our early-morning wanderings."

"We are all gathering," the priest said. He paused as the waitress brought coffee and left. "At least I hope we are all gathering."

"Why are we gathering?" Sheela asked. "I mean—you know what I mean."

"Are we being commanded by some higher power to

gather?" the priest asked. "I don't know. I like to think He has intervened."

"He with a capital H?" Sam asked.

"Yes." Father Debeau sighed heavily. "I left my home very early this morning. I spent several hours alone, in a small church not very far from here. In prayer. I have made my peace with God."

"Are you telling us you are ready to die?" Sam asked.

"Yes. And I probably shall do just that." He smiled. "I certainly hope not. But Nora despises me almost as much as she does you, Sam."

Sam looked up, and his eyes widened in shock and total disbelief. He half rose from his chair.

Phillip Baxter was standing in the door, motioning for Sam to come to him.

The big house on Maplewood Drive dominated the street. It always had, but today it seemed especially foreboding. It stood like an open challenge, daring anyone to enter. The house seemed almost *alive*. And it seemed to be waiting for something. The windows were like eyes, looking in all directions. Unblinking and unforgiving and evil. The house watched as Detective Archie Fremont drove past. It watched as Lieutenant Blassingham drove by. It watched as Dean Ellis drove past. And it watched as many others passed, driving slowly.

And Nora watched it all, from her bedroom window. The child shifted her gaze, her mind's eye seeing a classmate of hers playing in her front yard, enjoying this last day of vacation, on this Friday before school resumed on Monday. That stupid fool of a coach, Rich, had gone to the school to wait for his prey, and his foolish wife had wandered aimlessly about. Well, that was all right. She would allow them to wait; it would be good to have some fun on Monday as well.

Nora's mind's eye registered a car approaching her classmate's corner of the street. Nora smiled and took command. The girl straightened up and walked to the sidewalk. As the car drew near, the child stepped into its path. The startled and horrified driver slammed on her brakes. But it was too late. Both front and back tires rolled over the child after she was mangled on the bumper and grill. The heavy car crushed the life from her. She lay broken and bloody on the cold street.

Nora found it hysterically amusing. In her bedroom she laughed and laughed as the music played and the clown's head swayed back and forth to the somber dirge.

"I saw it all!" a neighbor yelled, running to the scene. He stopped as Nora's will took control of his. The man's face changed to hate. "You deliberately ran down that poor little girl. Goddamn you!"

"I did not!" the woman screamed. "She stepped right out in front of me!"

"Liar, liar!"

The man and woman were still screaming and cursing when the police arrived.

"Isn't this fun?" Nora cried.

"*Ja, ja!*" the clown head shouted. "Almost as much fun as killing.

"Contain yourself," she said. "That will come later."

"*Gut!* The sooner the better." The clown head looked at the girl. "What are you thinking?"

331

"More fun. Fun for mother. Oh my, yes."

Nora turned her head around and around, her eyes savage and lustful and wide. She laughed and projected her thoughts.

Downstairs, Jeanne rose from the couch and gathered up coat and purse. She left the house and got into her station wagon. She drove off.

"Where are you sending her?" the clown head asked.

"To Hell . . . ," Nora said.

"Sam! What's wrong?" Sheela asked.

Debeau did not look up. Instead he kept his eyes downcast, staring into his coffee cup.

Sam sat down. His face was pale. "Phillip was standing right there in the door."

Debeau sat very still and very silent.

Sheela looked at the priest. "Joe," she said quietly. "Is that possible?"

"All things are possible," he said.

"Joe, don't quote me drivel or Scripture. I don't want to hear it. What I want is for you, a man of God, a human being, to tell me if the dead can rise."

"Jesus did."

"I could argue that point," Sam said. "But I won't."

"I thank you for that," Debeau said.

"Can the . . . no. Have you ever known of the dead rising? You, Joe—*personally* witness anything like that?"

"I have . . ." He paused. "I have heard reports of it, yes. From very reliable sources. I personally have

332

never seen it."

"Do you believe it's possible?"

"Yes," the priest whispered.

"Under what circumstances?"

Debeau tried a smile that didn't quite come off. "What you saw, Sam, if you saw anything, was not the Phillip you and I knew. His body is still in the ground. Perhaps . . . perhaps you saw his spirit returning to assist us."

"What could a *spirit* do?" Sam found himself asking, incredible words coming from his mouth.

Debeau said, "Phillip now knows what lies on both sides of the veil, Sam. We are only cognizant of what lies on *this* side."

Sam nodded his head. "OK, Joe. I'm just a bushleaguer playing in your ball park. What next?"

"We wait here until the others gather."

"They're coming here?" Sheela asked. "Did you phone them?"

"No," the priest said.

"Then . . . ?"

"Have patience, child. They'll be here."

"I wonder which side Jeanne is on?" Sam blurted, not really knowing why he asked that question at this time.

"She is unwillingly—for the most part—a pawn of Satan. I don't know which side she'll eventually take."

Sam stared as Shawn Cosgrave entered the café. "Well, I'll be damned."

"I hope not," Father Debeau said.

32

Judy Gipson answered the front doorbell. She smiled and waved Jeanne inside. "Jeanne! How good to see you. Is something the matter?"

Jeanne stepped inside and returned her friend's smile. "Not really," she said, as the door closed behind her. "I've just come to kill you, that's all."

Judy looked startled for a second and then laughed. "Darling, your sense of humor is positively *morbid*. So early in the morning, too."

"Where is Matt?"

"Sleeping like a baby. Come on, let's have some coffee and you can tell me why you're out and about so early."

"The kids still away at their grandmother's?"

"Uh-huh."

"That's good." Then she picked up a vase and smashed it over her friend's head, knocking the woman to the floor.

Stunned, Judy crawled and wriggled her way across the floor. She pulled herself up and stood leaning against the wall, blood running down her face from the cut on the top of her head.

Jeanne hit her with her fist, knocking her to the floor. Judy's lips were mashed against her teeth as the blood dripped. She opened her mouth to scream and Jeanne kicked her in the stomach. Judy's mouth opened and closed in silent agony. Jeanne kicked her again, this time in the head, knocking the woman unconscious.

Jeanne went into the kitchen in search of a butcher knife. When she returned, the long knife in her hand, Judy was staggering to her feet.

She ran into the den. She was so frightened she was unable to scream, could only make little mewing sounds of fear.

Jeanne began slashing with the butcher knife. Blood splattered the floor and walls of the den as the sharp blade cut through the flesh of Judy's arms and shoulders and chest. One swipe of the heavy blade ripped Judy's lower face, slicing through her tongue. As Judy slipped from painful reality to unconsciousness, Jeanne stood over her, stabbing her again and again.

Satisfied with her work, Jeanne tossed the bloody knife beside the body of her friend and went into a spare bedroom, stripping off her clothes and taking a quick shower. She walked naked through the house, up the stairs to the master bedroom. She slipped into bed beside Matt and began fondling him.

Matt came wide awake with a startled look on his face. "Jesus Christ!" he said, looking at Jeanne's nakedness.

"Relax," she told him, feeling him harden under her stroking fingers. "Didn't you tell me at last year's club party you wanted to make love to me?"

"Well, yes. But good God, woman, Judy . . ."

"Judy is . . . out," Jeanne said. "She won't be back

any time soon. You don't think I'd be here if there was any chance we'd be discovered, do you?"

Matt laughed hoarsely as his fingers caressed Jeanne's flesh. "I suppose not." He groaned as Jeanne continued her ministrations. "Where'd she go?"

"For a ride."

"You're some baby!"

"Yeah, Matt, that's me, all right."

Matt panted and groaned and hunched. For at least three minutes. He rolled from Jeanne to lie by her side, his chest heaving from his exertions. "Was it good for you, baby?" he asked.

"Outstanding, Matt. You're a real tiger."

Matt didn't quite know how to take that remark. Now that the sex act was over, he was becoming very nervous. Now that it was over, he was wondering how and why it had happened.

"Uh . . . Jeanne?"

She rolled from his side and stood up.

"What's the matter, Jeanne?"

"I think I heard a car pull into the drive."

Matt jumped out of bed, showing more acrobatics in that one move than during the entire three-minute exercise in climactic futility. "Oh no!" he yelled. He ran around the room, not accomplishing anything except making Jeanne laugh.

"You think this is funny?" he shouted at her.

"Yeah, sort of," she said. "Oh, by the way, Matt. What is all that blood in the den?"

"I don't hear any car. *Blood!* What blood?"

"That's what I asked you. The den is splattered with blood."

"Oh my God!" Matt ran to the top of the stairs. Jeanne gave him a little help going down the stairs. She pushed him. Matt crashed down the stairs and lay at the foot of the staircase, one leg twisted under him. The whiteness of bone stuck out, glistening amid the spurting blood of a severed artery. He groaned once and then passed out.

Jeanne found the bloody knife and slashed Matt's throat, almost cutting off his head. She found jeans and shirt and dressed quickly. She wrapped the butcher knife in a towel and left the house, carefully locking the door.

"Did you have fun, mother?" Nora asked when she returned.

"I suppose so, dear," Jeanne replied. She could not remember anything she had done. "But I am rather tired. I think I'll lie down and take a nap."

"That would be nice, mother. But first I want to show you something."

"Oh? What's that, dear?"

Nora grinned and pointed to the second floor of the house. Phil Jr. hung by his neck, the rope tied at the base of the railing. His face was dark and swollen, his tongue protruding from his mouth, his eyes wide and bugging out from the pressure of choking to death. Blood that had leaked from his torn throat was dried now and crusted on his lips and chin.

Jeanne looked at her son. But she was mentally dead. Her soul was no longer her own. She looked at her son with no more interest than if he were a side of beef.

"Well, now," Jeanne said. "We'll have to do something about that, I suppose."

She climbed the steps and went to her bedroom, closing the door.

"You're moving too fast," Jane said. She had stepped out of the den.

Nora screwed her pretty little mouth into a pout. "I am not!"

"You're too impatient for power. You could have had so much, but soon you will have nothing."

"You can't speak to me like that!" the child squalled her outrage.

"You're a foolish little girl," Jane told her. "You're vain and much too sure of yourself. You should have waited. You . . ."

"Shut up!" Nora screamed. "Shutupshutupshutup!"

"*Ja, schweigen!*" the jack-in-the-box screamed harshly from the top of the stairs.

"It's not too late, Nora." Jane refused to be silenced. "Listen to me. We can repair all the damage. We can back off, right now, and salvage so much. Listen to me, Nora, we . . ."

Nora looked at the woman. Her eyes glowed. Jane's feet flew out from under her, toppling her to the floor. Nora began bobbing her head up and down. Jane's head began beating against the floor, faster and faster, harder and harder. The sound of the woman's skull popping was like gunshots. Still Nora kept the woman's head hammering on the floor. Bone and blood and fluid and brains began leaking from the shattered skull. Nora laughed at the sight. The clown's head bobbed and swayed, harsh laughter springing from the cruel mouth.

Nora's eyes ceased glowing. Her laughter died

338

away. The jack-in-the-box slowly sank into its wooden case, the lid closing with a click.

Nora climbed the steps to her bedroom and changed clothes, putting on her black SS uniform. She carefully hung the Nazi flag on the wall. She waited.

On the landing Phillip's sister lay dead in a pool of blood, her face unrecognizable from the battering.

Phil slowly turned at his rope's end, swaying gently.

Jeanne slept.

The big house sighed.

And time seemed to pause for a moment. The street grew silent.

Snow began to fall, the silent white hushing all things it touched and gently covered. All along both sides of the street, people sat in their houses, fear gripping them. They did not know what was taking place, only that they did not dare interfere.

"Are you out of your mind?" the sheriff asked District Attorney Dean Ellis. "You want me to do what?"

"Sounds stupid, doesn't it, sheriff?" Ellis said.

"Stupid is not the word for it. Dean, you're a very bright young man. And you're going to be one whale of a good lawyer. But you need some time off. You've been working too hard."

"Everything I just told you is true, sheriff," Dean hung on.

"All right, Dean. I'll send some people out that way to check it out."

"Don't patronize me, sheriff," Dean said.

"Is there anything else, Dean?"

Dean stood up. "I tried. God knows I tried."

The sheriff sat behind his desk and stared at the man.

Dean shook his head and slowly walked out of the man's office. He closed the door behind him. He knew that for some reason he had to head toward the state line. He couldn't explain it, he just knew he had to go that way.

"Haunted houses," Sheriff Collins said. "Devil-kids and hobgoblins. Nonsense!"

At the truck stop, Dean saw he was the last of the group to gather in the restaurant. He sat down at the large table and ordered coffee. He told the others about his session with the sheriff.

"That wasn't such a bad idea," Archie said. "You're on record, in a manner of speaking, requesting help."

Dean shook his head. "Weird weather," he said. "It's snowing like crazy just a few miles from here."

They all looked outside. The sun was shining brightly.

"Are you serious?" Shawn asked.

"I sure am. It's like a blizzard."

"Morgan's funeral is tomorrow," Sheela said.

"Might be a lot of funerals tomorrow," Steve Blassingham added. "They're still burying those kids."

"We're all stalling," Sam said.

Sheela gasped. Everyone at the table looked at her. Her face was very pale and her eyes were wide and staring.

"What's wrong?" Sam asked.

"Phillip Baxter," she finally found her voice. "He . . . he was standing right there in the front door.

Motioning at me. It . . . it seemed like he was trying to tell me something." She turned to the priest. "Joe. It wasn't my imagination. I *saw* Phillip Baxter."

"I know you did, Sheela. So did Sam. I, well, felt his presence about a half hour ago. What do you think he was trying to tell you?"

"He was holding up six fingers. Six fingers. What does that mean?"

No one knew.

Then it came to Sam. "The tapes," he said. "Nora must not be allowed to reach her twelfth birthday. Monday is her birthday. The sixth of January."

Lieutenant Blassingham looked at his men. At Mark Hopper. "We'll go in first. We can't all just bust in. I've been reading about . . . devil possession since this first came up. There is a theory that the person possessed can be weakened, the powers diminished by constant use. So we'll save the special troops, so to speak, for last. Me and Mark go in first. Then Shawn and Charlie. Archie and Dean go next." He looked at Bob Turner and Ed Weiskopf. "I can't give you guys orders. It's your decision to make."

"We'll go in next," the lawyers said.

"This might wipe out the firm," Sam said with a smile he did not feel.

Father Debeau looked at Sam. "You know you have to confront her alone, don't you, Sam?"

"Yeah," Sam said. "The Lone Ranger. You'll go in with Sheela?"

"Yes, Sam."

"A half hour apart sound all right to you people?" Sam asked.

"I feel like a fool," Dean said. "All these grown

men and women up against two kids."

"No, young man," Debeau warned. "Against the Devil."

Dean did his best to suppress a shudder.

Shawn waved the waitress over.

"Yes, sir?"

"Do you have any Bibles in the gift shop?" he asked.

"Oh yes, sir," she said. "A very wide selection."

Sam handed her a wad of bills. "Bring us a dozen of them, please."

The waitress looked shocked at the hundred-dollar bills he had pressed in her hand. "Do you want them gift-wrapped, sir?"

"No," Sam said. "Keep the change. I don't suppose you'd have the Old Testament alone?"

Debeau handed Sam a copy of the Old Testament. "I thought you might want this," the priest said.

"I'd rather you gave me the phone number of Samson, Joe," Sam fell back into character. He hefted the Bible. "But this feels pretty good."

Sheela touched Sam's hand. "I love you, Sam." She said it simply and sincerely.

Sam grinned. "Hell of a time for romance, babe."

33

"Where's all the snow the DA talked about?" Mark asked.

"That must be it just up ahead," Steve said. He shuddered. "You feel something . . . well, odd?"

"Yeah, and it's gettin' stronger, too. What is it?"

"I don't know. But I'll bet you it isn't anything good."

"You believe in time warps, Steve?"

"Mark, after all that's happened, I'm about ready to believe in anything."

"Nothing is moving, Steve," Mark pointed out. "No dogs, cats, people, nothing."

"I see it." He turned on Maplewood Drive. The Baxter house loomed up before them.

Steve was driving slowly and carefully, the street slippery from the crush of new-fallen snow. He stopped several hundred feet from the Baxter's driveway. The men sat for a moment, looking at the house, feeling the evil coming from it. The invisible force seemed to be directed straight at them.

Steve held out his hand. "Good luck, buddy."

Mark gripped the offered hand. "Luck, buddy." He

smiled. "Let's go give it hell!"

"Wonderful choice of words," Steve laughed. He opened the door. He looked back at Mark. "Do you have any idea at all how we're going to fight this she-devil?"

"Nope. Nothing." He looked toward the second floor. "There she is."

The cops walked toward the evil, silent, staring house.

The music began to play, drifting to them through the thick-falling snow.

I'm number six, Sam thought, waving away the offer of another cup of coffee. Six. I wonder what that means? If anything. The sixth team to enter that house.

Shawn and Charles had already left the truck stop, heading for Maplewood Drive.

"What are you thinking, Sam?" Ed asked. "You're very quiet."

"You guys shouldn't be in on this," Sam hedged the question. "You got no business here. You should head on back. Right now."

"The more the merrier," Bob said. "Come on, Sam. We were pulled here, just like all the rest."

"Messages from On High?" Sam said, much more sarcastically than he intended.

"Yes," Ed said solemnly. "I believe that. Don't you, Sam?"

"I guess so. Sorry I snapped at you." Something caused him to look around. He stared in disbelief.

The truck stop was empty. They were the only customers present. With one exception.

344

Phillip Baxter sat alone, at the table across the room.

Sam stood up abruptly, in his haste knocking the chair over. He looked straight at Phillip, not knowing if the others at the table could see him. Phillip smiled at him and held up one finger, pointing the finger first at Sam, then at himself.

"You and me?" Sam whispered.

Phillip nodded.

"All right," Sam said.

Phillip vanished.

Sam turned around and looked at the others. To a person they were staring in shock at the now-empty table where Sam had seen Phillip.

"So now you all believe, huh?" Sam said in a low voice.

They all nodded. "He indicated he was going to help you," Sheela said.

"Yes. But I don't know how he's going to do that."

"With God's help," Debeau said. "God is intervening. We have a chance."

"Why doesn't God just . . . well, wave His hand and put a stop to all of this?" Dean asked. "He could do that."

"God can do anything," the priest answered. "Michael is probably going into a rage watching all this. He would be eager to join the fight. But God won't let him. You all must understand that this is a human problem; we—all of us—brought it on, now we must combat it. Alone, for the most part."

"How did *we* bring it on?" Bob asked.

Debeau smiled, only then noticing that the big truck stop was empty of all other customers. He did not act surprised. "How many times has your law firm defended, successfully, pornographers, child abusers, pimps, whores, thieves, murderers, and all other kinds of human filth? Eh?" He looked at Archie. "How many times have you practiced selective law enforcement, detective? A double standard, if you will? Allowing your friends and the monied people in your community to break the law while arresting another, less-affluent person for doing the same thing? Turning your back when one of your buddies drives drunk, but arresting a stranger for doing the same thing? Eh?"

He laughed bitterly. "Oh, we're all guilty of that. Sins on top of sins. Everything foul and ugly that has visited this earth can be directly attributed to us. Everything of a human nature, that is. But we all pay for it, people. In one way or the other. Just as we are doing now."

"Good Jesus Christ!" Steven said, entering the house.

Jane's blood had leaked from the floor to the foyer, drenching the carpet with a dark crimson. One hand, pale and dirty in death, stretched out, balled into a fist at that last moment of painful life as death touched her.

The cops shifted their eyes up, toward the second-floor landing. They saw young Phil's body, swaying at the end of the rope. The boy's face was horribly swollen and dark.

Nora appeared at the head of the stairs. Evil seemed to spring from the child. Steve's mouth tightened at the sight of her. He knew that uniform. World

War Two Nazi SS. She held a wooden box in her hands.

The box slowly opened, an ugly clown's head appearing, bobbing and weaving forth. The jaws of the jack-in-the-box clicked and opened. Harsh words rolling from the mouth.

"Machen Sie di Tür zu!"

"What did he, it, whatever, say?" Mark asked.

"I don't know," Steve replied.

"My friend asked you to close the door," Nora said. Her voice was not that of a little girl. It was hollow and deep and evil.

Steven closed the door. Both men were immediately aware of a foul odor in the house. Not the odor of death, but something else, something neither man could describe.

"Welcome," Nora said. "You have a decision to make. Both of you."

Together, the men raised the Bibles purchased at the truck stop's gift shop.

"So you have made it," Nora said. "So be it."

"What do you hope to gain by all of this, kid?" Steve asked.

"I've already gained it," Nora replied.

"I don't understand," Steven said.

"Even should I lose, I've won," the girl told them.

"That makes no sense. *What* have you won? What have you gained by all this death and pain and suffering?"

Nora smiled sweetly. "Stupid, foolish men. You're going to die for nothing. You can't kill me. Nobody can kill me. I plan to destroy all of you. And then, because I'm just a little girl, what do you think will

347

happen to me?" She laughed. "Nothing. Your courts will institutionalize me until I'm eighteen, and then turn me loose. I can wait. I have lots of time to plan and organize."

The cops looked at each other, knowing the girl was right all the way.

"Clever of you," Steven conceded. "So now what?"

Nora smiled. "Look at your friend."

Steve turned his head. Turned his head just in time to see Mark jack back the hammer on his .357 magnum. "What . . . ?" Steven managed to say before Mark pulled the trigger. Steven's brains splattered on the foyer wall.

Mark put the pistol back in his shoulder holster.

"Go wait in the den," Nora told him.

The cop obeyed, moving as a zombie.

Nora sat down at the top of the stairs and waited, the swaying clown head beside her, its jaw clicking and snapping as it laughed and laughed.

"The Master is always right, child," the jack-in-the-box said. "It is good that he came to you. This way is better."

Nora did not agree, but she had no choice in the matter. The Prince had given her instructions. And the Dark One must be obeyed.

The child and her toy waited.

Shawn Cosgrave and Charlie Brewer stepped up onto the porch of the house. Like those who had preceded them, both men could feel the evil of the house. It was unnerving.

And both cops could smell the odor of fresh blood.

"I wonder whose it is?" Charles asked.

"One way to find out," Shawn said, and pushed open the door.

Sitting in the car parked in the driveway of a family the sheriff knew was gone for the winter, Sheriff Ed Willis sat with his chief deputy, Jerry Asminov. The men had been there for several hours. And they were both becoming more and more curious.

Ed lowered his binoculars. "Well, there go Shawn Cosgrave and Sergeant Brewer. Now what in the world is going on, Jerry?"

"Maybe the DA was leveling with you?"

"Jerry . . .!"

"You asked me, I told you. What if he is right, Ed? Have you thought about that? If we don't do anything else, we'd better check this thing out or we're liable to wind up looking like a pair of fools."

"Yeah." Ed's reply was anything but enthusiastic. "Did you log the time?"

"The second team showed up exactly one half hour after the first team. Ed? You wanna call the CHP?"

"No! You want to call the state police, Jerry? Tell them we're investigating a witch?"

"I guess not."

"That's what I thought. Look, we're close enough to hear any shots, right? We haven't heard any, right? No signs of any trouble, right? Let's just sit it out for a while longer."

Nora looked at Cosgrave and Brewer. She froze them rock-still. "Listen to me," the girl said. "I know neither of you wants to die. So I'm going to spare your lives. To serve me. *Look at me!*" she said sharply. The men could move their eyes, nothing else.

The eyes of the cops shifted, locking with the hard, bright gaze of the child dressed in black.

"You may speak when asked a question," Nora told them.

"Yes," the men said together.

"Do you wish to die?"

"No."

"Do you understand how you may live?"

"Yes."

"Is that agreeable to both of you?"

"Yes," Charles Brewer said. Shawn remained silent.

"I thought it might be you," Nora said. "You're a damned fool."

Shawn did not speak.

"Shoot him, Mark," she commanded.

Mark Hooper stepped out of the den and shot Shawn between the eyes. Bits of his brains joined those left on the wall by Steven Blassingham. Shawn's body tumbled to lie beside Steve's.

"Did you hear something?" Ed asked his deputy.

"I didn't hear nothing."

"Must have been my imagination."

"Thank you, Mark," Nora said. "Return to the den."

Yes, Princess," Mark said. His eyes now shone with an evil light.

Nora looked at Charles Brewer. "You may leave. Go to your and car and leave. Do not contact any of the others. You remember nothing. You will remember when you are told to do so. Who is your master?"

"Satan, Princess."

"Go."

"Now what?" Ed said, watching Charles leave the house.

"Weird," his chief deputy agreed. He reached for the mike, hesitated, then pulled his hand back.

"Go ahead," the sheriff told him.

"And tell dispatch what?"

Ed sighed. "Christ, I don't know. Pull a unit in here, Jerry. Unmarked. We'll take it from there."

Neither man noticed the elderly woman walking slowly up the street.

Archie and Dean were only a few miles from the Baxter house. Those five remaining at the truck stop had grown silent. There was not that much left to say.

No phone at the truck stop had rung. And all knew what that meant.

"I wonder if they're dead?" Sheela broke the silence.

"There are worse things they could be," Father Debeau said.

They all knew what that meant.

"Time for us to go," Ed said to Bob.

"You guys are nuts," Sam said. "You're over your heads in this thing. I wish both of you would just go on back to the city."

Before either partner could reply, Debeau said, "Don't go in the house, gentlemen. Drive to it, park outside and wait. If the police do happen to drive by and question you—although I don't believe they will—tell them who you are and that you are waiting for Jeanne Baxter. You have to go over some matters pertaining to your law firm. Do not enter that house."

"Then what good are we?" Ed asked.

"Witnesses," Debeau said. "There must be someone left alive to tell what happened—or at the very least, remember it."

"Be careful," Sam told his friends. "We'll see you in a little bit."

Sam looked across the room.

Phillip sat at that same table, staring at him.

34

"What's up, sheriff?" the deputy asked.

"We don't know," Ed admitted. He informed the two deputies about Dean's visit that morning. And of the people who had entered the Baxter house. Only one leaving. Thus far.

"Ghosts!" the younger of the deputies said. "Witches?"

Ed Willis sighed. "That's what the man said." He paused as another car pulled up to the Baxter house, two men getting out. "Look, There's Dean now. But who is that with him?"

"I've seen him a time or two at HQ. I think he's a detective from Bridgeport. Yeah, Fremont's his name."

Before Willis could hail the men, they had disappeared into the house.

The deputies got into the back seat of the sheriff's car. One said, "I feel weird."

"Weird, how?" Jerry asked.

"I don't know. Sort of, well, *creepy.*"

"So do I," the sheriff admitted.

"Holy cow!" Archie blurted. "Look at all this mess."

Dean looked at the dead cops and turned his head

353

away, puking in a corner of the foyer.

"Oh, you'll be easy," Nora said.

Both men jerked at the voice. They looked at Nora, sitting on the steps. "Who'll be easy?" Archie asked.

Before Nora could reply, a little girl's voice drifted down from the second floor. The voice was singing a nursery rhyme. "Pat-a-cake, pat-a-cake, baker's man. Bake me a cake as fast as you can. Pat it and prick it, and mark it with B. Put it in the oven for baby and me."

"What the hell . . ." Archie muttered.

Jeanne danced by on the second floor landing. Her hair was all done up in brightly colored ribbons. She had pinned up the hem of a dress high above her knees. She had applied makeup as a child might, smearing the lipstick and putting on far too much rouge, coloring her cheeks like a clown. Even from the first floor the men could see her eyes were mad.

Jeanne held a doll in her arms, cradling it protectively. "Here comes a candle to light you to bed," she sang. "Here comes a chopper to chop off your head."

Jeanne whirled and danced about the landing, holding the doll close to her. "Here's my little demon," she said. She stopped her dancing and looked at the men. "Isn't my little demon baby pretty? Pretty baby, pretty baby."

"Hi, Archie," Mark said, stepping out of the den.

Archie turned just in time to catch a glimpse of the meat cleaver in Mark's hand. That was the last thing in this life he would see. The cleaver split his head open from crown to neck, spraying the walls with blood and brains.

Dean stood jumping from one foot to the other,

354

making little grunting sounds.

"Uh, uh, uh," he said.

"Be still," Nora told him.

Dean stopped his hopping.

"Who saw him die?" Jeanne sang in her little girl's voice. "I, said the fly. With my little eye, I saw him die."

"That's enough, mother," Nora said. "Go to your room."

Jeanne danced off, holding the doll, singing, "Pease-porridge hot, pease-porridge cold, pease-porridge in the pot, nine days old."

The door to her room slammed. She was silent.

Nora looked at Dean. "Whatever you were, you will remain. Except for your mind. That belongs to me. Do you understand?"

"Yes, Princess," Dean replied.

"When this is concluded, I shall direct you on the proper legal course. Is that clear?"

"Yes, Princess."

"Tell those watching outside that nothing is happening in here. Now go. And wait for my orders."

"Yes, Princess."

Dean left the evil-filled death house and stepped outside. He walked to his car. The sheriff backed his car out of the drive, stopping Dean.

"What's going on in that house, Dean?"

"Just continuing our investigation of the murders, Ed. Fremont from Bridgeport had some new evidence. Mrs. Baxter is very helpful, and Phil is . . . hanging loose."

"Oh, I see. You need any help from us?"

"No. But thank you, Ed. Oh, tell your people there

355

will be men and women in and out of the house all day. No need for concern."

The sheriff looked relieved. "Good. Ah, Dean, you have, ah, changed your mind about that, well, little matter we discussed earlier?"

Dean laughed. "Oh, yeah. Sorry about that, Ed."

Ed patted Dean on the shoulder. "Good, Dean, good. See you around."

"Right, sheriff."

Once more the snowy street was deserted.

Bob and Ed had stopped along the way and bought a large thermos, filling it with coffee. They had sandwiches prepared and topped off the gas tank. They settled down for a long wait, parking on the snowy, deserted street.

"What's with this neighborhood?" Bob asked. "It's eerie."

"Yeah, but I want to know what's going on inside that house," Ed replied.

"Look!" Bob said, pointing toward the second floor.

Nora stood at the window, staring out at the men. The silver death's-heads on her collars caught the light and glinted at the men. She was smiling and motioning for the men to come on in.

Ed opened his door.

"Where are you going?" Bob said.

"You take that side of the street, Bob. I'll take this side. Let's go to every house. Bang on the door. We're investigators working on the kids' murders. Come on."

The men tramped through the snow up and down

356

three full blocks. No one would come to the door. When they got back to the car, their feet were soaked and cold. They turned up the heater and took off their shoes and socks, placing the socks next to the blast from the heater to dry them.

"You get any response?" Ed asked.

"Not a peep. I could see people in the houses. But they acted like they didn't hear my knocking. And I really hammered on the doors."

"Yeah. Me too. And I could see dogs in some of the houses. They didn't bark; didn't even look up at my knocking. It's like, well, something is blocking out reality. You know what I mean?"

"Yeah. And I know who is doing the blocking." Bob let out a yelp of fear, dropping his cup of coffee.

"What's that?" Ed asked. Any further words forming on his tongue were frozen there as his eyes riveted on the form outside the car.

Phillip Baxter stood on the snowy street, looking at the men.

"I still feel I should go in there with you," Sheela said.

"No," Father Debeau said. "You wait with Bob and Ed. I must confront the Dark One alone. It's something I have known for some time."

"Can you win?"

"No. But I can weaken his force. The rest is up to Sam."

Sheela and Debeau parked behind the two lawyers and got in the back seat. They could tell the men were badly shaken still.

"Phillip?" Sheela asked.

"Yes," Ed said. "He was standing right there!" He pointed.

"So lifelike," Bob muttered. "It got to me."

Debeau picked up his small leather bag and opened the door, stepping out into the snowy cold. He opened his mouth to speak just as a scream came from the house.

"That's the first sound we've heard from that house," Ed said.

Nora appeared at a window of the second floor. Everyone could see her mouth was bloody. She grinned in a macabre leer and lifted one arm. She held a dripping bloody head in that hand. The head of an elderly woman. She raised the other hand, showing off the bloody knife. She stepped away from the window, disappearing from view.

"My God!" Sheela said.

"Phillip's mother, I would guess," Debeau said. "The old lady tried to help. Perhaps her dying did help."

"How?" Ed asked, real anguish in his voice. He felt sick at his stomach at the sight of the severed bloody head.

"Nora is aided by Satan, certainly," Debeau said. "But she is still a child. This much strain on her powers has to be taking a toll. I can sense the evil enamating from the house has abated. And more than slightly. The girl herself is weakening." He looked at those seated in the car. "God be with you all." Then he was walking toward the house.

Debeau's stride was firm and determined. Reaching the front door, he did not hesitate. He pushed open the door and stepped into the stinking house of evil and death.

He looked at the dead man sprawled bloody on the floor and said a small prayer. Lifting his eyes, he looked at Phil dangling. "Poor possessed boy," the priest said. He prayed for Phil's soul, softly but firmly. He lifted his head at the sound of derisive laughter.

Nora stood at the top of the stairs, still holding the bloody head of Mrs. Baxter. She tossed the head, and it bounced and fell down the stairs and rolled lopsidedly across the foyer floor, coming to halt only inches from Debeau's shoes.

"My dear granny," Nora said. "Isn't she lovely?"

Debeau ignored the sarcasm and began praying. Nora reacted as if someone had slapped her in the face. She recovered and glared at the priest, pointing a finger at him.

"You're dead, Debeau. Dead, dead, *dead*!" she screamed.

Debeau felt a heavy, invisible weight settle on his chest, forcing him back a step. He straightened up and continued his praying, ignoring the pain of the weight.

"Die!" Nora screamed, spittle flying from her mouth.

Debeau stepped forward, slowly, painfully.

The music began its morbid tune, but the music was draggy and off-key.

Debeau took a vial of holy water from his bag and hurled the glass at the girl. The vial broke at Nora's feet, some of the liquid splashing on her boots and black trousers. Smoking holes appeared in the leather and cloth. Nora screamed in pain.

The priest smiled, knowing he had been correct in thinking the girl's powers were strained to the limit.

Debeau heard the door open and close behind him. He did not look around.

Nora shifted her gaze to Sam. "Welcome to the party," she hissed. "I've been waiting."

"I brought someone to see you, Nora," Sam said.

"I love surprises," the girl said.

"Look behind you," Sam told her.

Nora turned and began screaming as her father moved toward her, his arms outstretched, a smile on his face.

35

Nora squalled her fear and hate and revulsion at the sight of her father and rushed toward him, fury blazing from her dark eyes.

She ran right through him and smashed into the wall. She was knocked backward, stunned, and fell to the floor, her nose broken and bleeding. Before she could recover, Debeau and Sam were by her side, pinning her down. Debeau quickly opened his bag and removed several lengths of chain and three padlocks. Sam rolled the girl over on her stomach and helped the priest secure Nora's hands behind her back, twisting the chains tight and padlocking them securely.

Nora was kicking and squalling and cursing the men. Both Debeau and Sam were bruised from the heavy boots before they could chain Nora's legs.

Wild, mad, hysterical laughter came from Jeanne's room.

A red mist began slowly encircling the men and the howling child.

Debeau threw holy water on the mist. A silent scream almost deafened the men, the howl of pain so high-pitched it caused Debeau and Sam to wince in pain.

The mist pulled back, leaving the second floor landing. Debeau drove it further away with quiet prayers. The house became steamy hot and smelled of sulfur. The lights flickered off and on, dying down to a brownout. The brown-amber glow cast shadows about the house.

The house seemed to breath and sigh, almost in despair.

A million tormented screams filled the house, accompanied by the odor of burning flesh. The stench became almost unbearable.

"Ignore it," Debeau said.

"Ignore it?" Sam cried. *"How?"*

"Faith, Sam." Phillip spoke for the first time, his voice very deep, as if coming from a long distance.

Nora hunched and jerked on the floor, the verbal filth rolling from her mouth as she cursed God and her mother and father. She twisted and flung herself onto her back. She spat at the men and at the image of her father. Then she laughed as the mist deepened and thickened, once more encircling the gathering on the landing.

"Get away from me!" Sam told the mist.

The mist abruptly stopped.

"Help me!" Nora screamed.

The mist began another tentative approach.

The front door slammed open. Sheela stood framed in the open door, the snow swirling around her. She looked up at Sam.

"I love you, Sam!" she called.

The mist backed up.

Nora slumped back, her head resting on the carpet of the landing.

"Sam!" Sheela called. "Tell me."

Sam looked at the woman and smiled. "I love you too," he said. "I really love you."

The mist backed farther away.

Sam straightened up from his crouch. He looked at Debeau. "Is that it?" he asked. "After everything that's happened, this is all? No trumpets blaring? No great booming voices from the sky? We just talk about love and it's over?"

"It's just beginning," Debeau said quietly.

Phillip had vanished, leaving nothing behind to signify he had ever made an appearance from out of the grave.

Nora raised her head and bit Sam savagely on his ankle.

Sam yelled and jerked his foot away from her sharp teeth. He resisted an urge to kick the kid in the teeth.

"What do you mean?" Sam asked the priest. "Just beginning?"

Suddenly men filled the foyer, running through the open door, almost running into Sheela. Connecticut state police and sheriff's deputies.

"Jesus Christ!" Sheriff Ed Willis said, his eyes traveling from the dead men on the floor to Phil's dangling body.

Mark stepped out of the den and emptied his pistol into the knot of cops before a Connecticut state police SWAT member shot him dead with a single shotgun blast. The sheriff was down with a gunshot wound in his leg. The chief deputy fell with a wound in his side, and two state police went down with wounds.

Before the gunsmoke had drifted out the open front door, the men stood in shock and horror watching Jeanne drift out across the second floor. She drifted through the air, still holding on to her dolly. Her feet were several inches off the ground. She drifted down the stairs, her feet not touching the steps. She hovered in front of the cops.

Jeanne sang, "Ladybug, ladybug, fly away home. Your house is on fire and your children will burn."

She laughed insanely and sank slowly to the floor unconscious.

The rope holding Phil broke, dumping the stiffening body to the floor with a lifeless thud.

Nora began laughing.

"It is not over," Phillip's voice rang deeply throughout the house.

"What in God's name is *that*?" Ed Willis spoke from the floor, his hands holding onto his wounded and bloody leg.

"Phillip Baxter," Sheela said.

"Phillip Baxter is *dead*!" the chief deputy said with a groan.

"Well, there he is," Sheela said, pointing.

The deputies and highway cops looked up. Phillip Baxter stood on the landing, misty and sparkling as he began to fade, once more making his way through the veil. His voice came to them all. "This is only the beginning. It is far from over."

Then he was gone.

"Goodbye, Daddy dear!" Nora said with a laugh.

36

"You said you couldn't win, Joe," Sheela said. "But you did. We did."

The survivors were sitting in state police headquarters.

"We won a battle," Debeau said. "But the war is far from over."

Sam felt drained. He was very tired. He wanted to go back to his apartment, take a long, hot bath, and lie down beside Sheela. He wanted to forget. But he knew that was impossible. He would never forget.

None of the survivors would.

But of them all, only a handful knew that what they had witnessed that day was only the beginning.

"Did anybody find that jack-in-the-box?" Sam asked.

"No," Ed said. "It's gone."

A state police investigator entered the room. He looked confused. He sat down and looked at the five of them. "Here's the way it's going down, folks. Alec Tremain has been released from custody. Phil Baxter killed all those kids, and we can prove it. We're still trying to unravel who killed what cop in that house.

Mark's prints are all over that meat cleaver and gun."
He sighed and shook his head. "Jeanne and Nora
Baxter will be declared insane. Bet on that. Arrangements are being made to have them sent to a private
institution for the criminally insane. We could charge
you with killing those three members of that neo-Nazi
group, Mr. Sobel. But making it stick would be
another matter. As to . . . what you people claim to
have seen in that house . . . well," he once again
sighed, "that just isn't going to be made public. If any
of you bring it up, it will be denied. Do I make myself
clear?"

All agreed it was very clear.

"You will be notified when, or *if*, you are to testify.
Good day."

And that was that.

Or was it?

"A lot of loose ends still flapping in the wind," Sam
said to Sheela.

Spring was welcomed in the city; it had been a very
harsh winter. Sam and Sheela had been married for
exactly one month. They had honeymooned briefly,
then returned to work, living in Sam's remodeled
apartment. Remodeled to Sheela's specifications.

"What do you mean, Sam?"

"Judy and Matt Gipson. That little girl who one
neighbor says was run down by that lady, who says
she didn't do it. I believe the woman. Something is
very much the matter with Dean Ellis and Charles
Brewer. That coach who went berserk and raped that
young girl. And his wife; did you see that medallion
around her neck? Six six six. It just . . . it's all wrong,

Sheela."

"Joe said it was only the beginning, remember?"

"How could I forget? But the beginning of what? And where is Joe?"

She shook her head. "I don't know. He called me and told me he had to go away for a time. To recover his strength for the next battle."

"Again? We have to do all this again?" He smiled. "You wanna move to Seattle, honey?"

"I would if we could."

"But we can't. Is that it?"

"You know it is."

Sam walked to the window and looked out. "I don't want to have to fight the devil again, Sheela. I really don't."

"But you will," she said softly. "Won't you?" She brushed back the hair off her neck, just for an instant revealing a tiny birthmark there. It was in the shape of a pentagram.

"Probably so," Sam said.

37

"And how is our little patient this evening?" Dr. Kent asked a nurse.

"Same as always, doctor. She just sits on her bed, smiling."

"Ummm," the doctor said.

"A package came for her this morning, doctor. I wanted you to see it."

"What is it?"

"It's a jack-in-the-box."

"Ummm. Who sent it?"

"A Mr. Gunsche, I believe it was. Oh, and doctor, the patients seemed to be rather restless all afternoon."

"Probably the weather."

"About that jack-in-the-box?"

"Oh, give it to Nora. What harm could a toy do?"